Praise for the works of

"Whip-smart, subversive, and infinitely charming. [...]
beautifully messy work of falling in love on purpose[...]
—Becky Albertalli, #1 *New York Times* bests[...]

"At once raw, charming, messy, and heartfelt, *Save the Date* capitalizes on its hooky premise to tell a deep story about tenaciously going after the life you want. With fantastic romantic tension, delightfully well-drawn side characters, and a protagonist to cheer for, Raskin crafts a stunning debut and is absolutely a new romance author to watch."
—Emma R. Alban, *USA TODAY* bestselling author of *Don't Want You Like a Best Friend*

"Laugh-out-loud funny and searingly vulnerable, *Save the Date* is for the hopeful romantics, the wary romantics, and the romantics who throw caution to the wind. A captivating tale about a woman who isn't afraid to go after her happy ending, even if it means defying her own expectations in the process."
—Alina Khawaja, author of *Maya's Laws of Love*

"*Save the Date* is funny, relatable and beautifully told. With an unforgettable cast of loveable characters, not only will it make you laugh, think and feel, but it might just change your life. Allison Raskin sweeps you up on a joy-filled journey, offering a profound insight into love, values and authenticity along the way. This is a must-read and I challenge you not to have a warmer, happier heart by the end of it. I absolutely adored this book and I already miss it."
—Tessa Bickers, *USA TODAY* bestselling author of *The Book Swap*

"*I Do (I Think)* is a must-read for anyone and everyone that may be curious about the intricacies of modern marriage."
—Nick Viall, TV personality, host of *The Viall Files* and bestselling author

"[Allison's] writing is so funny and so thoughtful, and eased me into a view of marriage I had never considered."
—Jamie Loftus, *New York Times* bestselling author of *Raw Dog*, on *I Do (I Think)*

"Allison illustrates that, for the most part, we're all fundamentally good people doing our best, but our baggage, past trauma, and mental illnesses impede us. That's why she approaches marriage and all relationships with empathy, understanding, and curiosity."
—Zachary Zane, author of *Boyslut: A Memoir and Manifesto*, on *I Do (I Think)*

"Allison Raskin is a warm hug in the world of mental health."
—Kelsey Darragh, author of *Don't F*cking Panic: The Shit They Don't Tell You in Therapy About Anxiety Disorder, Panic Attacks, and Depression,* on *Overthinking About You*

"A warm and thoughtful guide to an under-discussed topic."
—Mara Wilson, writer and actor, on *Overthinking About You*

"Raskin's book is a powerful reminder that while mental health can be all-consuming, it doesn't define you—and it certainly doesn't have to define your relationships."
—*Teen Vogue* on *Overthinking About You*

Also by Allison Raskin

Overthinking About You
I Do (I Think)

Coauthored with Gabe Dunn

I Hate Everyone But You
Please Send Help

Look for Allison Raskin's next novel
available soon from Canary Street Press.

Visit Allison at allisonraskin.com.

ALLISON RASKIN

SAVE the DATE

CANARY STREET PRESS

**CANARY
STREET
PRESS™**

Recycling programs
for this product may
not exist in your area.

ISBN-13: 978-1-335-08132-2

Save the Date

Canary Street Press
22 Adelaide St. West, 41st Floor
Toronto, Ontario M5H 4E3, Canada
CanaryStPress.com

Printed in U.S.A.

To My Parents,
for helping me get up off the floor

A Note from the Author

Here's where I admit that the idea of *Save the Date* is based on my own life.

After getting engaged in May 2020, my ex-fiancé announced he was leaving me six months later because "something was missing," and I haven't seen him since. To say I was shocked would be an understatement. I also felt like an idiot. How could I not have seen this coming!? I'd been giving relationship advice on the internet and through my podcast for years. I was in the process of getting a master's degree in psychology. I even had a book set to come out in 2022 about the intersection of dating and mental health! I was supposed to be an expert in love, and yet I had no idea my partner didn't love me anymore. Mortifying. And quite a slap in the face!

As I sat in my parents' house editing my ex out of my book, *Overthinking About You*, I floated above my body and realized how ridiculous (and objectively hilarious) the situation I found myself in was. Not only was I faced with having to completely rebuild my life, but I also had to actively cut sentences about how wonderful and healthy our relationship was from my own manuscript. My private mistakes were a part of my public life—making them even harder to ignore. I had to delete my engagement announcement from my Instagram and replace it with an *I got left* announcement.

Quickly after the breakup, my dad started making jokes about how he still had the wedding planner if I wanted to find another guy to marry. And then my mom genuinely asked me if there were any guys from my past I could date instead. They both seemed to think that I could simply sub in a new person and continue with my married life on schedule. And while I didn't think this was a good idea for a real person, I thought it was a perfect idea for a book.

But for the book to work, it had to be about more than wanting to save face and save money. It had to tackle the all-too-common conundrum of not wanting someone else's unilateral decision to interfere with your life's trajectory. Because as much as I grieved the loss of my fiancé, I grieved the loss of my future more. I was ready to be engaged. I was ready to be married. And to be thrust back into an earlier life-stage didn't seem fair. It made me feel powerless.

So while Emma's motivation might appear ridiculous at first, in reality she is fighting for the life she wants and deserves. She is taking the power back—she just happens to be going about it in a strange way.

I might not have subbed in a new groom myself, but I did eventually get my happy ending. And I wanted Emma to get hers too to show that you don't have to give up on love just because one person gave up on you. (Not to spoil anything, but this is a romance after all!)

One

"I JUST DON'T UNDERSTAND WHAT HAPPENED."

Emma Moskowitz lay face down in her parents' office as they talked above her inert body. The carpet irritated her sensitive cheek, but getting a rash was the least of her worries at the moment. She was used to rashes. What she wasn't used to—at least not yet—was the staggering pain of betrayal.

"He didn't explain *why* he was doing this?" her father, Alan, asked for what had to have been the fifth time in as many minutes.

Instead of verbally responding, Emma let out a long groan to signal that she wasn't yet in the mood to psychoanalyze *why* her carefully planned life was falling apart. She was still very much in the *maybe I could just lie here for a few years and then die* stage of grieving. That stage wasn't talked about nearly enough. It was important.

"What did she say?" Alan looked to Emma's mother, Debbie, for an interpretation of what could best be described as an animalistic, guttural moan.

"I don't think she wants to talk about it just yet," Debbie offered, despite knowing this explanation likely wasn't going to appease her type-A husband.

"Can I have some water?" Emma interjected, finally moving into a seated position from a full-body sprawl. She wasn't entirely confident that she was capable of drinking anything yet, but she thought she owed it to her family to try. She knew her mom hated seeing her in pain and her dad hated not having a clear solution to offer. Now that he was retired, Alan wasn't sure what to do with himself. Emma didn't want her recent upheaval to become his newest pet project (along with pickleball, online poker and brewing his own root beer). Despite her mother's endless complaints of being smothered by her loving husband, Alan was the busiest retired person Emma knew. And as a couples therapist, she knew quite a few. Having a recently retired spouse was the new seven-year-itch—except this version of an itch appeared to be an overwhelming desire to be left alone. Emma wished with all her might that she was someone who wanted to be left alone instead of being herself: a person who as a child found a way to play "wedding" at every single playdate.

"Do you want bottled or from the tap with ice?" Debbie asked as though the right form of H_2O could fix a broken heart.

"Doesn't matter." Emma sighed for effect. "Nothing matters anymore."

Through a brief exchange of eye contact, Alan and Debbie mutually agreed it wasn't safe to leave their youngest daughter by herself. So Alan went to retrieve the requested water, while Debbie did her best to sit on the floor, ignoring her numerous knee issues and bad back. Her hand hovered over Emma's leg; she was unsure if physical touch would cause comfort or alarm.

"I am so sorry this is happening to you," Debbie whispered.

Emma thought about all the other times in her life that her mother had said this. There was the time Emma fell off a chair when she was six and broke her collarbone. The time in her early twenties when her "best friends" planned a weekend trip without informing or inviting her. And there were the far too many times Emma had been unceremoniously dumped by a variety of men.

Although her present situation technically fell into the latter category, Emma felt that having her fiancé walk out on her for no apparent reason warranted its own classification of suffering.

This time was different than when her college boyfriend left her to date a high-schooler. Or when her adult boyfriend left her for a college student. This felt like the sort of pain you couldn't get over with a laugh and a puff of medical-grade marijuana. This felt like the sort of pain that changed you forever.

Alan returned with both a cold glass of ice and a plastic water bottle. When Emma didn't move to take either one, he set them on the side table and declared, "I think I should call him."

"Call who?" Debbie asked with the cautious optimism of someone who hoped her husband wasn't a total moron.

"Ryan! Maybe I can talk some sense into him. Or at least get some answers."

Fear overtook Emma's nervous system at the mere thought of that conversation occurring. She reached out and grasped her father's ankle to let him know she meant business. "Please do not contact him. He won't tell you anything useful," Emma pleaded. "All he told me is *something is missing* and there is *no point in working on it because it can't be fixed.* I just need to *move on.*"

Debbie and Alan looked at Emma with a mixture of compassion and concern. Emma couldn't blame them—not after showing up the previous evening crying and shouting "It's over! He left me!" before abruptly passing out on the couch to avoid her feelings. Emma felt a pang of guilt that she'd left her parents with such confounding uncertainty for almost ten hours. She knew more than most that not knowing was a special form of torture. It was time to fill them in.

"It only lasted twenty minutes." Emma moaned as the painful memory hit her again. They had been eating dinner in front of the TV when she noticed something was off. As soon as she asked about it—expecting to hear that Ryan's stomach hurt or his boss was annoying him again—the floodgates opened. Apparently, he'd been having doubts for months but didn't know how to tell her. Emma tried her best to fight for them, but a switch had been flipped in Ryan's brain and it was like trying to reason with a concrete wall. Every suggestion she flung out to try to work on their relationship was met with steely resistance. It was obvious that once the words were finally out of Ryan's mouth, he had no intention of taking them back. He had been set free while Emma was left crushed and disoriented. Their engagement was unceremoniously over in less time than it took to watch a network sitcom.

"What were the doubts? Do you know?" Alan asked in a rather accusatory tone. Despite being retired, he would forever be a lawyer combing through details in search of a win. He didn't seem to understand that social contracts could be broken far more easily and with fewer repercussions than legal ones.

Emma shook her head. "Unless *something is missing* is a clarifying answer for you. Because it's not for me!" She could feel that she was losing control of her emotions. Within a minute or two, any attempt at coherent speech would be usurped by streaming tears and a horrifying amount of snot. She tried to get a handle on herself as her brain went into overdrive, poking and pinching the most vulnerable parts of her psyche, her insecurities finding every possible way to punish her for someone else's decision.

The entire breakup had felt surreal from start to finish. Emma hadn't even fully realized she was experiencing a breakup until about halfway through. She'd known things had been off between them for a few months, but it seemed to be more of a Ryan issue than a Ryan-and-Emma issue. He was unhappy with his job. He was struggling with anxiety. He had less interest in his hobbies than normal. To Emma, a licensed marriage and family therapist, it was pretty obvious he was in the midst of a depressive episode. She tried her best to be supportive while her partner was going through a tough time—and she used every ounce of self-esteem that came from her newly earned secure attachment style to not take it personally.

Turns out, she should have taken it personally. Because, according to Ryan, the issues in his life were not related to anxiety or depression after all. He was miserable because he was in the wrong relationship. *She* was the source of the problem, not *him*. And once he realized that, he had to end things right away. Or, you know, once Emma dragged it out of him on a random Monday night.

As Emma recounted this to her parents, somehow managing to make it through without dissolving into incoherent sobs, she felt slightly vindicated by the looks of confusion on their faces. This was objectively confusing, right? To ask your live-in partner to marry you and then walk out six months later completely certain that there was nothing to be done to salvage the relationship? Emma was a couples therapist, for Christ's sake! She made a living salvaging relationships and Ryan wasn't even willing to *try*? It was both a personal and a professional slap in the face.

Emma had a bunch of clients in far worse situations than hers who'd been tirelessly working on fixing things for years. One notable client had slept with his wife's second cousin for three years and they were still together. Yet Ryan—who only a few months ago had cried with happiness as he put an engagement ring on Emma's finger—insisted there was no point in even attempting to repair whatever he thought was broken. He had too many "concerns," so it was best to just move on. What those concerns were exactly remained a mystery that would likely haunt Emma until she died in what she anxiously feared would be an untimely and possibly gruesome fashion.

While on the topic of unfortunate demises, Emma briefly considered murdering Ryan before news of her abandonment became public. That way she would be perceived as a grieving fiancée instead of a rejected loser, which felt much more palatable. While murder would never be her first choice when dealing with a crisis, her reputation was on the line. It is one thing to get blindsided by your partner when you're a civilian. It's quite another when you have a master's in clinical psychology and make a living giving relationship advice. It was the professional equivalent of a cardiologist not realizing she was having a heart attack: mortifying. For the first time, Emma regretted her inability to hide in obscurity due to her hard-earned success.

Oh, fuck.

"My book deal!"

Debbie stopped stroking Emma's back, unsure of what this seemingly random declaration meant. But like any good mom, she remained determined to be supportive. "That's right. You have a book deal, a YouTube channel, and a thriving private practice. I know your heart is shattered right now, but you have a full life. Ryan was just a part of it, not the whole thing."

Years of therapy talk had clearly rubbed off on her mother by osmosis, but Emma wasn't in the position to take any of it in just yet. So instead, she channeled her teenage self and shouted, "No, you don't get it! He's ruined my book deal. How can I write a book about the secret to maintaining healthy relationships when mine just imploded? I'm going to have to give the money back and die from shame instead." She looked at her father pleadingly. "Can I slowly die at home? In my old room? You won't even notice!"

"I think we would notice if you were slowly dying in the guest room."

"*Guest* room? You said it would always be *my* room! This is even worse than I thought!"

And with that, Emma collapsed once again on the carpet. Face rash be damned.

Two

IT HAD BEEN THREE WHOLE WEEKS SINCE RYAN WALKED out, and Emma was proud of her ability to not let her heartbreak interfere with her work. Sure, she was a complete shell of herself outside of client sessions and had basically abandoned her apartment because it felt too sad to live there alone—not that she could afford to live there alone anyway. But finding a subletter was rather low down on a to-do list that included things like "shower without crying" and "remember how to smile."

On top of her struggle to complete basic tasks, Ryan had finally called last night for the first time since they broke up and she kept replaying their interaction in her head. Emma had answered on the first ring, completely confident that he'd changed his mind and wanted her back. Why call and not text if it wasn't to declare he'd made a huge mistake? She'd even answered the phone like she used to when they were a couple and not mortal enemies.

"Go for Emma," she'd said hopefully into the phone, expecting him to finish their normal call-and-response with "Go for Ryan."

Instead, he had replied with a stoic "Hey."

Emma felt the hope drain out of her but, like an idiot, she forged ahead instead of hanging up. "I'm glad you called. I miss you so much."

"Yeah, so I'm just calling because I need to get my stuff. And I was wondering when would be a good time to come by. I'm assuming you don't want to be there."

"Why would you assume that?"

"I don't know. It just seems like it would be…unnecessary. It's better if we both start to move on, right?"

Move on? It had only been two weeks. Images of Ryan on dates with girls who weren't as picky about food as she was flashed through Emma's mind, but she squashed those thoughts so she could focus. She had to be strategic if she had any shot at changing his mind.

"Don't you think we have things to discuss? Like why you suddenly can't stand to be in the same room with me? This whole decision seems pretty impulsive."

Ryan sighed like Emma was a coworker who had gotten the wrong message after a particularly friendly happy hour and he now had to bring her back to reality. "I'm trying not to give you any false hope. I know how you operate. I don't want to show up to get my stuff only for you to launch into a preplanned speech to convince me I'm making a mistake. Because I'm not. This is what's best—for both of us."

Emma felt shocked by his coldness and insistence that there was absolutely no wiggle room. Ryan was famously indecisive. He had once returned a pair of Banana Republic pants *two* different times before deciding to keep them. If only he had given their relationship that amount of consideration, they might still be getting married.

"You clearly have no idea what's best for me. I think that's evident by the careless way you have handled this whole thing."

"Fine. Then I'm doing what's best for me. I hope you can—"

Emma didn't hear the rest of his request because she had chucked her phone across the room.

An hour later, once she was done hyperventilating, they emotionlessly agreed over text that he would grab his stuff the following Saturday while Emma stayed at her parents' house. She didn't mention she had been with her parents every night since Ryan left—she knew it would make him feel better about the whole thing. He'd assume he didn't have to care about her well-being because her family was there to pick up the pieces of what he'd left behind, as if heartbreak was something that could be evenly distributed between a group to reduce individual suffering. If that were true, she'd have a lot fewer clients.

Now that she was living with her parents again, she had reverted to angsty teenage behavior outside of the office, which included a lot of rage-singing along to breakup songs and refusing to eat anything other than bagels and pizza. At work though, she'd been able to compartmentalize and keep it professional. Until now, apparently.

"At least he hasn't left you yet," Emma blurted out to the couple in front of her without thinking.

"Excuse me?" Leah, the wife, asked with a bit of a bite.

Emma rearranged herself into a more professional stance in her therapist chair and tried to correct her completely inappropriate comment. "I just mean, despite all the arguments and the fighting and the periods of not speaking to each other, you have both stayed. And that is no small feat."

Emma waited with bated breath to see if her reframe would stick. She figured flattery would work on Patrick, a hotshot tech executive with the emotional intelligence of a seven-year-old, but Leah was smart. Emma might need to repair this therapeutic rupture by disclosing her broken engagement and she wasn't sure she was ready to do that yet without sobbing; no one comes to couples therapy to comfort their lovesick therapist.

"I guess that's a good point," Leah conceded, reaching over to take Patrick's hand. He squeezed hers back and cracked a grin.

"Good luck getting rid of me," Patrick said to his wife before turning back to Emma and adding, "We have an airtight prenup and I don't want to lose the house."

Emma smiled in response to the tasteless joke, praying her face didn't reveal her disdain. As a therapist she cared about all her clients. As a person she hated a good ten percent of them. "Why don't you tell me more about how your date night went? Were you able to get a babysitter in time?"

As Leah launched into a tirade about the lack of "good help" in the area, Emma let her mind wander. Her eyes drifted to Patrick's cell phone on the couch, and she felt a now-familiar pang of guilt that she hadn't posted anything on YouTube since Ryan walked out. Part of the reason her audience had grown so much was because she'd let them see inside her own relationship while also providing mental health advice and debunking myths around psychology. What had started as an educational channel about couples therapy—hence the name Neutral Third Party—had slowly transformed into something far more personal and expansive without Emma even realizing it. Her most popular video wasn't when she'd spent over an hour breaking down the Gottman's four horsemen of the apocalypse in relationships (criticism, stonewalling, defensiveness and contempt); it was when she and Ryan played the newlywed game for seventeen minutes because they were bored one night. Over the last year, she'd somehow gone from posting occasionally to getting yelled at in the comments if she went a week without uploading. And now she had almost skipped an entire month.

Emma knew she'd need to make more content soon if she wanted to keep her large fan base, but the idea of publicly announcing her broken engagement made her want to hurl. Why had she made Ryan a part of her channel? At the time it had seemed innovative—including her actual partner to teach people about healthy relationships—but now it seemed more misguided than Patrick signing that airtight prenup. Even if Ryan's involvement had skyrocketed her subscribers from a few thousand to nearly half a million. Maybe all those colleagues who talked shit behind her back at mental health conferences had been right the whole time: fame does ruin your professional credibility. And maybe your sanity.

"I just don't get why it's so hard to find someone comfortable with our indoor security cameras," Leah lamented. "It's not like I want to watch you picking your nose. We only have them for emergencies. You understand that, right?"

Emma found herself nodding even though she was barely listening. Her mind had once again returned to her phone call with Ryan as Leah continued to bemoan Gen Z's obsession with privacy in the background. Emma found herself stuck on whether Ryan had always had this capacity for coldness and she had just missed it somehow. But as her mind flicked backward all she saw was his kindness. Like how he had spent months trying to prepare vegetables in a way that didn't make her scrunch her nose at the sight of them (Szechuan sauce and a lot of garlic). Or how he bought a Kindle so he wouldn't keep her up at night with the light on when it became clear her (extremely) early bedtime was not sustainable for him. He was the kind of guy who called his mom on the ride home from work and helped clear the table when everyone else was still chatting. He was a *good guy*. Even their shared dentist had told her so!

"Can we talk more about Leah's aversion to blowjobs?" Patrick interjected, breaking Emma out of her spiral. "Because babysitter or no babysitter, I think that is really getting in the way of our connection."

Clearly now was not the right time for an existential crisis. She'd have to fit one in later.

★ ★ ★

"Do you think I should just give back the book advance?" Emma asked her older sister, Jackie, as they waited for their parents to serve dinner.

Jackie was only five years Emma's senior but was already ten years into a fulfilling marriage with her college sweetheart. Jackie had spotted Chris at a bar her senior year, declared to a friend, "I'm going to marry that man," and had then managed to pull it off. It was classic Jackie; everything she ever wanted for herself came true with minimal to no effort. She genuinely didn't seem to know what it meant to struggle outside of strenuous exercise. Meanwhile, all Emma had ever wanted—and still failed to procure—was the safety and security of a life partner who was legally bound to her. The ache of her singleness hit harder now that she had come *so* close to never having to attend a family event alone again. But here she was, back to being a perpetual fifth wheel at the Moskowitz dining room table. Even her two nieces had each other.

"Why would you ever give money back?" Jackie asked, perplexed. She looked at her husband for back-up. Chris was furiously typing something on his phone next to her. When he didn't immediately agree, she nudged him with her elbow.

"Never give back money," Chris declared, finally looking up. "Especially if you haven't been sued yet." Chris owned his own trading firm after stumbling into commodities by accident. Now he and Jackie had a huge house, multiple babysitters and a large willingness to dispense financial advice whenever appropriate (or inappropriate). Unfortunately, little of it was applicable to someone on a therapist's income who no longer got to split her bills with a partner. Yet another unfair aspect of singledom.

"I don't *want* to give it back. But let's be real. I'm in no position to write about sustaining healthy relationships. I should just change professions. Do you think I'm too physically weak to work with my hands?"

Jackie and Chris seemed to be seriously debating the question when Debbie appeared out of nowhere with a large salad and a hefty dose of motherly encouragement.

"You are not changing professions. You help your clients every single day." She put the salad down and joined them at the table. No matter what the family was eating for dinner, it was always preceded by a large salad.

Alan appeared next, holding a water pitcher for the table and one can of Coke for himself. Alan's dinner Coke was another sacred Moskowitz ritual.

"I feel there's an opportunity for a joke here," Emma said with a sigh. "Something like those who can't do, teach, and those who can't maintain a relationship, give relationship advice for a living."

"What about 'relationship coaches don't play'?" Chris generously offered.

"Oh my god, I bet I'll have to become a *life coach* after this because no one will take me seriously anymore."

There was nothing worse in the professional mental health community than a nonlicensed life coach who told people what to do without any proper training. Although, at the moment, Emma could see the appeal of not having to make her own decisions. Maybe she should dump her own rational, measured therapist for a twenty-three-year-old wellness influencer who would take complete control of her life. Seemed easier than properly processing her grief.

"Stop it," Debbie interjected. "You are more than capable of maintaining a healthy relationship." Debbie was now serving the salad and dropping large pieces of lettuce all over the place despite years of practice.

Emma smiled at her mother's clumsiness. She knew despite everything that had happened, she was lucky to have such a strong support system. No one important in her life had reacted to the news of Ryan abruptly leaving with anything other than bloodcurdling rage on Emma's behalf. Even her own normally stoic therapist had broken character to indignantly call him an asshole. Emma kept waiting for someone to suggest that he must have left for a *reason*, but so far no one had blamed her in the slightest. Now if only she could figure out a way to stop blaming herself. But that kind of unbridled self-compassion was hard to come by, even with the assistance of psychotropic medication.

"I'm confused," Jackie interjected. "Didn't you already write this book? Isn't that why you couldn't watch Amelia when I had to get my face waxed? You told me you were 'near the end of the book' and couldn't risk 'losing steam' months ago."

"Wow, I didn't realize you listened closely enough to quote me," Emma teased.

Jackie ignored the subtle jab. She was the aloof one in the Moskowitz family, but if there was ever a crisis, Jackie was the first to arrive on scene, often with retail therapy shopping bags in hand. She had even threatened to "confront" Ryan on multiple occasions without explaining what that would entail. Luckily for Ryan's fragile ego, and maybe his windshield, Emma had said it wouldn't be necessary.

"But you're right," Emma said. "I did finish the first draft of the book. The only issue is that half of it is about how wonderful my relationship is with Ryan."

"Can't you just cut those parts?" Chris asked.

"And fill it with what exactly? How many hours I've spent psychoanalyzing the characters in *Friends*?" Emma was only half joking. She had once spent an entire afternoon making a YouTube video that proved Phoebe was actually the most emotionally mature and resilient one in the group. Rachel fans had come for her, but the Joey fans got it.

"I guess when you really break it down—which I have during many early-morning hours when I should be asleep—I no longer feel qualified to write this book. I feel like a fraud who couldn't even make a relationship last long enough to walk down the aisle."

"Please!" Jackie responded with the authority of a world leader. "What happened to you wasn't your fault. Ryan didn't leave because you were a bad partner—he left because he's a spineless coward with no concept of what commitment actually looks like. Do you know how many times I've fantasized about leaving Chris when he's snoring so loudly I want to rip my extensions out?"

"Uh...no." Emma sneaked a look at Chris, who didn't seem offended in the slightest.

"About a billion times." She turned to Chris. "And how many times have you wanted to leave me during my ninety-minute skin-care routine that keeps the lights on in the bathroom?"

"Every single night," he responded. Chris pointed at his head and said, "My mind needs total darkness to shut down or it keeps generating the goods."

Alan nodded in agreement as though he didn't often fall asleep under the fluorescent lights of the mall while waiting for Debbie to try on yet another chunky sweater.

"See!" Jackie exclaimed. "Just because you have moments of wanting to flee doesn't mean you actually do it. You suck it up and wait for the feeling to pass. Because we are adults."

"And we love each other," Chris added.

"Right. And that," Jackie agreed.

"I have never once wanted to leave your mother," Alan proudly proclaimed, reading the room wrong.

"Well, you're weird, Dad." Jackie gestured at her parents. "You two are like obsessed with each other."

"No, we're not," Debbie protested.

"Fine. But Dad is obsessed with you."

Debbie nodded in agreement, causing Alan to shout, "Hey!"

"We're just teasing, honey. Of course I'm obsessed with you too."

"My point is that you don't need to learn anything because you didn't do anything wrong, Emma. You just need to date someone else. Someone better."

Emma couldn't help but snort at the notion of dating again. She wasn't exactly feeling desirable. "I seriously doubt I'll date anyone before my rewrites are due in a few months. Unless you happen to know someone interested in pursuing a hollow shell of a human being?"

"Actually, there is this one guy at my gym—"

"Jackie! It's way too soon for me to even *think* about dating someone else. Right?"

Emma looked to her parents for confirmation but failed to find it. This was strange because her parents had spent years of her twenties trying to get Emma to focus on anything other than locking down a husband. This was likely due to her younger self's tendency to completely fall apart whenever a relationship ended; it was historically safer for everyone when Emma was single. But now that her mental health was in better shape, were they suddenly yearning for more grandkids?

"I don't know if it would be such a bad idea to venture back out there," Debbie suggested with the tentativeness of a mother whose head had been bitten off too many times. "You've done a lot of work on yourself to get to this point. Who says you suddenly have to put your entire life on hold because your fiancé got cold feet?"

While Debbie had asked the question in a hypothetical way, Emma felt something substantial shift inside of her. She was having what those in the therapy biz called "a moment of clarity." Up until a minute ago, Emma had had one very clear idea of the world: if your fiancé abruptly leaves you, the appropriate response is to close yourself off and hide for *at least* eight to twelve months in order to heal properly, and maybe *one day* move forward. Now, she wasn't so sure that was her only option. Plus, her mother was right. Emma had spent her entire adult life figuring out how to get her anxiety disorder in check so she could be a good partner and eventual wife. After countless therapy sessions, multiple medications and one very helpful social skills class, she didn't want to lose steam on all her progress just because Ryan turned out to be a spineless coward.

"You don't think I need to wait, I don't know, like six months or something?"

"Six months! I don't think you have to wait six weeks!" Jackie decried with the conviction of someone who had had only one serious relationship before getting married at twenty-seven. "Everyone knows the best way to get over someone is to get someone else."

"I think the phrase is, 'The best way to get over someone is to get *under* someone else.'" Jackie stared at her blankly, so Emma clarified further, "You know, in a sexual way."

"Ew! We're with Mom and Dad!"

"*You* brought it up!"

"I'm just saying, you go on all the time in your videos about how easy it is to find a 'good enough' relationship if you're willing to put in the work. Maybe it's time for you to start putting in the work."

Emma was startled and flattered to realize that her sister seemed to be a real fan of her content. Jackie also had a point. Emma had built her career around the concept that love wasn't based on a magical connection. It was something two (or even three or four) people worked on together. Romantic love was about compatibility on some level, but it was mostly about dedication and commitment. It was picking someone who treated you well and then treating them well back. You couldn't have fire and passion all the time. But you could—and should— always have mutual respect. And looking for someone you

respected and enjoyed was far less of a tall order than finding
The One.

Not that Emma believed in The One in the first place. Or at
least not in the traditional sense with certain connections being
preordained from above. Emma thought people became soulmates over time. True, enduring love couldn't just be found—it
had to be built, making it more attainable than people thought.

A wild idea started to percolate in her brain, but she wanted
to get a better sense of her audience before sharing it. So, as
nonchalantly as possible, Emma asked, "Don't you think people
will be freaked out when they learn I was engaged to someone
else a few weeks ago?"

"Eh, shit happens!" Debbie waved her hand in front of her
face as though she was casually swatting away a fly instead of
a widely held societal expectation. "I'm sure the right person
would be understanding. You're a catch. Anyone would be lucky
to have you."

"Ryan didn't think so," Emma replied, unable to resist an
opportunity to poke at her wound.

Alan scoffed. "Ryan thought the Padres had a real chance
of winning the World Series. He was delusional from the start.
You're too good for him." He reached across the table and
squeezed her hand for emphasis.

Emma knew that her lifelong obsession with marriage had a
lot to do with her parents. She equated marriage with family so
she was always eager to take the leap from dating to *I can trust
you with my life.* She had seen her parents consistently show up
for each other and she craved that for herself. And to be perfectly honest, she wanted to wear the Oscar de la Renta wedding dress she'd already purchased at a huge discount.

"So none of you think it would be too early for me to start
dating?" Emma asked.

All four heads swiveled side to side.

"Would it be too early for me to get into a serious relationship?"

Again, four shakes of the head, although Chris's was less emphatic since he was back to sending emails on his phone.

"What about finding someone who not only wanted to date me but also marry me—" Emma paused for dramatic effect "—on August 29?"

"Of this year?" Debbie exclaimed with enough shock for the entire group.

Emma nodded.

"As in, six months from now?" Alan added as if that couldn't possibly be right.

Emma felt a smile creep across her face as everyone stared at her in disbelief. She knew she was about to head down a path that would completely blow up everything she'd been taught about love, marriage and party planning. But maybe it was time for her to hit the detonator for once instead of being collateral damage.

"I'm not going to call off the wedding," Emma declared with more conviction than she had any right to feel. "I'm just going to find a new groom."

Three

EMMA'S FAMILY HAD EVENTUALLY COME AROUND TO THE idea once she made the appropriate arguments. Jackie had been the first to fall; all Emma needed to do was reference reality TV shows like *Indian Matchmaking* and *Married at First Sight* to prove that the Western standard of dating—meet, date for years, have a long engagement—wasn't the only way to go about finding a suitable partner. Emma had barely gotten the words out before Jackie was on board and clamoring to help set up her dating app profiles.

Alan and Chris were convinced by a more practical approach. Emma brought up all the nonrefundable deposits that had already been made: the band, the venue, the flowers, the multiple outfits! From a financial standpoint, it simply made more sense to at least try to find a groom than give away all that money without a fight. Plus, it was far easier to exist in LA in a two-income household. Why should Emma's quality of life drastically decrease if it didn't have to? Maybe she could find a really nice guy who was also really rich—wouldn't that be a nice twist for everyone? Chris and Alan thought so.

Unfortunately, this angle didn't move the needle for Debbie.

Apparently, she didn't want her youngest daughter to "marry a stranger just to save some money." So Emma shared the other big part of her motivation that had quickly formulated in her mind as her plan took shape. As much as finding a new groom was something Emma wanted to do for herself and her future, she also saw it as an opportunity to influence the Western narrative around marriage—a narrative Emma had already been fighting against in her career. If she pulled this off, she'd be sending a message to all her followers (and maybe the world) that the length of time two people knew each other wasn't what made or broke a relationship. And neither was the amount of lust and attraction couples felt at the beginning. What mattered most was a certain level of compatibly paired with a commitment to making it work.

If Emma's practice had taught her anything, it was that following the traditional rules of courtship didn't protect people from divorce. What did protect people was a willingness to work through their issues. Love didn't stay alive because you had great sex on your third date forty years ago; love was something that needed to be tended to and maintained. Emma just needed the *start* of something wonderful with someone. They could grow the rest of their partnership once they were married. And after about forty minutes of listening to Emma make her case, Debbie reluctantly agreed.

But her best friend Imani, who had just finished listening to a truncated version of the exact same spiel Emma gave her family, wasn't convinced.

"This is a horrible idea," Imani said, with her arms folded across her chest, sinking further into their shared office couch.

Emma had met Imani the first day of her master's program. They'd become fast friends and had managed to turn their dream of co-running a private practice into a reality after years of working at clinics to get their required hours for licensure. Sure, the office space was small and smelled faintly of body odor despite being professionally deep cleaned three times, but it was their own. And none of their clients had complained—at least not about the smell. They complained about everything else constantly.

"I appreciate your honesty," Emma said. "But that's not what I need right now. I'm currently in the market for unbridled support."

Imani raised her eyebrows and clicked her tongue with distaste. She had an expressive face that went well with her equally expressive outfits. Imani had never met a color too bold and she changed her hairstyle almost daily to align with her mood. Emma knew her pragmatic best friend would be the hardest to convince that finding a new groom in time for her original wedding was a good idea. Or at least not a completely terrible one. But she was up for the challenge, and/or willing to beg.

"Sorry. Still a no. You're going to need to find your unbridled support elsewhere."

"But didn't you like the part about changing the narrative—"

Imani put her hand up to stop Emma from saying another word. "It doesn't matter if I like it or not. We are living in the real world where six months isn't enough time to know if someone is a psychopath or not. That's just a fact."

Imani had a point. It had once taken Emma nearly ten months to figure out one of her clients was a malignant narcissist with violent tendencies—and she was a professional.

"Now, if you were trying to pitch me on this with someone you already knew but had never dated, like that guy Bryce from—"

"Oh my god." Emma sprung up from the couch and started pacing their shared office. "You're so right! I don't need to start from scratch with someone completely new."

Images of Tony began to flood Emma's thoughts. Tony in the car. Tony in the shower. Tony catching and then immediately falling off a wave. She hadn't seen the guy in years and suddenly it felt like he was in the room with them.

"I can just reach out to one of my exes and try to make it work this time!"

"Whoa." Imani grabbed for Emma's leg as she marched by her. "That's not at all what I meant. I meant someone you already know but have never dated. People getting back together never works. Couples break up for a reason."

"But what if *I* was the reason? And now I've changed?"

"Explain."

"Do you remember what I was like before Ryan? I was an anxious mess who self-sabotaged pretty much every relationship I could force my way into. But now, I'm more confident, I have better coping tools and I'm securely attached. It wouldn't even be like returning to an old relationship because I am basically a completely different person. I'm Emma 2.0."

"I caught you crying in your car thirty minutes ago."

"Because I'm grieving. Emma 1.0 would have been hysterically calling Ryan over and over and demanding he return to me. Now, I just cry in random places by myself. That's progress, baby."

Imani narrowed her brown eyes in thought. Emma sensed she might be on the verge of winning her best friend over. She just had to stick the landing.

"Do you already have someone in mind? And you better not say—"

"Tony."

"Absolutely not. Nope. Unsubscribe."

Imani had never met Tony in real life, but she had heard enough about him over the years to form a strong (negative) opinion. He and Emma had officially broken up about a month before Emma started her grad program six years ago. But Emma had kept tabs on him, occasionally sending a flirty message or birthday greeting, obsessively dissecting their failed dynamic with Imani over many a late-night drink. There had also been a few whirlwind weekends spent together that never resulted in anything other than hurt feelings. She'd finally stopped reaching out once she was with Ryan, which she'd privately viewed as a major indication of her growth. Except now Emma was right back where she was at twenty-six: thinking about Tony.

"I don't get it. The biggest issue you had with this guy was that he couldn't commit and now you think he's going to want to marry you in six months? Why in the world would he want to do that?" Imani said before half-heartedly adding, "No offense."

"Offense taken. But I'm not completely delusional. I know Tony has a habit of jumping from girl to girl with more than the occasional overlap. But what we had was different. I know it sounds arrogant and maybe completely misguided, but I genuinely think that if given the explicit choice, he would take the leap with me rather than lose me forever."

Imani sighed, her reason and resolve dwindling in the face of Emma's fanaticism.

"As your friend, I hope you're right. As a therapist, I have to tell you that's very worrisome to hear."

Emma laughed. It was also a bit worrisome to feel, but she felt like she owed it to her heart and her twenty-six-year-old self to at least see what might happen. If Tony turned her down, well, she'd experienced worse.

"Thank you for pretending to support me."

"I just don't understand the hold this guy has over you. I've seen his Instagram. It's nothing special."

"I think he was the first person I ever really loved," Emma confessed, knowing this was only partially true.

Emma had fallen in love with pretty much everyone she had ever dated for more than three weeks. And one guy on vacation. The real difference, she knew, was that Tony had left his hooks in her. While past loves had faded into a distant memory—she couldn't even remember the first name of that guy in Tulum—Tony remained ever present in her mind. It always felt like only a few days had passed since she'd last seen him, even though it had technically been two years. She told herself that must mean something. Even if this type of magical thinking was exactly what she urged her clients to avoid.

"Well, the first person I ever loved is dead. You don't see me trying to crawl into her coffin to reconnect," Imani scoffed.

Imani had decided to become a therapist after her high school sweetheart died in a car accident and her school's counselor helped her navigate the pain. It was a huge turning point for Imani, and she hoped her own lived experience could help others better navigate their own grief. It was also endless fodder for exceedingly morbid jokes. The only thing Imani liked more than using humor to cope was using it to make other people squirm. Fortunately, Emma was mostly immune to be being shocked at this point—with the exception of the "Great Abandonment" as she'd taken to calling it.

"I think our situations might be a bit different given that Tony is still alive. And, from my internet stalking, still single."

"You mean to tell me a guy with overwhelming commitment issues hasn't put a ring on it yet? Have you alerted the proper authorities?"

Emma chuckled despite herself. Imani might not have known Tony in the traditional sense, but she'd heard enough about him over the years to put together a fairly accurate picture. While Tony was undoubtedly a great guy in that he was funny, caring and creative, he was also a serial monogamist with an avoidant attachment style. This meant he often fell into relationships without really thinking. For him, having a girlfriend was basically like having a good friend you slept with sometimes. It didn't mean he had to plan his life around a partnership or progress the relationship in any way. This would all be fine if his various girlfriends were on the same page. Instead, they spent months and sometimes years not understanding why their boyfriend didn't seem to care about them all that much—Emma included.

But toward the end of whatever one might call their situationship, Emma had seen a flicker of real emotion. Tony hadn't wanted her to leave, and she'd been secretly clinging to that high ever since. Tony also brought out a playfulness in Emma that she missed almost as much as she missed him.

"I guess I don't actually know if he's single. I just know he hasn't posted about dating anyone lately so whatever he's up to can't be that serious."

"Does he *ever* post his partners on social media?"

"He posted me once! After I threw a fit and threatened to date his friend. To this day I'm the only person he's ever gone social media public with."

"That's not the slam dunk you think it is."

Emma knew Imani was right. But one of the benefits of having your life blown up was that you could take a big risk without it ruining everything. Because everything was already ruined.

"Tony Moretti is not who I had in mind when you pitched me this scheme," Debbie complained as Emma searched her childhood closet for a good outfit. It was surprisingly hard to find a something that said, *I'm appropriately heartbroken but also eagerly looking to marry.* Maybe she could borrow something from Jackie.

"You always liked Tony," Emma argued as she sifted through the meager offerings she'd brought from her apartment. The apartment she still had to pay rent on despite being too heartbroken and poor to live there alone. Maybe her dad could help her find a subletter; he loved a task.

"I liked Tony as a person. But I never liked him for you."

"I never liked Tony as a person *or* for you." Jackie had magically appeared in the doorway eating one of those big bars of ridiculously expensive dark chocolate from Whole Foods. Jackie lived on a diet of fruit, vegetables, grilled fish and massive amounts of chocolate. It seemed to work well for her.

"What are you doing here? Is that mine?" Debbie gestured to the nearly devoured sweet treat.

"No, I brought it from home. I came by to help Emma find an outfit for her date. Even though I think Tony is weird and needs a real job."

"He has a real job," Emma exclaimed in defense of a man who once forgot to pick her up from the airport because his new neighbor—who was also a model—needed help moving in. "He's a freelance video editor."

"Freelance means he doesn't have a job!"

"No, it doesn—" Emma took a deep breath. She had already spent too much of her relatively young life trying to explain to her sister that there were huge contingents of the population who didn't have traditional nine-to-five jobs but still worked and supported themselves.

Even though they had grown up in the same house, it often felt like Emma and Jackie had had completely different lives. Jackie had managed to go from living in the bubble of a Jewish private school to living in the bubble of Beverly Hills as a stay-at-home mom. Emma had also attended Milken Community School growing up but had then ventured out and built a life filled with people who weren't exclusively Jewish or generationally wealthy. It gave Emma a different perspective that Jackie often found baffling.

"I'm thinking of wearing this." Emma held up a black jumpsuit in an attempt to change the topic. Both her mom and sister crinkled their noses although Debbie had the decency to try to hide it.

"I think we can do better," Jackie declared as she started to rifle through Emma's limited wardrobe. As someone with sensory sensitivity issues, Emma was reduced to only buying clothes that didn't pinch, rub or itch—which meant almost everything remotely fashionable was off limits, much to her older sister's horror. "How did this whole thing happen anyway? You just asked him out after not talking for two years?"

"I texted him and asked if he wanted to catch up." Emma attempted to avoid their incoming scrutiny by examining a pair of jeggings that were slowly but surely falling apart—much like her own mental state.

"Wait. A catch-up is not a date. Does he even know you and Ryan broke up?"

"I don't know. I didn't mention it. But I haven't reached out to him since I first told him about Ryan, so he probably put two and two together. Plus, I've been posting cryptically sad quotes on my stories."

Jackie and Debbie exchanged a look that could only mean they had been having secret conversations behind Emma's back. Emma's suspicion was confirmed when Debbie patted the bed for Emma to sit. Jackie sat down on the floor. Some sort of intervention was brewing whether Emma was ready for it or not.

"Sweetheart, have you thought at all about when you're going to go public with the breakup? I know your fans would want to support you through all of this. It might even help you move on and start fresh."

Emma felt a tug on her heartstrings that her mom thought of her 410,000 followers on YouTube as fans. To Emma they felt like vultures who were going to pick her apart once they found out she'd been unceremoniously left. She wouldn't even blame them for devouring her. She'd been cocky and foolish thinking that after years of failed relationships she, of all people, had finally figured it out. What kind of couples therapist couldn't even stay in a couple? (Actually quite a few from what she'd observed at professional conferences, but the internet had little tolerance for nuance.)

"I thought that maybe I would just stop posting until the plan is further along. That way it can sort of be a one-two punch."

"Like when celebrities have a surprise baby? One day you'll just announce you're married to a different guy?" Jackie asked.

"Exactly! Yes. Exactly like that."

"It's not the worst idea," Jackie consented. "But I think I have one better." She paused for dramatic effect. "You should tell them about the plan and then make them a part of it."

"Absolutely not!" Debbie nearly shouted. "We are not letting random people on the internet choose Emma's husband for her. That is where I draw the line."

"Mom, relax. We're not going to let YouTube pick the guy. Emma will just make some videos about the process. People go bananas for this kind of thing," Jackie said, as though she had a master's in social media marketing and not just hours and hours of Instagram consumption under her belt.

"I don't know. I already feel like an idiot for including so much of my personal life online. If I had never shown Ryan in a video, I wouldn't even have to address the broken engagement at all. I could just keep making informative videos about attachment styles until I die alone."

"Yeah, maybe," Jackie conceded, "But then you wouldn't have a book deal. People like your stuff because it's authentic. You've gone viral because you feel like a real person. And what's more real than being left at the altar?"

"I wasn't left at the altar," Emma pointed out. That was one kindness Ryan had extended her. Although it probably had less to do with her feelings and more to do with him wanting to start his new life away from her as quickly as possible.

"Fine but we want to play into the drama here. Your fiancé left you so you're going to stick it to him by marrying someone else on the same day you two were supposed to get married? That's incredible content and you know it."

"I'm not doing this to 'stick it to Ryan' though. I'm doing this for myself."

"Absolutely," Jackie agreed without really meaning it. "And if you happen to gain a ton more followers and release a best-selling book as a result, then that's just a happy accident, right?" Jackie winked at Emma, which was far more disconcerting than she would have expected.

"How would this help the book?" Debbie asked.

"The more followers Emma has before the book comes out, the more people potentially buy the book. And if she announces what she is planning to do, and why she is planning to do it, people will get invested. It'll blow up," Jackie explained.

"That would be great for your practice too," Debbie said, with sudden enthusiasm. "If your book does well, you'll always have a waitlist of clients. It's financial security."

"Aren't we at all concerned that I might not be able to pull this off? What happens if I don't find another groom in time?" Emma asked.

"You will. And if not, we spin it," Jackie declared, her missed calling as a publicist becoming more and more evident.

"I get what you're saying. I really do. And from a business perspective, it makes a lot of sense—"

"Perfect!"

"Wait. I… I'm just worried that if I share my plan publicly, I might start doing it for the wrong reasons. I might, I don't know, marry the wrong person just so I won't look like a loser online."

"Emma," Jackie replied, "people have gotten married for much worse reasons than that."

In the end, they decided on a multitiered approach. Emma had quickly filmed a YouTube video announcing her broken engagement, but she didn't share anything about what had officially been titled Operation: Save My Date. Debbie had come up with the name after Emma vetoed Jackie's suggestion of

Groom Swap. In the approximately three-minute recording, Emma had steered away from bashing her ex and instead focused on the importance of prioritizing herself after heartbreak.

About halfway through filming, though, Emma had found it hard to maintain her normally hopeful and upbeat online persona. Her eyes drifted away from the large poster board filled with the talking points they'd meticulously discussed. It was suddenly all too polished to accurately describe the current of emotions coursing through her veins (and stomach). Overwhelmed, Emma had rubbed her face in frustration and opened her mouth without thinking too much for once.

"Look, I'm going to be honest, it is *really* fucking hard to love yourself when your heart is broken. Your brain wants to collect all this evidence that proves you *deserved* to be left because it likes to make sense of things. It likes to point to a *reason* for all the pain. And the easiest reason my brain can come up with is that I suck. That I am not good enough to marry. But I want it on record, for both me and you, that I reject that reason."

Emma quickly wiped a tear from her right eye that had had the indignity to escape. "I'm not perfect. I know I'm not cool or chill or low maintenance. But that doesn't mean I am unlovable. Because despite everything, I continue to love myself. That's why, even with this massive shock I'm *still* trying to wrap my head around, I don't want to die. I don't even want to give up. Which is a huge improvement from how I felt the last time someone left me behind. So I'm going to celebrate that win— even if I'm crying while I do it."

Emma signed off by swearing that she wasn't going to give up on love or marriage and to stay tuned for more updates. The video was a wonderful mix of genuine emotion and clever clickbait. She had somehow managed to share the worst news of her life through a lens of hope and self-compassion. Maybe it would even help someone in a similar position. Or, at the very least, not paint her as a total fraud. At this point in her increasingly public career, Emma understood that sharing her life online required walking a fine line between authenticity and proactive damage control. It was both exhausting and exhilarating.

By the time they were done and the video was officially uploaded, Emma realized she was running late for once in her anxious life. She was so panicked about beating traffic and finding parking, she didn't even have the brain power to process what was about to happen until she arrived. She was going to see Tony again. And she was maybe going to ask him to marry her.

Four

AS EMMA SCANNED THE COFFEE SHOP, SHE REMEMBERED that Tony had a habit of being a hair past fashionably late to everything. So instead of ordering at the counter and opening herself up to the possibility of being surprised, she maneuvered her way through the cramped tables to snag a seat with a view of the door. As she sat waiting for what might be a life-changing moment, she felt an overwhelming urge to check her new video's view count. She genuinely wasn't sure if she wanted the video to flop so Jackie would lose interest or for it to catch the algorithm wave and make the whole project more real.

At exactly seventeen minutes past the time they had scheduled to meet—and approximately twenty-eight months since they had last seen each other in real life—Tony Moretti walked through the door. Their eyes found each other and suddenly Emma Moskowitz felt eerily certain that despite everything that had happened, despite the heartbreak that was still very much alive and propagating, she was meant to be here in this moment—with him.

"Look who it is," Tony said with more charm than any single man should be allowed to have.

As he enveloped her in his sinewy arms, Emma was trans-
ported back to when they first met, at a rock show. For Emma,
a lifelong Blink-182 fan, the fact that for a moment in history
she had actually been saved in someone's phone as "The Girl
at the Rock Show" was still a thrill. Whether or not the local
indie band they were both casual fans of at the time counted
as actual rock was beside the point.

"It's so good to see you," Tony gushed as he gave her a playful shove.

Emma's therapist brain tried not to attach too much meaning to him physically pushing her away so quickly into their
reunion. She understood that part of Tony's appeal was never
knowing if he was about to surprise her with the perfect gift or
completely disappear into the ether. It kept her on her toes. It
also didn't hurt that with his jet-black hair, short thick beard and
classic yet simple wardrobe, he was the epitome of Emma's type.
She loved a man in a flannel shirt and nice jeans. So sue her.

"Thanks for agreeing to meet. I know it was probably out
of the blue for me to text you like that."

Tony shrugged as though it hadn't even occurred to him
to question her invitation. "We're old friends. Old friends get
coffee every few years—that way we can still pretend to know
each other." He pulled out a chair and sat down without ordering any coffee. Emma joined him and launched into her best
impression of playing it cool. All while secretly panicking that
they were going to get in trouble for loitering.

"You probably heard that I got engaged—"

"You got engaged? Emma, that's amazing! I know that's
what you've always wanted. I think you even said that on our
third date. And most of our dates after that." Tony laughed at
the memory of her inappropriate behavior. Emma suddenly
had more insight into why she had romantically struggled for
so many years, but right now wasn't the time to unpack that.

"Yeah…well. It didn't work out. Ryan…left."

Tony's face fell and Emma worried that any lingering affection he had toward her was about to turn into pity, which rarely brought about sexual desire—at least not healthy sexual desire. She needed to change the narrative and take back control.

"Work has been good though and my dad's trying to get me to try pickleball—"

"Wait. Sorry. What do you mean Ryan left? Are you okay?"

It was a good question. Was she okay? In the immediate sense, yes. She was still alive. She was still breathing. She was able to feed herself when she was hungry and bathe herself when she was dirty. But in a larger sense, Emma feared she would never be the same again. Unless she managed to pull off the impossible and convince this man to marry her in approximately five and a half months so she didn't have to give up on love. Or herself.

"It's been tough. I didn't see it coming—at all—so the last few weeks have been...hard." By which she meant soul crushing and completely destabilizing. "But my support system has been great. They've really encouraged me to move forward and not let Ryan's complete lack of empathy ruin my life for any longer than it has to."

"I agree with them. Fuck that guy. You deserve better." Tony smiled at her, and Emma felt her insides move.

"I just realized I'm not actually thirsty. Do you want to get out of here?" The words were out of her mouth before she even understood the implication, but Tony seemed unfazed.

"Sure."

Emma smiled. When it came to Tony, "sure" was the most enthusiastic commitment one could get. Not bad for a pity hang.

Everything looked exactly the same, from the *I Love Lucy* memorabilia to the Urban Outfitters record player she'd bought him for their one-year anniversary. The only indication that any time had passed since Emma had last been in Tony's Hollywood apartment was his receding hairline. And her extra seventeen pounds. It seemed bodies changed far faster than stuff needed to be replaced.

"Is a bowl okay? I also have some joints."

Emma broke away from trying to see if he had at least added any new books to his bookshelf to find Tony holding the same pipe they'd used back when they were together. She tried not to think about how many other women's lips had sucked on it in the interim.

"Let's do a joint."

"You got it, toots."

Tony went to rummage through a drawer in his brightly tiled kitchen and Emma was reminded that despite being born in 1987, Tony was a relic from another time. He worshipped Lucille Ball and almost exclusively listened to music from before 1965—with the notable exception of Blink and a few other pop-punk bands. Unlike most Angelenos, Tony never wore sweatpants or sneakers and actually dressed up for air travel. He firmly believed everything in society went to shit after Nat King Cole died. Minus, you know, all the newfound civil liberties. Tony seemed to long for a version of the past that had never actually existed. Emma wondered if, in some way, she was doing the same thing.

"Here." Tony went to hand her the weed and lighter before stopping himself. "Oh wait, let me start it for you."

Emma smiled and didn't mention that since they last smoked, she had finally learned how to light her own joint at the ripe age of thirty. It was nice to have someone do it for her. And even nicer to feel the effects of the drug strip (some of) her anxiety away. They sat next to each other on the couch, passing the joint back and forth, neither acknowledging that their legs were touching.

"Is it weird that this doesn't feel weird?" Emma eventually said.

"Why would it feel weird? We've smoked on this couch like hundreds of times."

"We also haven't seen each other in person in over two years. I lived with someone else and almost married him."

"That's not saying much though. You try to marry everyone."

Now it was Emma's turn for a playful shove—although it wasn't that playful. She'd always known she'd wanted to get married. She just hadn't been aware of how loudly she had been broadcasting it.

"What was he like?" Tony asked while removing some ash from his tongue.

"Ryan? I honestly don't know. My whole conception of him has changed since he left. The way he acted at the end, leaving like that without any warning. It's made me think I didn't know him at all." Emma let out a long puff and shared the thought that had slowly been burning a hole inside her soul. "Maybe it's not possible to *really* know anyone."

Tony rolled his eyes. "Of course you can't really know anyone. That's what makes life interesting." He turned to face her on the couch. "Like right now. I can listen to you and nod and say the right stuff, but you have no way of knowing that at the same time I'm also trying to figure out how I can get a burrito."

"You're thinking about a burrito right now?"

"Among other things, yeah. That's what's great about the brain. It's just for you."

"That doesn't freak you out? That you can share your entire life with another person and not know what they're actually thinking or feeling?"

"Depends on the person. I pretty much always knew what you were thinking or feeling because you couldn't stop yourself from saying it out loud."

Emma's face got hot. Oversharing wasn't something she was

particularly proud of. "I keep my true thoughts from my clients all the time—that's like ninety-five percent of being a therapist."

"I'm sure they can still tell. You don't have much of a poker face."

"That is blatantly untrue! I have spent years of my life learning how to keep a neutral but open face."

"Show me."

"Okay. Go sit on that chair and tell me something shocking."

Tony obliged, moving to his midcentury modern teal armchair. Emma shifted her body upright and planted both feet firmly on the ground, something she made sure to do at the start of each new session, although this was her first time doing it high. She had to stop herself from rubbing her socks on the carpet over and over again.

"I had a threesome with two of my sister's friends when I was still in high school."

Emma nodded in response, keeping her facial muscles calm.

"One of those girls still texts me all the time even though she's now a lesbian."

"And what do you think compels you to keep responding to Angela?"

"How do you know her name is Angela?"

"Because you tell everyone this story within like five minutes of meeting you. I said tell me something shocking, not your greatest achievement to date."

"Fuck! Okay, I got something else."

Emma retook her therapist pose as Tony shifted nervously in his seat. He took a deep breath and locked eyes with her.

"Sometimes, when I'm bored or really lonely, I think I made a mistake letting you get away." Emma's mouth dropped opened at the same time Tony's broke into a grin. "See! No poker face!"

"That's not fair!"

"Why not?"

"Because…" Emma couldn't think of a reason. She was too

busy trying to figure out if what Tony had said was true or just meant to shock her. "Do you really think that?"

"Maybe. I think all kinds of stuff. I try not to read too much into it."

"Tony..." Emma braced herself for what would be a full confession. She was going to tell him all of it. That deep down she was afraid that she'd never stopped having feelings for him. That she wanted to give their relationship another try. And that, if he acted quickly, he could probably get a bespoke suit in time for their August nuptials.

But when she picked her head up to look him meaningfully in the eye, his phone was out, and a burrito menu filled the screen.

"Want to order some bean and cheese?"

Emma released a breath she didn't know she was holding. "Definitely."

Confession could wait. It wasn't like it was Yom Kippur.

Five

SINCE THEIR REUNION A WEEK AGO, EMMA AND TONY
had started texting each other every day. Nothing too serious,
just a lot of memes and old inside jokes they had managed to
dust off. She kept waiting for him to initiate another meetup,
but he seemed content to never share physical space again. So,
after seven excruciating days, Emma had suggested trying a
new pizza place near his apartment. He'd instantly agreed, and
they'd met up that very night.

Emma's nerves got the best of her during her first slice, but
by the time she'd torn into her second it felt like old times. One
thing she loved about Tony was he could always take a joke.
Since she was a teenager Emma's favorite form of flirting was
a lighthearted tease. But Ryan had often been too sensitive to
handle it. She'd had to learn how to tame that part of herself in
exchange for Ryan's gentle kindness. Across from Tony though,
she was back to firing on all cylinders and roasting him for having so many parking tickets.

"They can throw you in jail if you're over a certain number," Emma warned as she tried not to fixate on his hands. For

whatever reason, male hands excited Emma in a way that was usually reserved for bulging biceps and six-pack abs.

"What number?"

"I don't know."

"Exactly. No one knows. And that's why I will never reach it."

"And if you somehow do, you'll just sweet-talk your way out of any hard time?"

"Absolutely. I've sweet-talked my way out of much worse."

"Like the night I found those texts on your phone?"

Tony was mortal enough to look embarrassed. "I plead the Fifth."

"Oh, so you are no longer sticking to your story that your mom's friend has dementia and thinks you're her dead husband, so it would've been cruel of you to not respond?"

Tony grinned. "Come on. That was pretty good for thinking on my feet."

"Except I'm not totally convinced it was the first time you used it."

"I forgot you were such a detective." Tony reached across the table and snagged a fallen olive off Emma's plate. "I know you have no reason to believe me, but nothing happened with that girl. I was just worried you were going to get the wrong idea so I panicked."

"And made up an elaborate lie that made you look even more guilty?"

"Hey, you're the expert. How often does panic lead to good decisions?"

"Fair enough." Emma took a sip of her Diet Coke and wondered how she would have reacted if he had told her the truth back then—that it was just some friendly flirtation and nothing to be worried about. Emma of today would have understood that flirting isn't the same as cheating. Sure, sometimes it can lead to infidelity, but more often than not it simply scratches an itch. An itch that is perfectly normal to have when you are a three-dimensional adult who doesn't completely disconnect from the outside world just because you're in a monogamous relationship.

Emma of yesteryear though? She would have thrown a fit.

"I'm sorry you felt like you had to lie. I wasn't exactly... confident in our connection back then. I saw everything as a threat."

Tony shrugged. "I'm sure I wasn't helping things by being so shady all the time."

Emma smiled. It seemed like they'd both changed. Which meant this time around would be different—and Imani would be wrong for the first time in her insightful life.

"I think we both made a lot of mistakes when we were together."

"Really? I mostly remember getting stoned and watching *Nathan for You*."

"I hope that's not *all* you remember," Emma said flirtatiously.

He raised his dark eyebrows at the implication. "I guess there were a couple other things that stand out. Like your animal pajamas."

Emma laughed at the memory. She'd gone through a phase where she'd been obsessed with this comfy, cozy nightgown covered in different safari animals. Tony had started to name each one and often acted out little scenes between them; he was surprisingly good at voices.

"I still have it, you know. If you wanted to say hi."

Before Tony could respond, his phone buzzed. She wondered if it was a sign from the universe to not go through with pitching him her master plan. Good thing she wasn't the type to take signs from the universe.

"Oh fuck." Tony looked up from his phone with a guilty expression. "I totally forgot my buddy needed to grab something from my apartment tonight." He started cleaning up their paper plates and discarded napkins. "I've got to run."

"No worries," Emma lied. Maybe she had read their new connection all wrong. Maybe he was only interested in finally trying New York–style pizza with a Middle Eastern spin—whatever that meant; it had just tasted like regular pizza to her. Another disappointment.

"Hey." Tony grabbed her shoulder on the way to the garbage. "What are you doing Monday?"

Emma's heart skipped a beat as she blurted out "Nothing. *The Bachelor* is on hiatus."

"Great. We're doing after-work drinks at Sassafras. You should come. See the old gang, hang out."

"That sounds fun," Emma said while wondering if a group hang was a good sign or a platonic one. Either way, he had remembered her animal pajamas and that felt like a win.

Emma peered into the bar through its big glass window, hoping to spot Tony so she would know where to go. For all her work to combat her social anxiety over the years, nothing made her feel more on display—in a bad way—than the act of looking for someone in a crowd. What if that person wasn't there? What if there was never a person at all and her entire reality was a figment of her imagination as her body hung stagnant in a bunch of goop somewhere else in the universe? What if—

She felt her neck relax and her anxiety spiral stop as she spotted Tony's signature posture near one of the high tops in the back. He was half leaning on the table with one hand out, wildly gesticulating—both calm and vibrant at the same time. He wasn't the kind of guy who would necessarily catch your attention from far away. Average height. Small to medium bald spot. Simple wardrobe. But the moment he started talking, it felt like a movie star had entered the room. Tony exuded the kind of effortless confidence that Emma had been searching for her whole life. And failed, so far in her personal growth journey, to find.

Emma flung open the surprisingly light door and headed toward the man who she hoped would be her salvation. Even if it took him hours to return a simple text.

"Emma!" Tony embraced her in a bear hug. She tried to feel if his heart was pounding as fast as hers was, but it was impossible to tell through his well-made flannel. "You remember everyone."

Emma looked at the surrounding faces. A few formerly mutual friends stood out from their time as a couple, but at least two of the five were complete strangers. "Sure! Hi, I'm the ex-girlfriend. Approximately one of six hundred."

Everyone laughed the right amount at her gentle jab. Tony's storied dating history was the perfect low-hanging fruit for almost every awkward occasion.

"Let me get you a drink." Tony headed for the bar and after a moment of hesitation, Emma followed him.

"It's so nice you all still do this." She gestured to the group, who seemed to be letting pretty loose for a weeknight. But then again, her barometer might've been off considering her 10:00 p.m. bedtime.

"After-work drinks are a lot more fun when you don't actually work together. Plus, as a freelancer, it's important for me to put in the time to make my own community."

"*I* told you that."

"And I listened." Tony grinned.

Emma let the spark sizzle through her before reaching for his arm. "I want to get back together," she blurted without thinking.

Tony's head snapped back from looking for a bartender, his expression one of shock. Not ideal but workable. At least it was out in the world now, before some sort of natural disaster could thwart her.

"And I don't just want us to date and break up and date and break up. I want us to give it a real go."

Tony stayed quiet but Emma figured that was better than active protest. She plowed forward, boldly ignoring everything she had been taught about social cues. No one ever became president without making at least a few people uncomfortable after all. "This is going to sound a bit bananas so bear with me, but I actually still have my wedding venue booked for this summer and—"

"I have a girlfriend."

"What?"

"I have a, you know, a girlfriend." Tony looked over at the group, where one of the unfamiliar faces, a tall blonde, was glaring at them. He waved. She raised her eyebrows as if she knew exactly what they were talking about.

Tony's confession, paired with his girlfriend's incredible body and frizz-free hair, felt like a punch in the face. Pretty soon Emma was going to get used to men ripping the rug out from under her and shattering her world. It had already happened twice in one month, which seemed excessive.

"Why didn't you tell me?"

"It didn't come up. And it's not that serious."

"How long have you been together?"

Tony's face looked strained as he tried to recall a number that was most certainly on the top of the tall blonde's mind. "I dunno. Eight, maybe ten months."

"You're unbelievable." Emma knew she should leave but she was too riled up to stew in her car alone. Her latent fear that Tony brought out the worst in her was being confirmed in real time, but she would have to unpack that later. Right now, she wanted a fight and hoped he would at least do her the honor of having one.

"What was I supposed to do? You texted me out of the blue to catch up and then tell me your engagement fell apart and

I'm supposed to start talking about how great Naomi is? That's not nice."

"So she didn't mind we hung out alone in your apartment the other day?"

"I didn't mention it. I'm allowed to have friends. You're my friend."

Suddenly everything clicked. The whole time Emma had been with Tony he put other people's needs above her own. Emma's love for him had been a given so he didn't need to tend to it. Instead, he spent his energy on pleasing every other female in sight. Now Emma was the random woman he was prioritizing over his girlfriend, and her presence was causing his new partner pain. It made her feel unbearably icky.

"I think I should go." Emma waited for him to protest. Part of her still thought the connection they had was stronger than all his bullshit, that in the end he would see she was worth taking a leap for. She wasn't just another ex-girlfriend in a sea of ex-girlfriends; she was his and he was hers and all the bullshit she'd been through would be worth it when they ended up together. Her broken engagement would be a blessing, not a curse, because it led her back to Tony. The one she never got over. The one who never got over her.

"Okay. Get home safe," Tony said simply. His world seemed only mildly shaken while hers had collapsed.

Emma turned and walked out as Naomi watched her with relief. Not for the first time, Emma wondered why she was so easy to let go.

Six

———————

THE VIDEO HAD REACHED ALMOST THREE MILLION VIEWS in eight days. Emma never had these many eyeballs on her content before and she was shocked to find all the attention exhilarating. Once Emma realized her breakup announcement was garnering sympathy and encouragement instead of insults and attacks, she'd had a hard time putting her phone down. The tidal wave of engagement was also helping heal her humiliation over Tony. So what if she'd been rejected—again? Thousands of strangers cared enough about her broken engagement to write a heartfelt message or a heart-filled sequence of emojis. Her YouTube comments overflowed with stories of other people who had been abruptly left. Some had found love again and some... Well, no one's story was ever truly over until they were dead. And maybe not even then! What did little old Emma know about the rules of the afterlife?

Returning to Tony had clearly been a mistake. An emotional relapse. But that didn't mean Emma needed to give up on her plan, which was why she now found herself in her sister's second living room—yes, Jackie's house had *two* living rooms—

surrounded by ring lights so she could announce it to the whole world. Or at least a small corner of the internet.

"You look stunning," Jackie cooed as she finished applying another layer of lip gloss to Emma's now extremely plump lips.

"I'm worried it will look like I'm trying too hard."

"I've never understood that expression. Why is it bad to try to look good?"

Emma stared at her sister with something akin to awe. Yet again Jackie had managed to diminish a widely held societal belief without really trying. "You're right. I just still want to look like me."

"Obvi. Go look."

Emma got up from her sister's exorbitantly expensive armchair and went to check herself out in the bathroom mirror. The face glowing back at her was completely recognizable yet somehow entirely elevated. Her normally boring brown eyes popped. Her long brown hair looked intentionally wavy instead of confused. And her lips glistened with invitation. She felt like Emma 2.0 in the flesh.

"You're a magician," Emma declared as she retook her place in front of the tripod.

Jackie waved the compliment away. "I just work with what I've got. And you're already beautiful."

Emma felt her face flush. Growing up, Jackie was the pretty one and Emma was the smart one. Maybe they'd each been a mix of both this whole time without realizing it.

"How should I do this? I'm worried that if I launch right into the plan I will seem—and I do not use this term lightly—completely crazy."

"Maybe you take the audience through your thought process? Like, how did you even come up with Operation: Save My Date in the first place? And then you can do that thing where you list all the reasons it seems like a bad idea before revealing that it's actually a great idea. That way if anyone says anything bad about it you can be like, *Um… I already addressed that.*"

"That's brilliant. Your talents are being wasted."

"Not anymore!" Jackie smiled. And for the first time, Emma realized that what she was about to do, whatever mess or success she was about to get herself into, she wasn't doing it alone. She had her big sister to help.

"Rolling!" Jackie declared. "No, wait. It's filming me." She hit a few buttons. "Rolling take two!"

As Emma went to sleep that night, one full hour after her normal bedtime, she felt as though the Earth had shifted. Within moments of uploading the video, feedback started flooding in. While there were plenty of comments calling her "desperate" or "delusional" or "delusionally desperate," there were far more applauding her courage. One follower had commented that it had been over five years since her husband left and she hadn't been brave enough to move on yet but that Emma's announcement felt like a sign for her to get back out there too. Many others echoed the same sentiment.

Emma no longer felt like she was going through with this bizarre plan just for herself; she was now doing it for her followers, which was both motivating and terrifying. Through one YouTube video, she had become a role model of sorts. A guinea pig in the search for love. She fantasized about victoriously sharing footage of her wedding day—it would be the social media equivalent of returning home from war with the evil dictator as your captive. Or scoring the winning basket in whatever was the most important basketball game of the year. But in many ways, it would be bigger than either of those things, because it would inspire other people to be brave and not wait around for love to "find" them. She was helping people put aside societal expectations around the "right" way to walk down the aisle and commit their life to another person. Marriage would no longer be something people felt they had to wait patiently for even when they were already ready for it; it would become an accomplishable goal and not an otherworldly mystery that *only happened when you least expected it.*

Emma had felt so empowered after explaining her plan to find a new groom through a combination of online dating and old-fashioned setups, she'd let Jackie sign her up for all the apps. Including a new app for divorcees called Leftovers, whose tagline was misguidedly, "One person's trash is another person's future." She'd only agreed to that one because Chris's friend had cofounded it and apparently divorced men were a hot commodity. They weren't afraid of commitment and, as a bonus, often knew how to effectively save for retirement—something Emma quite frankly did not understand how to do.

In the wake of all this possibility, it no longer seemed to matter as much that the two men she had loved the most in her life—Ryan and Tony—didn't love her back. What were two lone people in an endless sea of profiles? For this all to work, she needed to focus on the future. The more she was willing to open herself up to complete strangers, the better chance she had at finding the best fit. She just had to rip off the Band-Aid. Who knows, maybe she'd nail it on her first try.

"So many people have a favorite food. But I find it hard to pick one because I like all foods."

Emma tried not to look at her date in confusion. She hadn't asked him to identify his favorite food. Tim was a thirty-four-year-old accountant who didn't smoke but moderately drank; he was also her very first match and she was trying to keep an open mind.

"I do have a favorite movie though," Tim said. He leaned in as if sharing a secret. "It's *Dreamgirls.*"

Emma tried not to laugh at how proud he seemed to have an

"unconventional" favorite film for a straight white man. "Oh, really? I've never seen it."

"You've never seen *Dreamgirls*?" Tim looked the most animated he'd been throughout their nearly forty minutes of first-date platitudes. "It's incredible. Great music."

Emma nodded and wondered if she was going to be asked to contribute to this conversation in any meaningful way.

"In terms of sports, I'm definitely a football guy. But I'll also watch basketball or hockey when it's on." Tim continued to answer a series of basic questions about himself without being prompted. It became clear that he was a Hinge veteran who thought the best way to get to know a complete stranger was to monologue about what (she hoped) were the most boring parts of his personality. Emma's eyes were starting to glaze over when Tim suddenly looked at her expectantly. Unfortunately, she hadn't been listening to him in over a minute.

"What about you?"

"What *about* me?"

"Do you have any living grandparents?"

Emma felt her poker face faltering. What kind of a conversation was this? She hadn't been out of the dating game long enough for everyone to become this painfully dull, had she? "I have two, both on my dad's side."

"Lucky."

Emma guessed it was lucky to be her age and still get to go to her grandparents' *chachka*-filled house for Passover. But right now, she felt a little cursed. She was clearly going to have to keep searching for Mr. Right-For-The-Plan. If she didn't die from boredom first.

"I'm not really that close with them," Emma confessed. "My grandma is kind of a bitch." The shocked look on Tim's face was almost worth the twenty dollars she was going to have to pay for an Uber home. "She once told me that my face would be perfect if I got a nose job."

"That's horrible. What did you do?"

"I got a nose job to prove her wrong. See?" Emma gestured to her face. "Still not perfect!"

Tim forced himself to smile but it was clear he was reassessing the seemingly normal girl in front of him. He not so subtly looked at his phone. "Oh, wow. It's getting late," he announced.

Emma, tickled by the experience of no longer trying to be a "good date," ignored his attempt to wrap things up. If this wasn't going to be a romantic success, she could at least conduct some field research. "Tim, can I level with you?" Her second drink, which she ordered only because he ordered one, was catching up with her. "Can I put it all on the table for your honest reaction?"

"Uh…sure."

"Great. You see, Timothy—"

"It's actually just Tim. My mom thinks all names should be five letters or less."

"Wow. Okay. You see, *Tim*, I was engaged. Until my fiancé decided to walk out on me six weeks ago." Tim opened his mouth to speak but Emma put up her hand to stop him. Better to get it all out at once. "And while I was initially heartbroken, I've decided that I'm not going to let another person's callous actions stop me from moving forward with my life. So, I kept the wedding venue and I kept my dress and I am officially on the hunt for a new groom."

"That's…surprising to hear," Tim mumbled.

"I know. Pretty brave," Emma said, although they both knew that wasn't what Tim had meant. "What I'm asking of you, Tim-not-Timothy, is how you think I should go about explaining all this to potential grooms in the future. Because I don't want to scare them off, but I also want them to know what's up." Emma sat back, ready to hear his insight. She was also pretty drunk at this point, which prevented her from feeling anything resembling embarrassment.

"Wait. Are you asking me to marry you?"

Emma burst into laughter. "God no. We aren't right for each other. I haven't even seen *Dreamgirls*."

Tim nodded in agreement.

"I'm just asking your opinion, as a man in the dating pool, how I should best go about this delicate, but ultimately life-affirming, situation."

For a moment, Emma thought Tim was just going to get up and walk out. But after what felt like an eternity, he said, "Honestly? I wouldn't tell him a thing. Just date him and have a lot of sex with him and never do anything annoying. And then, the night before the wedding, you get him really drunk and say something like, 'Wouldn't it be epic if we got married tomorrow?' Forty percent chance he'll go for it. And in the game of love, forty percent odds ain't bad." He took a swig of his beer as Emma wondered whether she had underestimated this man in front of her. His plan was brilliantly diabolical.

"Tim, I'm not going to do any of that. But I will buy our drinks."

"Works for me."

As they clinked their glasses, Emma asked, "Do you happen to have any single friends who would be open—"

"No."

Well, at least she asked.

Seven

———

EMMA STARED AT THE CLOCK. IT WAS 12:02 P.M. AND HER book editor was supposed to call her at noon. She wondered if the delay was a bad sign. Or if she was just making assumptions without having any real information and evidence. It was hard to be a therapist with generalized anxiety disorder; sometimes she just wanted to let her brain misbehave without feeling any pressure to act rationally.

When the phone rang at 12:03 p.m., Emma answered on the first ring. She had given up trying to seem aloof years earlier. It didn't suit her.

"Hi, this is Emma!" Her voice reached the level of pitch reserved for awkward phone calls and unsettling interactions with strangers on elevators.

"Hi, Emma, it's Michelle."

Michelle was around Emma's age and had been the one to reach out about the potential of writing a book after finding Emma's content on YouTube. Michelle was a younger editor and was hoping to use her social media fluency as a leg up in her old-school industry. Emma had been unbelievably flattered when Michelle reached out and immediately sent over a flurry of potential book ideas. They ultimately decided on *The Good-Enough Relationship: How Unrealistic Expectations Get in the Way of Love*. The first draft was a blend of Emma's experiences as a couples therapist, the latest evidence-based relationship research and snippets of her own love story with Ryan. That last part was the problem.

"How're you doing?" Michelle asked with the gentleness of someone who expected a long and harrowing answer.

"I'm, you know, still processing. But I'm excited to dive back into the manuscript," Emma lied. She wondered if Michelle was going to bring up Operation: Save My Date or if she'd stopped watching Emma's content once they had a signed deal. She secretly prayed for the latter even if it meant one less view.

"I'm glad to hear that. I know we'll have to make a lot of changes given what happened, but I still think the book has good bones. I really enjoyed the read."

Emma sighed with relief. After she'd rushed to meet her deadline right before Ryan left, it had mostly been radio silence as Michelle worked through the draft. This was the first she was hearing that it wasn't a complete disaster.

"That's great. I was worried you hated it!"

"If I hated it, this would be an email not a phone call. I hate confrontation."

"Good to know. The next time I see an email from you, I'll be sure to panic." Emma let out a nervous giggle that didn't enhance her awkward joke.

Michelle, smart enough to bypass the minefield of Emma's writing insecurity, replied, "So, what are you thinking for the next draft? I know it would be easiest to cut Ryan out completely, but I don't want to lose the personal narrative. We've found people engage with advice better when it seems to be coming from a real person and not just an expert."

"Yeah, I get that. I'm just worried that if I include what really happened, my premise will sort of fall apart," Emma replied.

"Maybe. Or maybe it will prove it. Did Ryan have unrealistic expectations about love?"

"Oh. I hadn't really thought about it."

"Really? That's the first thing I thought when I found out he left without any real reason. I mean why do you do that unless you think there's something better out there?"

For someone who hated confrontation, Michelle didn't have any aversion to being blunt. But it was a good point: could Emma's own relationship have fallen victim to the very type of thinking she railed against? Had Ryan convinced himself he could "do better" or "love more" when really what he should have been doing was pouring more effort into what he and Emma had already built together? The possibility made Emma's heart sink. But it did lend itself to a compelling book narrative. If only it wasn't about her own life.

"You could be right," Emma confessed. "I clearly didn't know what was going on in his head."

"Well, it's a theory. And one that could work well for the book. You could even do a thing where you don't reveal until the very end that he left you. And then it's like, *Boom, unrealistic expectations ruined my relationship too!*"

Emma felt a sob almost escape her body, but she managed to turn it into a fake cough instead. While she understood where Michelle was coming from, the delivery could've used some work.

"Totally. Yeah. Let me think on the right approach and get back to you." If Emma could make it off this call without bursting into tears, she deserved a medal in composure. And maybe some ice cream.

"Perfect. In the meantime, I'll send you all my notes on the current draft in the next few days. I've been highlighting every time you mention Ryan, so we know what needs to change."

"Sorry to make you do that."

"It's no problem. Maybe it will feel nice to delete him."

Emma laughed to be polite, but she knew that she would never get to fully delete the remnants of Ryan from her book or from her life. That's not how the mind worked.

"Oh, and Emma?"

"Yeah?"

"If you pull off this whole Save My Date thing, I want it as the epilogue. Or, depending on how things go, maybe it's juicy enough for its own book. Like an unconventional follow-up or sequel."

"Wow, that would be amazing," Emma replied, trying not to convey her quickened heart rate. Her mind flashed forward to one year in the future. Best-case scenario she would be a new-lywed on a major book tour with a second book deal. Worst case... Well, worst case was almost too terrifying to think about. "And just for curiosity's sake, what would happen if I don't, you know, pull it off?"

"Then we pretend it never happened. And hope it doesn't completely ruin your credibility." Michelle paused. "But who knows! Wilder things have happened. My aunt met my uncle after falling off a cruise ship."

Emma wasn't sure what that peculiar love story had to do with anything, but she was sure that the stakes of her little ex-periment were now at an all-time high. She had to get to work, both on and off the page.

"Do you want organic bananas or regular bananas?" Debbie asked as Emma scrolled through Hinge in the produce section of the Westwood Whole Foods. Emma didn't care that she was shamelessly scrolling for love in public—she had to find a new match soon if she wanted to keep her career and will to live.

"What do you normally get?" Her thumb hovered above a surprisingly intriguing profile. The man in the photos, who claimed he was a podcast producer named Will, looked secure but not cocky with his blond hair and bright blue eyes. He had an easy smile that ate up half his face and an entire photo dedicated to the books he had recently bought and wanted to read. Emma was delighted to see psychiatrist Viktor Frankl's *Man's Search for Meaning* in the pile; it was one of her favorites.

"I normally get regular because I don't think the pesticides can make it through a banana peel, but I don't want to get a lecture about it if you prefer organic."

"I think you have me confused with Jackie. I'll eat whatever."

Debbie nodded and put a few of each kind in the cart anyway. Emma didn't care though. She was too busy reading Will's answers to the app's often cringe-inducing prompts.

In response to "Two Truths and a Lie," he had written "My mom thinks I like her homemade jam more than store-bought jam and now I can never have good jam again." Emma chuckled. The answer was not just endearing but showed he was willing to disobey authority by ignoring the rules of the prompt. Emma appreciated that kind of independence when it came to things that didn't actually matter. She kept scrolling. In response to "The Dorkiest Thing about Me," Will had written, "If I make you breakfast, we can only use my mom's homemade jam and it is not very good." And finally, in reply to "This Year I Want to…" Will wrote, "This year I want to work up the courage to buy jam from someone other than my mom but that was my resolution last year too and I couldn't find the strength." Emma was officially laughing out loud to herself in a supermarket, which would be a perfect start to their love story as long as he didn't end up being a serial killer.

"Mom, look at—" But before she could shove Will's profile in her mom's face, Emma noticed she was being watched by a tall guy wearing a *Rick and Morty* T-shirt. When they made eye contact, he waved. Terror shot through Emma's body. The last thing she needed was a random client seeing her in her pajamas with her mommy. This could be worse than when Imani was high at Disneyland and ran into a client's entire family in the hour-long line for Space Mountain. Actually, that one was impossible to beat. Emma could always flee and wait in the car.

But as the man approached, Emma realized he wasn't a client after all. It was Rob... Something. The nice guy who lived next door to her at her first apartment after college. A guy who had tried, rather relentlessly, to make the move from neighbor/acquaintance to full-blown love interest only for Emma to dodge his advances at every turn.

As he confidently made his way past the oranges and apples, Emma had a hard time remembering why she had turned him down—multiple times. He had floppy brown hair and looked like he would fit right into one of Emma's favorite pop-punk bands with his thin frame and skinny jeans. He was middle-school Emma's epitome of a man. And adult Emma had similar taste.

"Emma Moskowitz! I thought that was you."

"Rob! Hi! It's been forever." Emma knew the next move was to hug but she suddenly felt shy. So she turned to Debbie, who was already staring at Rob with more interest than was socially appropriate.

"Mom, this is Rob. We lived next to each other in Silverlake."

Emma nearly shuddered at the memory. After graduating, Emma had thought living in the "coolest" part of Los Angeles would rub off on her. Instead, her immediate distaste for the area had further proved Emma's suspicion that young adulthood didn't suit her, and she moved west as soon as her lease was up. She felt more at home with the sixty-five-and-up crowd with their clean sidewalks and chain restaurants. And that was perfectly okay.

"Rob, so nice to meet you. I remember that building. It was..." Debbie searched for a diplomatic description as Rob stepped in to save her.

"A total eyesore. Which was why we could all afford it."

Both women laughed as they exchanged a knowing look.

"Why don't you two catch up?" Debbie suggested. "I need to find a few more things anyway. Meet at the car?"

Emma nodded as Debbie pushed her cart away. She and Rob watched in suspense as Debbie narrowly missed a pyramid of cantaloupes before turning back to each other.

"How have you been?" Emma asked, secretly hoping her life wouldn't pale in comparison.

"Good, thanks. I'm officially a doctor of radiology. So, if you break a toe or swallow something metal, I'm your guy. I mean I couldn't fix it or anything, but I could identify the problem and help you find a better doctor." He smiled and Emma remembered what the issue had been almost ten years earlier: Rob liked to shit on himself. Despite everything he had going for him, he was painfully insecure.

"They didn't cover how to fix a broken toe in eight years of medical school?"

"Sure, they did. But I specifically went into radiology so I wouldn't have to touch anyone's feet."

Emma laughed. Maybe what was once insecurity had morphed into flirtatious self-deprecation.

"Enough about my raging success. What's up with you? Are you living with the fam?" He vaguely gestured in Debbie's direction although she was now hidden behind the cereal aisle.

"Sort of. I have my own place—I've just been spending some more time at home. Kind of alternating between the two." This was an exaggeration bordering on a lie. Emma hadn't been back to her old apartment in weeks and her father was actively looking for someone to take over her lease. The misrepresentation gnawed at her. She decided to abandon the niceties of small talk. "I actually went through—or am going through— a broken engagement. So, it's been nice not to come home to an empty apartment every night."

Instead of looking shocked or uncomfortable by this overly vulnerable admission, Rob's eyes lit up. Despite his apparent pleasure in the news that she was single, he managed to say, "That must be really tough. I'm sorry."

"Thanks. But I'm doing okay. Trying to, you know, get back out there and flourish."

"You look fully flourished to me," he replied, and Emma felt her heart twitch.

"Rob seemed nice," Debbie said as she pulled out of the panic-inducing parking lot. Emma nodded, waiting to see if her mom could resist saying more. "What'd you two talk about?" Debbie stole a look at her daughter.

Debbie was big on respecting boundaries, mainly so she could enact her own and never have to address any potentially nosy questions about her personal life. So, while Emma was incredibly close to her mom and had spent an immeasurable amount of time with her, she knew very little about Debbie's childhood. Whenever she'd tried to ask, Debbie would say something like "Who cares about that!" and then change the subject to the latest *Bachelor* drama. As a daughter, Emma found this frustrating. As a therapist, Emma also found this frustrating. And a bit pathological.

"We were just catching up. He's a doctor now." Emma sneaked a glance at Debbie, who despite all her progressiveness was still a Jewish mother at heart. As expected, Rob being a doctor had brought a grin to her face.

"That's wonderful. Is he…um…seeing anyone?"

"I hope not. Because he asked me out. We're getting dinner on Thursday."

Debbie pumped her fist in the air like she had personally scored a touchdown. "How exciting, Emma! I have a great feeling about him."

"Great enough that you think he'll agree to marry me in five months?"

Debbie's face briefly revealed her skepticism about the entire plan, but she recovered with a grin. "I guess we'll just have to find out."

Eight

EMMA WAS FINISHING UP EDITING A NEUTRAL THIRD PARTY video when her phone buzzed. With Jackie's help, she'd filmed a Q&A where she answered questions from her audience about their relationship issues. She worried she'd been too harsh to a fan who wanted to know if it was okay that her boyfriend never said "I love you" unless it was a special occasion. Emma had gotten rather fired up during her response and was trying to finagle a more measured take in the edit. Clearly this man was withholding affection as a power move, but Emma didn't need to be on record saying he was a terrible partner—especially now that she had more eyes on her than ever. The sound of an incoming message was a welcome distraction from her limited editing skills.

Her home screen showed she had a new notification from Hinge and she immediately hoped it was from Will. After matching over the weekend, they'd been chatting on and off. He'd tried to lock down a time to meet in person but Emma was being cagey. She wanted to go on her first date with Rob before committing to anyone else. While others had no problem seeing multiple people at once, Emma knew herself. And she didn't want a nauseating sense of guilt—justified or not—hanging over her head as she tried to secure a husband.

Emma did her best to tamp down her excitement when she saw the message was, in fact, from Will. He had sent her a link to an article about Edith Wilson, the focus of his latest podcast project. Emma hadn't believed him when he told her Edith secretly acted as president for over a year while her husband, Woodrow, was recovering from a stroke. But a cursory glance at the article proved Will had been right. Emma sent back a mea culpa followed by multiple questions regarding how this was legally allowed.

As Emma stared at her phone longing for a response, she noticed the time and realized she was supposed to be across town in forty minutes—something that was nearly impossible in Los Angeles. Normally Emma was overly vigilant of the time, arriving most places early and ending every client session at exactly five to the hour (unless someone was in crisis). She wondered if it was a bad sign that she hadn't even left enough time to brush her teeth before her date with Rob. Or maybe it was good that she didn't feel the need to overly primp and prepare. They already knew each other; it wasn't the same as a normal first date. She didn't need to have nervous butterflies to fall in love—in fact, in some ways, she'd prefer not to. Romance and anxiety were experienced a bit too similarly in her body for her liking.

Emma arrived at the trendy wine bar about fifteen minutes late, which might have been the latest she had ever been to anything. She'd wasted some valuable time trying to parallel park in a spot that far exceeded her parking abilities. By the time she got through the door her bangs were damp with sweat and she irrationally felt like she was in a lot of trouble. But when Rob saw her, he didn't look mad. He looked delighted.

"I'm so sorry! I have no excuse," she blurted out as she barreled into Rob for a less than graceful hug. She noted that he had forgone another graphic tee for an overly tight button-down that didn't look comfortable or flattering.

"Don't worry, you're well within the acceptable range of lateness."

"Still. I hold myself to a different standard. Moskowitzes are never late. Except for my sister, which is why we made her take her husband's last name."

Rob laughed loudly. While Emma had always found her own jokes to be hilarious, she didn't know if this one warranted such a reaction. But she was happy to take it.

The waiter arrived and provided an extensive tour of the wine list. Rob and Emma both selected an Argentinean Malbec, mostly so they could be left alone. Emma wasn't even sure if Malbecs were red or white but she had discovered that the snooty waiter thought anyone who liked Riesling had no respect for themselves—and anyone who didn't like Bordeaux somehow had daddy issues. It was one of the strangest interactions she'd ever had with a person outside of her office; Emma was dying to dissect it.

"Well…that was *interesting*," Emma said, barely holding in her laughter as their waiter walked away

"I thought so too. I know almost nothing about wine," Rob remarked without a hint of sarcasm. Emma looked at him to decipher if he was just being polite or if he genuinely hadn't found the waiter's three-minute monologue about the evils and sadistic nature of organic wine to be off-putting.

"He was a bit intense, don't you think?"

"Maybe. But I always love when people are passionate about what they do. So many people hate their jobs. It's nice to find someone who cares."

Emma nodded. It was a good point. But her brain couldn't help but jump ahead to the possibility of a lifetime of not being able to connect over other people's weird behavior. If Emma got hassled by a man on the street about the restorative power of accepting Jesus into her heart while he flung a handwritten pamphlet in her face, was Rob just going to politely say how wonderful it was to see someone with such a profound spiritual life? One of the perks of having a partner was always having a safe space to trash-talk other people. She and Ryan had spent as much time dissecting what other people had said at parties as they did at the actual party. If Ryan had experienced that exchange, he would have made fun of their waiter for at least the next four to five months.

But Emma wasn't with Ryan anymore. And maybe the type of guys who didn't poke fun at other people's general existence also didn't abruptly leave their partners.

"So where are you living these days?"

Rob looked at her strangely. "You know where I live. You used to live there, too, remember?"

Emma did her best to hide her shock. "You're still at Baxter?"

Baxter was the name of their old street in Silverlake, and what she had taken to calling the hellhole apartment complex where she met Rob. The twenty-unit monstrosity was managed by a woman who seemed to hate both humans and material goods. Emma had once caught her kicking the lobby garbage can for no apparent reason other than "it was asking for it," which, quite frankly, was a pretty unhinged thing to admit. During the year she lived there, Emma had lost hot water about fifteen times and had three roach infestations. It was hard to believe anyone would stay if they had a better option. Or a medical license. But Rob merely nodded.

"Twelve years and counting. I think I'm officially the longest tenant other than that married couple in 3C."

"Oh my god. I can't believe they're still married."

"I don't think they can either."

The fights in 3C were a thing of legend. The combination of thin walls and booming voices meant everyone in the complex was always up to date on the latest drama between two people who looked like librarians and fought like reality TV stars. The night before Emma moved out, there was a huge blowout because the wife had bought the wrong kind of toilet paper—again!

"Do you like it there? I feel like all we did back in the day was talk about moving."

Rob shrugged and took a sip of the wine that had mercifully been dropped off by a silent busboy. "I don't hate it. And it's such a hassle to find a new place. I'd rather do that once I'm in a relationship and we're moving in together." Rob's eyes quickly met Emma's before diverting elsewhere.

Emma smiled to let him know he hadn't scared her off. Quite the contrary. "That's smart. It's always better to move in somewhere new together instead of one person having to claim space in the other person's home."

"Is that what you and Ryan did?"

Emma laughed in response—caught. "No, he moved into my apartment after my roommate left. Maybe that was the beginning of the end." Emma made a mental note to return to that possibility in therapy.

"Look, I obviously don't know the guy, and maybe this isn't my place, but he must have been an idiot to leave someone like you. I mean…" Rob gestured in Emma's general direction.

The compliment caught her off guard and emboldened her to admit, "You know what? I've thought the exact same thing a few times." *Wow.* It felt good to confess that, even if it made her seem arrogant. Why pretend she didn't have a lot going for her—including access to all her parents' various timeshares? The one in Mexico was breathtaking.

"I'm glad we're in agreement." Rob reached across the table

and brushed some hair out of her face. Emma felt herself float out of her body and observe the moment from above. Everything was objectively perfect.

Except for a gnawing sense that she should bat his hand away and run.

"You're not a real person to him. You're a trophy. A beautiful, midsize, trophy." Imani was spread out on their office couch, while Emma was perched in the therapist chair, although their seating arrangement didn't stop Imani from doling out advice.

"No, no. Rob's a good guy," Emma protested.

"How many times have you heard a client use those exact words to describe someone who was definitely *not* a good guy?"

Emma rolled her eyes as memory after memory popped up. She tried not to think about one woman who had said that *after* her boyfriend had stolen all her savings to start an exotic animal business. The things people do for love (and large reptiles).

"I get why you would think that, but I don't think he's the problem," Emma said. "I think I have an aversion to romance or something."

Imani looked at her with enough skepticism to turn a Catholic agnostic. "What do you mean by that?"

Emma shifted in her chair so her legs were tucked under her butt. She knew her body language was betraying any sense of authority she hoped to convey over her own experience, but it was more comfortable.

"Okay," Emma said. "So, you know how I love love?"

"Yeah, it's like half your personality."

"Well, I think I love love in the sense that it is wonderful to have a partner and someone to share your life with. But I don't want to stare into anyone's eyes or have them say sweet nothings in my ear for hours on end. To me, the best kind of love is more like a friendship where you also hold hands sometimes."

Imani nodded. "That tracks."

"But I think Rob might be more of a 'I made you this mix-tape because these are the songs I listen to when I think about you' kind of guy."

"What makes you say that?"

"He made me a mixtape."

"Stop!" Imani was so thrown she sat up and stomped the floor in disbelief. "For your first date?"

"After the date. And it wasn't a mixtape so much as a Spotify playlist."

"Show it to me."

"I can't. I'd die of mortification."

"Fine. Describe it to me."

Emma scrunched up her face. "I don't think I can. I'm too embarrassed." Mostly about the Coldplay. Not to mention the Celine Dion.

"So, what are you going to do, immediately break things off and change your number?"

Emma shifted her legs around again, essentially curling herself into a ball. "Not quite. We're going out again tomorrow."

"Emma!" Imani reached out and flung the tissue box at her. "Why would you do that?"

"Because I'm trying to break my old habits! Sure, maybe Rob can be a little cringey, but he's a freaking doctor who seems to be obsessed with me. I could do a lot worse."

"Since when is that the only barometer for finding the vice president of your life?" Imani asked, using Emma's own terminology against her.

Emma picked at an angry cuticle in response, wincing at the searing pain. "I think I should examine why outward displays of affection and romance make me so uncomfortable. And I think Rob is a safe person to do that with."

"Mm-hmm. And you also think he might just be nutty enough to agree to your ridiculous plan?"

"Don't say words like *nutty*. It's not nice."

Imani glared at her. "Do you know what's not going to be nice? When you find yourself married to a guy you can't stand."

"That's why they invented divorce," Emma joked back, even as a sense of dread took over her body.

Nine

AS EMMA HUFFED AND PUFFED UP THE STEEP HILL, SHE wondered how she'd ever had the stamina not only to live at Baxter, but park on the street every day. By the time she reached her former apartment complex, her calves hurt and her temples were moist. She thought she'd have a warm sense of nostalgia upon entering the worn-down lobby, but all she felt was relief that this was no longer her life. She made a mental note to try to remember that feeling since it was so distinctly different than her other thoughts of late, which were more of the *if only I could go back in time* variety.

Emma pushed the elevator button and prepared to wait an unseemly amount of time, but the doors opened immediately as though it had been sent down to retrieve her. She entered the small space and was hit with the interlocking smells of weed and cologne. It was surprisingly pleasant. Within moments she was standing outside Rob's door trying to figure out the best way to greet him. Considering they hadn't even kissed yet, it seemed like a friendly hug would be the way to go—unless he went in for a cheek kiss, which was one of Emma's least favorite social conventions. She didn't desire random people's lips on her skin in a nonsexual way. And, unlike other features of her personality, this didn't feel like something she needed to change about herself.

"I see you!" Rob's voice came through the still-closed door.

Emma jumped in response. If there was anything Emma hated more than a cheek kiss, it was being startled. She tried to calm herself down as Rob flung open the door, smiling. He wore an apron that said Talk Nerdy to Me. A small amount of vomit came up Emma's throat, but that could've just been the effects of afternoon coffee on her fragile esophagus.

"You made it." Rob embraced her as if they hadn't recon-firmed their plans only a few hours earlier.

"Of course. Thanks for making dinner."

"For you? Anything! Including pasta."

Emma followed Rob into his large studio apartment, which thankfully didn't look exactly the same as it had ten years ear-lier, like Tony's place. She was pretty sure the couch was dif-ferent and the walls that had once been covered in taped-up movie posters were now covered with framed movie posters. The overall vibe was very much one of a bachelor with a strong interest in the arts and no favorite sports team.

"Can I get you something to drink?" Rob asked as Emma had yet again wandered over to the bookshelf in search of rev-elations about its owner.

"I'll take some white wine if you have it." Her eyes returned to shelves filled with medical textbooks, graphic novels and a box set of *West Wing* DVDs that looked unopened.

"Saving President Bartlet for a rainy day?" Emma asked as she joined Rob in the kitchen area. His counters were a mess and already covered in pasta sauce. She tried not to think about the hygiene, or lack thereof, involved in home cooking.

"Saving who for what?" Rob looked over at her, more stressed than seemed necessary for penne.

"I saw your unopened *West Wing* DVDs. Are you a fan of the show? Or just a collector?"

Rob picked up a dull knife and began ineffectively chopping some onions. "Neither. They were a gift and I guess I just never got around to watching. I'm not that into politics."

"Not into politics as in not into watching acclaimed political dramas, or not into politics as in you don't vote?" She'd tried to be casual but her tone revealed the importance of his answer.

"I vote! I vote, like, every time I'm allowed to. It's part of being a citizen and everything. But..." Rob struggled to find a description that wouldn't make him seem like a privileged straight white man who didn't need to care about politics in order to survive and thrive. "I guess it's just not my passion or anything. I'd rather read a medical journal than try to follow which senator is the most racist of the day."

Emma nodded, content enough not to pry further. She had already ruined many a date night fighting about racist senators. Most notably when she had accidentally gone on a spring break trip with a Young Republican in college.

"Do you need any help?" Emma gestured in the direction of an overflowing pot of boiling water.

Rob jumped back before turning the heat down. He looked like he had been through war and still had to fight his way home. "No, no. You sit. I'll be done soon." He motioned to the sofa and returned to what was quickly becoming the greatest challenge of his adult life.

Emma wondered why he hadn't just bought a can of sauce instead of attempting to make his own. Maybe he hadn't realized she was surprisingly easy to please in the sauce department. That was one of the many strange parts of dating—you find yourself doing intensely intimate things for people you barely know.

A memory of Ryan holding her hair back while she puked from acid reflux on their third date popped into her head. It had been her first time at his place, and he hadn't even hesitated. He'd just rubbed her back and pretended the sound of her hurling wasn't a huge turnoff. Emma had barely known the guy but after that moment she felt safer with him than she had with anyone. He'd even sent her a bunch of articles the next day about how to reduce acid buildup. His genuine desire to find a way to help her feel better made her fall in love with him. It also allowed her to burp freely instead of holding it in.

But maybe it was time to let that love go to make room for someone else. Plus, Rob probably already knew a lot about acid reflux; he was a doctor.

Dinner was finally ready nearly an hour later. Emma stood awkwardly while Rob set the table, not letting her so much as lay down a mismatched fork. As he scavenged his kitchen drawers for matches to light two rather formal candlesticks, Emma wanted to point out that he was focusing on the wrong things. She wasn't there to be wooed by some archaic standard of romance; she was there to get to know him—and they'd barely said ten sentences to each other since she arrived.

But she also understood that nerves could get in the way of logic. That's why she nonsensically shouted, "Autograph my foot!" the one time she ran into Mark-Paul Gosselaar outside a popular restaurant. She hadn't been thinking clearly because she'd been overcome with nerves at meeting her childhood crush. Maybe something similar was happening now. Rob probably didn't date much, which would explain why their interactions always had a level of performance to them. She needed to make him comfortable enough to open up and be normal with her. Criticizing his "moves" wasn't the way to get there.

"Sorry, this took a bit longer than expected. I guess I don't have the red thumb I thought I had," Rob said.

"Red thumb?"

"Like a green thumb but in the kitchen."

Emma laughed, which made him break out into a splotchy blush.

"Oh, no. Have you never heard of that? Is this another thing my parents led me to believe was universally used but is really a made-up saying?"

Emma tried to suppress another laugh. She couldn't tell if Rob was going to be able to joke about this or if he was on the verge of tears. "I think they made it up. But I also think it's brilliant and I will be using it moving forward."

"Really?"

"Definitely. I mean, sayings have to start somewhere! Why not in your own family?" Rob looked at her with such relief it made her uncomfortable. She wanted to move away from the intensity of the moment. "What else have they made up?"

Rob leaned back in his chair, letting his brain whirl. "They call stomachaches 'ouchies.' If you said you had an ouchie, you immediately got a ginger ale and some crackers."

"Your parents sound awesome."

"Yeah, until you go to the nurse's office in high school and announce you have an ouchie in front of Steven Bombardo and get called Ouchie for the next two years like an idiot."

"Who is Steven Bombardo?"

"Just the most popular guy at my school. Quarterback, but could also make these incredible ceramics. Really cool dude." Rob looked off into the distance as though he was summoning the image of his high school idol/tormentor.

"But didn't he give you a mean nickname?"

Rob shrugged. "I was an easy target. You can't blame the guy for taking advantage of the situation. I mean, I thought *ouchie* was a medical term until I was fifteen—I deserved to be made fun of."

"I don't think anyone deserves to be made fun of. Except Republicans. And maybe those people who dye their dog's hair without their consent."

Rob smiled and reached for her hand. "You're a really nice person."

Emma smiled back. While the compliment felt sincere, she knew she hadn't earned it from him. For all he knew, Emma stole money from old people or left trash on the highway.

"I thought gunpoint was an actual place until I was an adult," Emma confessed. "Like when Cher from *Clueless* said she got robbed at gunpoint, I thought that was just a dangerous place in LA and people shouldn't go there."

She waited for Rob to laugh but instead he nodded, somewhat solemnly. "I can see how that would be confusing," he replied without a hint of irony.

Emma put some overcooked pasta in her mouth to keep from screaming. After a few more minutes of polite eating, Emma excused herself to the bathroom and immediately dialed Jackie.

"I've got to get out of here," Emma whisper-shouted into her phone as she climbed into the shower for added sound protection.

"What's wrong? Is he trying to murder you? Because you should try to leave strands of your hair around as evidence—"

"No! No. He's just… He doesn't get when I'm joking. And every time I say something, even if it's not that smart, he looks at me like I'm the greatest thing since sliced bread."

"I'm having a hard time locating the problem here," Jackie replied. "Are you complaining because Rob likes you *too* much?"

"Yes! No. I think Imani was right and he just likes the idea of me, not me as an actual person. Also, I think I maybe hate him." Emma hadn't meant to add that last part, but now that it was out, she knew it to be true and her desire to flee quadrupled. "I need an excuse to leave right away that won't completely destroy his already dangerously fragile ego. And you lie better than me. I need your best stuff. Please."

Instead of responding, Emma heard Jackie talking to someone else in the background, followed by a distinctly male murmur.

"Emma, we think you might be overreacting a bit. Isn't this guy a doctor?"

"Yeah…" Emma replied, already nervous as to where this was going and vaguely annoyed that Chris was involved in what she had hoped was a private conversation.

"And your main issue is that he likes whatever you're saying too much?"

"It's more than that. I don't think I'm attracted to him."

"Because of his looks?"

"No. He's good-looking."

"Because of his smell?"

"I haven't noticed his smell."

"Well then, you are definitely overreacting. He's probably just nervous. If you find a good-looking, nice doctor who doesn't smell and is obsessed with you, you don't just walk away because things are a little awkward at first. That would be insane."

From what sounded like a far distance she heard Chris shout, "Super insane!"

"Don't say 'insane.'"

"We won't if you act normal for once. Now go out there and get a better sniff." Jackie hung up the phone, leaving Emma to fend for herself. Which, quite frankly, Emma was not prepared to do.

When Emma left the bathroom—far too many suspicious moments after she went in—she was shocked to see Rob had moved over to the couch and dimmed the lights. He patted the seat next to him as though this was the inevitable progression of a great evening. Emma looked longingly toward the front door before making her way over to the neutral-smelling radiologist. She tried to remind herself that sometimes a physical barrier needed to be broken in order to break down an emotional one—or at least she'd been told some version of that at summer camp when her bunk mates had pressured her to kiss a boy she had never even *talked* to before. She'd gone for it, and they had somehow ended up "dating" the rest of the camp session even though they continued not to speak. It was a confusing lesson at the time.

But this wasn't the summer of '02 anymore; the stakes were higher. She wasn't just looking for a boy to hold sweaty hands with while avoiding eye contact during the talent show—she was looking for a life partner. And sometimes that required searching in unexpected places. She decided to push through her growing sense of ick and sat down.

"Hi," Emma said.

"Hi," Rob replied.

As he stared deeply into her eyes, Emma wondered why she had never enjoyed the lead-up to a first kiss. She always felt anxious to get it over with. That's why her favorite ones were when she was taken by surprise and didn't even have time to panic. Like how on the night she met Tony he had simply leaned in and kissed her goodbye as though they were already a couple. Her brain didn't even get to process what had happened until she was safely tucked in her Uber on the ride home. No anticipation anxiety, just the afterglow of realizing something magical had happened to her without her having to orchestrate it first.

"Can I kiss you?" Rob asked with a slightly deeper voice than normal. It reminded her of the guy from Moviefone, which was not an association that put her in the mood to do anything other than see a blockbuster.

"Um...sure."

Rob closed his eyes and leaned toward her mouth. As their lips connected, Emma tried to be in the moment and shut off her overactive brain. But all she could think about was the repetitive motion of Rob's tongue. She wondered if he knew that not all kissing had to be of the French variety. After about fifteen seconds of more of the same—like *exactly* the same—

Emma knew she had to get home to her toothbrush. And she realized she might have just the right play to get herself there.

"I want to get married," Emma blurted out as she pulled away from his still-open mouth.

Rob took a moment to process what she had nearly shouted before breaking into a grin. "I want to get married someday, too."

Emma shook her head, leaning into the role of a slightly more unhinged version of her true self. "No. I want to get married soon. Like on the same day I was supposed to get married the first time."

Rob sat back on the couch. "Okay…" He seemed interested instead of repulsed, which wasn't what Emma was looking for.

"Like I want to find a replacement groom and sort of just swap him in for Ryan so I can continue with my life as planned. I already have the venue and everything. It would be exactly the same wedding as I was previously planning with someone else."

Rob nodded as though what she was saying wasn't completely bonkers. She needed him to see the light and kick her out.

"I know that probably sounds a bit intense."

"Not necessarily. Weddings are expensive. And if you already have the venue…" Rob gazed at her with what appeared to excitement. "When's the date?"

"August 29. Of this year."

Rob looked at his Apple watch and seemed to do a quick calculation. "That should be more than enough time to get my family out here. That is—" he leaned in and cupped his giant hand under her chin in what she guessed was supposed to be a romantic gesture, but ultimately felt infantilizing "—if you're asking *me* to marry you."

Emma felt her stomach turn as she jumped up from the couch. "I have to go!"

"What?"

"I'm sorry. I'm really sorry. I thought… I don't know what I thought but this isn't going to work out."

Rob's eyes flashed with hurt. "Then why did you just ask me to marry you?"

Emma searched around for her purse, located it and made her way toward the door. "I didn't mean to! I thought if I told you my plan in the bluntest way possible you would be freaked out by it and ask me to leave. But I can see now that was misguided."

"Why do you want to leave? And what do you mean your 'plan'? Are you really trying to find a replacement groom or not?"

"Sort of. Not a replacement though. More of an upgrade."

Rob followed her to the door. Emma was quickly learning that all her professional training on delicate delivery of tough information went away the moment she was the one in crisis.

"I see. And I'm not an upgrade so you were trying to get rid of me?" Rob appeared on the verge of tears.

Emma took a deep breath and tried to regain some control over the deteriorating situation. She reached for his hand as a rush of thoughts shot through her. "Rob, I swear this isn't about you. I'm a mess right now. I came up with this completely delusional idea that if I could find a different groom in time for my original wedding, I could avoid all the hurt and pain that comes with being left." Emma barked out a laugh. "I even let myself think I could be an inspiration to other people. I thought I could reinvent marriage, for Christ's sake! But saying it all out loud to you just now made me realize how bananas the whole idea is. I clearly need to take a break from dating and get back to healing. I hope you can understand."

A moment passed and then Rob squeezed her hand three times as if they had some sort of secret signal. "I understand. Thank you for being honest. And if you ever feel ready to get back out there, you know where to find me." He opened the door, and she looked back at him one more time.

"Thank you. For everything."

He nodded solemnly before blowing her a kiss.

As Emma walked toward the elevator, she sent a mental thank you to her high school drama teacher whose years-old guidance had just allowed her to give the performance of a lifetime. It had been so convincing she'd almost believed it herself.

As the elevator descended, Emma opened Hinge and sent Will a quick message officially asking him out.

She was ready to meet. And she was ready to marry.

Ten

EMMA DIDN'T KNOW WHAT TO DO WITH HER ARMS. NOR-mally she was on her phone or holding client notes or gesticu-lating wildly as she told a story. But now that she was standing alone on a sidewalk waiting to meet Will, she felt the burden of having to look calm and casual. She didn't want his first image of her to be her head buried in Instagram, because she didn't want it to be extremely obvious that she needed con-stant stimulation to avoid an overwhelming sense of dread. He could learn that about her later.

Emma decided to try holding and stroking her own hand. It was a self-soothing technique that worked more often than she expected. As her right thumb caressed the stretch of skin between her left thumb and index finger, she felt the pound-ing in her chest start to calm down. Emma tried to remember that she was physically safe. Even if her body wanted her to flee and never go on a first date ever again.

"Laura?"

Emma turned and found a guy who looked exactly like Will staring at her. He was dressed in a fashionably understated light sweater and jeans. His combo of blond hair and blue eyes looked like it was right out of a J.Crew catalog.

"Are you Laura? Because I got this mysterious letter in the mail that said if I showed up here on this day and time and met a girl named Laura, I might be able to save the world."

"No, sorry." Emma smiled, catching on. "I'm actually here to *destroy* the world."

"Just my luck! Have a good one. And please spare my family." The guy took off down the street and for a very brief moment, Emma wondered if that actually was Will's doppelgänger on some sort of magical quest. But then Will spun around and grinned at her.

"I got you for a second."

"No way. I was just going along with the bit."

"If you say so," he teased before putting his arms out. "Should we hug?"

Instead of answering his question, Emma instinctively stepped into his embrace. Unlike with Rob, there was nothing awkward about the way they folded into each other. Will was on the shorter side, around five-eight or so, which helped their bodies line up. He also smelled clean and freshly shaven, two things Emma loved in a man given her obsession with hygiene and her overly sensitive skin. She overrode her desire to keep nuzzling and pulled away.

"It's so nice to finally meet you," she admitted.

"I wasn't sure this day would ever come. You certainly know how to give a guy the runaround."

"We matched like two weeks ago!"

"It was at least three, Laura." Will gestured for Emma to lead the way.

As she headed inside with Will right behind her, she wondered if this was the story she would get to tell her grandchildren. Probably not, her anxiety replied. Anxiety always liked to bet on the worst possible outcomes—and it was destructively easy for Emma to catastrophize given her brain's faulty wiring. But instead of falling into her old habits, she urged herself to ignore the pessimistic voice in her head and instead focus on how cute Will looked in his jeans. The side view of his butt cheeks helped her stay present.

"Welcome to Color Me Mine," a bubbly young woman or mature teen (Emma couldn't tell) called out from the back of the store. Emma was finding it difficult to guess people's ages now that she was officially over thirty. "Please select what you'd like to paint and then I'll help get you all set up."

"Thank you," Emma and Will sang in unison. It was good to know they were equally polite. Shared values went a long way in forming a healthy relationship.

"So, is this how you separate the wheat from the chaff? By seeing who can paint within the lines?" Will asked as they perused the store's ceramic offerings.

"This pottery doesn't have lines. That's how I can tell if someone does well under pressure."

"Smart." He held up a unicorn-shaped plate. "Think I can handle this bad boy?"

"Impossible to say. I barely know you," Emma teased even though it didn't feel true. She was having one of those rare experiences where it felt like she'd known Will far longer than she actually had. Which in this case meant more than six minutes.

After some excruciating decision-making and a brief tutorial on how to select and use the paints, Emma and Will were set up at a table for two. Emma had decided to tackle a practical tic-tac-toe set while Will had stuck with the unicorn plate.

"Should I be scared that you're a therapist?" Will asked as he mixed hot pink and navy blue on his palette.

"Only if you have something to hide."

"Nothing to worry about there. I'm what you professionals would call 'incredibly normal.'"

"I find that hard to believe. This place has a selection of over forty colors and you immediately decided to try to create your own." They both looked at the streaky mush of color that Will was trying to improve by swirling his brush.

"That was just me trying to impress you. You know, show off my creative and untamable spirit."

"When do you think you'll actually start painting?" Emma had already finished her first X. She'd gone with a light blue that reminded her of her favorite water bottle.

"In due time. I don't want to rush and mess her up." Will stroked the head of the unicorn plate in a way that would have been incredibly creepy if Emma hadn't already found him so charming. That was the real law of attraction: if someone already liked you, you could pretty much get away with anything.

By the time Will put the finishing touches on what they now referred to as Laura the Unicorn, Emma had already been done with her project for thirty minutes. But the extra time allowed for more conversation. So far, Emma had learned that Will was a podcast producer for one of the bigger networks. He'd also hosted a few midlevel shows of his own and hoped to one day create an audio empire full of important information and relatable narrators, because good stories changed the world. Emma loved the way he talked about his work. She'd never thought about how podcasts were basically an extension of the oral storytelling tradition before; it was clear Will thought about his impact on the world as much as she considered hers.

"So what do you think?" Will held up his plate. His meticulousness had paid off.

"She's beautiful."

"She's yours." Will handed Laura to Emma, who was more shocked than she should have been considering the unicorn's strong female energy. And the fact that Will had asked for her favorite colors while picking out the paint.

"Thank you so much. Do you want mine?"

Will considered the sloppily painted mess that was Emma's

tic-tac-toe set. She'd decided halfway through that she didn't like the orange she'd picked for the Os and mistakenly thought she could just paint over it with a different, brighter orange. The result was pretty awful.

"That is so sweet, but I don't want people to come to home, see what you made and think I'm a serial killer."

Emma shoved his shoulder in mock offense. She wanted to keep touching him but was socially aware enough to know now wasn't the time.

"All done here?" The upbeat employee from earlier hovered over their table. Up close, Emma still had absolutely no idea if she was over eighteen or not. "I'll take them in the back to get finished up and you can come get them any time after 4:00 p.m. on Monday."

"That sounds great, thank you," Will replied. He waited until the employee was safely out of earshot to whisper, "Is that a child? Or an adult?"

"I have no idea! I've been trying to figure it out this whole time."

"Same. Her face is very young, but her essence—"

"Is like a forty-year-old's."

"Exactly."

For a moment Emma and Will just sat there smiling at each other. It was wild how easy it was to connect with the right person. No uncomfortable silences. No second-guessing if she should make a certain joke or not. A second date felt like an inevitability—in the best way.

It reminded Emma of how simple it was those first few months she was with Ryan. Until everything went wrong.

"You okay?" Will had noticed the shift in Emma's mood. Her anxiety was back and she wasn't sure what to do about it. It felt like the fantasy of their potential relationship was crashing down around her even though nothing bad had actually happened.

"Yeah. Yes." She let out a fake cough to try to recalibrate. "We should probably get going." She gestured to the employee who was clearly cleaning up for the night. "Let her get back to her math homework."

"Or her three kids."

"Maybe both," Emma joked, feeling a bit more grounded in the moment instead of spiraling about the possibility of Will one day proposing and then breaking her heart.

"Not to be too forward, but would you want to get some ice cream?" Will asked as he held the door open for her.

"Will—" Emma turned to him and looked deep into his ocean-blue eyes "—if I ever tell you that I don't want to get ice cream, take me to the hospital. Because something is very wrong."

"I knew I liked you," Will said before bopping her on the nose in a move that seemed to surprise both of them. "Sorry. I don't know why I did that."

Emma laughed. It felt nice to not be the only flustered one for once.

Eleven

What's your last name?

EMMA HAD BEEN STARING AT WILL'S TEXT MESSAGE FOR multiple minutes while unintentionally holding her breath. She tried to think of a witty response that could evade the question without seeming suspicious. But so far all she'd come up with was "I don't have one" and "You first," which wouldn't really solve the problem for more than a few seconds.

"Have you seen your mother?" Alan asked as he entered the industrially designed open concept living room and found Emma splayed out on the couch. Debbie and Alan had done a full renovation five years ago and Emma's childhood home now felt like an edgy *Architectural Digest* spread filled with black doors and exposed brick. It was unlike any other house on their cookie-cutter, suburban-feeling street, and Debbie took a lot of pride in that.

"She went for a walk," Emma shared while hiding her phone under a heavy woven throw—as if that would make her problems go away.

"Without me? What the hell." Alan flopped himself on the

armchair perpendicular to the couch. "I told her I wanted to go. The Millers got new landscaping and I hear it's terrible."

"I think she wanted to be alone, maybe."

"What makes you say that?"

Emma wasn't sure how to respond. From a family systems point of view, she should let her parents figure this stuff out on their own to avoid triangulation. But as a meddler since birth, she couldn't resist telling her dad the truth.

"She might have said, 'Don't tell your father but I want to be alone,' before racing out of the house."

"Oh." Alan sighed, dejected.

"I wouldn't take it personally. She's always needed a lot of alone time."

"Why? I never need to be alone."

Emma laughed, even though he wasn't kidding. "You two are wired completely differently. You must know that by now."

"I guess I'll never understand her."

"You're in an adjustment period. For the last forty-four years of your marriage, you were at work every day. She got used to having a lot of space. Now she has to actively carve it out for herself."

"Why does she need space from her own husband?"

Emma sighed. This conversation was quickly turning into a full-blown session and she needed to tread lightly. "I don't think that's what's going on. But if it's upsetting you, maybe you should ask her about it."

Alan shook his head. Emma knew it was always easier to vent than communicate.

"Do you want to go look at the Millers' terrible landscaping with me? I hear it's full of hydrangeas." Alan shuddered at the thought.

"I'd love to, but I'm in a bit of a pickle at the moment. That guy Will wants to know my last name."

"How does he not know it already?"

"We met on an app. You don't have to share it on your profile if you don't want to."

"That seems incredibly dangerous."

"Definitely," Emma conceded. "But it also means he hasn't
been able to google me and find out about my not-so-secret
plan."

"You haven't told him about it yet?"

Emma squirmed. She had intended to bring it up from the
outset to avoid wasting anyone's time. If Will thought the whole
idea was absolutely bonkers, Emma wanted to know sooner
rather than later. But as the night had gone from painting to
ice cream, Emma failed to find a good window to share. It was
one of those dates where there wasn't ever a chance to change
the subject because the conversation just kept going. The only
moment of silence had come right before Emma had gotten in
her car and both of them were wondering if Will was going to
kiss her or not. After what felt like an eternity, he decided to
go for what Emma could only describe as a sensual hug.

While part of her had been disappointed, another part was
relieved. Unlike her failed make-out with Rob, kissing someone she actually liked felt like it would be the final lock on a
door she hadn't wanted to close. Rationally, Emma knew Ryan
was never coming back whether she slept with the entire city or
not. But for now, it felt safer to remain unkissed and delusional.

"It hasn't come up yet," Emma explained. "I just want to
make sure he hears about it from me and not the internet."

"Why not give him a fake name then? Like Bond. Emma
Bond."

Emma smiled at one of her father's favorite jokes. She couldn't
count how many times Alan had approached a hostess stand at a
restaurant and given his requested name as "Bond. Alan Bond."
Nine out of ten times the host had no reaction, but that didn't
stop him from continuing the bit.

"I think he might see through that."

"Smart guy. Well," Alan said while standing up, "as the monks say, honesty is always the best policy. Just tell him you don't like to be googled before you get to know someone in real life." And with that incredible piece of advice, Alan left to call his wife for the fourth time.

"Do you want to get a few things to split?" Will asked as they each perused the extensive menu at Genghis Cohen. The restaurant was an LA fixture that inexplicably combined Chinese food with a Jewish last name. Emma had grown up going every few months with her family but Will had never been.

"I have to tell you something," Emma confessed. Will put his menu down and looked at her expectantly. "I am not good at sharing food."

Will breathed a sigh of relief. "That's all? I thought you were going to tell me you were married or only had ten months to live."

"Which would have been worse?"

"Great question. Probably married. You can get a lot done in ten months."

Will was clearly joking but his take on time was promising. Maybe he wouldn't think five months was too rushed to get married after all. Or maybe Emma was grasping at straws to calm her nerves.

"I know in comparison being a bad food sharer doesn't seem like a big deal. But I want to warn you now, it will grate on you."

Will laughed, clearly unconvinced. "How so?"

"A myriad of ways, really. Group dinners? I'm a nightmare at those. Have to order my own separate thing that always confuses the waiter. New restaurant where you want to try a bunch of different things? Too bad. You have no one to share them with."

"Sounds pretty rough."

"It is. So feel free to get out now." Emma said this part lightly, like she couldn't care either way, but her insides proved otherwise. Every muscle from her toes to her shoulders tensed up as she waited for Will's reply. It was a clear signal of how much she already liked him.

"I think I'll take the risk. But I do need to know why you are so antisharing before I make my final decision."

"Fair. I guess it's a combination of being a picky eater and not liking to be surprised. My anxiety makes me have all these weird fears around food and I do better when I know exactly what I am going to eat. Otherwise, I spend the whole meal worried I'm not going to take the right amount of brussels sprouts or whatever is being split. If I order my own thing, I don't have to go outside my food comfort zone *and* I don't have to worry about portion control."

Will stared at her with an indiscernible expression. "I take it you're one of those therapists who also goes to therapy?"

Emma laughed, thrilled that he had poked fun at her instead of clamming up or taking it all too seriously. "Oh, absolutely. Almost since birth."

"Really? What do babies have to talk about?"

"Not enough milk. Difficulty communicating. Separation anxiety."

"Touché."

"Thank you. Although I was actually closer to eight when I started. It's sort of been on and off ever since."

Emma knew plenty of dating coaches and women's magazines would advise against sharing one's mental health struggles on the second date, but she always encouraged her clients to be open about the things that mattered to them—it was a good test to see how the other person received information. Like the time she told a college hookup she was on antidepressants and he tried to convince her to sell him some. This showed not only a lack of empathy for her psychiatric needs but also a fundamental misunderstanding on how antidepressants work. He was clearly thinking of Adderall.

"Why'd you go?" Will asked, looking genuinely curious and not at all judgmental. It made Emma want to tell him her entire mental health history, complete with a full list of medication side effects, but she restrained herself.

"I was having trouble sleeping because all I could think about was death."

Will nearly choked on his water. "I'm sorry. I just did not expect that to be the reason for an eight-year-old."

"It's okay. It *wasn't* normal for an eight-year-old, which is why I needed help. I'm lucky my parents took it seriously."

"That's awesome. I grew up with parents who think therapy is for quacks and drug dealers."

"Not sure I see the connection there."

"Neither do I. But Fox News isn't known for evidence-based theories." Will saw the look of concern on Emma's face and quickly clarified, "*I* don't watch Fox News, by the way, which is one of the many reasons my father doesn't talk to me. Apparently unintentionally raising a progressive son with a liberal arts degree wasn't on his to-do list."

"Having different politics than your family is hard. Especially right now."

"It actually makes it easier. At least for me. I can just tell people my dad is a Trumper and no one questions why we're estranged."

"I'm assuming you don't want me to question it either?"

"Maybe after a few drinks," Will said with a smile that didn't quite reach his eyes. Emma used all her restraint not to push. She felt strangely confident that he would tell her more when he was ready.

"So you've never been to therapy? And you live in Los Angeles?"

"I actually went a few times in college. My school offered some free sessions so my parents never found out."

"Did you like it?" Emma was always curious how other people felt about therapy since her own relationship with it had fluctuated so much over the years. As a kid, it had felt like punishment for being broken in some way. As a teenager, it had often felt like her only lifeline. And as a young adult, it felt like a professional calling that could help save the world. Now that she was usually the licensed expert in the room instead of the client, Emma was more aware of its limitations. Talking about feelings couldn't solve systemic issues like poverty or racism or completely change a family's dynamic. But, for some people, it did make a big difference.

"It was helpful. My girlfriend had just broken up with me and I was a wreck. My friends wanted to help me through it but twenty-year-old college radio DJs don't always give the best advice. So I went to a professional. He helped me realize my entire life wasn't over just because Cassey Richards didn't want to sleep with me on my twin bed anymore." Emma laughed as Will blushed. "I can't believe I just admitted I went to therapy over my college girlfriend."

"Hey, breakups are brutal. There's even a diagnosis in the *DSM* called Adjustment Disorder that's used when people go through a rough time following something like a breakup or a death and need some help getting back to baseline."

"That makes me feel better," Will said with a real smile this time. Emma loved that he was someone who openly wore his feelings on his face, unlike other men who had what she referred to as resting-nothing-face. Those guys always seemed more like moving statues than red-blooded humans. "What about you? Any therapy-inducing breakups in your past?"

Emma was keenly aware that this was the exact opening she'd been looking for. Will had just given her a chance to explain not just her humiliating broken engagement but her reasoning behind Operation: Save My Date. But just as she was bracing herself to potentially ruin everything that was growing between them, the waitress appeared, giving Emma the perfect opportunity to be a total coward.

After they ordered their separate appetizers and entrées, Emma deftly navigated the conversation away from breakups and into embarrassing stories about interactions with customer service people. Emma shared how she had once threatened to never return to a nail salon only to have to awkwardly sit there for another thirty minutes as they finished her manicure. Will confessed he had once spent two hours on the phone with an insurance agent because he seemed like a cool guy.

"How is that embarrassing for you? That seems lovely."

"At the end of the conversation I invited him to my birthday party."

"Did he go?" Emma asked, excited at the prospect of being able to make new friends through random phone calls.

"No. He laughed at the offer and quickly hung up."

"Wow," Emma exclaimed. "That's really embarrassing for you."

"I know! I had to change insurance."

"If it makes you feel any better, I would have gone to your birthday party."

Will grinned and she felt her stomach do a flip. He was a combination of all her teenage crushes come to life. If *Teen Beat* was still a thing, he could have been on the cover. She couldn't believe her luck, that in all the Jewish/Chinese restaurants in all the world, he was here with her.

Now if only she could figure out a way to legally keep him until one of them died. Then she could really relax.

Twelve

"I DON'T WANT TO BE PRESUMPTUOUS, BUT DO YOU HAVE any interest in going to my place to watch a movie?" Will asked as they walked out of the restaurant over an hour later. "Or maybe a sitcom we've each already seen ten times?"

Emma tried not to show how utterly thrilled she was at the prospect of taking things to the inside-each-other's-apartment level. "That depends. *Friends* or *Seinfeld*?"

"Ah. The Sophie's Choice of our generation."

"What if we went rogue and—"

Before Emma could finish her pitch, her right leg collapsed out from under her and she screamed in pain. "Oh my god! Oh my god!"

On the ground, Emma could see that her right kneecap was poking out the side of her leg. It was both disgusting and excruciating.

"Are you okay?" Will crouched down next to her, confused and shaken.

"I think I need to—"

WHACK. In one fluid motion, and completely on instinct, Emma hit her right hand against her patella, shoving the dislocated knee back in place. She felt immediate relief as the pain went from an eleven to around a six. She could handle a six.

"What just happened?" Will asked as if he had just seen an alien abduction or the passage of universal health care in America.

"I think my knee dislocated." Emma lifted herself into a seated position. She tried not to think about the fact that she was on a disgusting city sidewalk.

"Is that normal?"

Emma laughed, a little hysterically, as tears from the shock and pain started to roll down her face. "I don't think so."

"Okay, so we will get you to a doctor. Yes. That is what we will do." Will's panic was clear despite his new robotic-sounding voice.

Emma could only nod her agreement because she was now fully sobbing. She was keenly aware there were globs of snot coming out of her nose, but she didn't have the energy to do anything about it. If Will couldn't take her at her most vulnerable, well, she would understand.

"Can you stand up?"

"I can try." She put her arm out for Will to help her up. Her right leg felt weak and definitely injured, but with Will's support she was able to hobble.

"I'm parked like a block this way. Can you make it, or should I come back to get you?"

Emma's heart sped up at the thought of being left alone—even for a few minutes. What if a murderer came and she couldn't run away? Given how many terrible things had happened to her in a row lately, she couldn't risk being bludgeoned to death on a sidewalk.

"I can make it. We just have to go slow."

Will nodded and tightened his grip around her waist. It was the most physical they had been with each other so far, and even though Emma was still reeling from her dramatic collapse, she couldn't help but notice that her shirt had bunched up and his fingers were touching her bare skin. Even through the moderate pain, she knew she wanted more of this later.

"My car's not huge, but maybe we can fit you in the back seat." Will stopped in front of a dark green, two-door Mini Cooper.

"That's your car?"

Will laughed at the obvious surprise in her voice.

"Sorry... It's just very small. Like maybe it's not even a car at all."

"I assure you it is in fact a car. With a manual transmission, if it impresses you that I drive stick. But it only has two doors so getting you in the back seat might be a little tricky." Will watched as Emma assessed the situation and tried to put on a brave face.

"Maybe if you pull the passenger seat all the way up—"

"Better plan. Where are you parked?"

About fifteen minutes later, Will was expertly driving Emma's SUV toward the nearest urgent care center while she was spread out in the back with her leg up. The immediate shock was wearing off and Emma had officially stopped crying. For now at least.

"How you doing back there?"

"Good. It doesn't hurt if I don't move it," Emma said just as she shifted and winced. "Thank you so much for driving me. I know this isn't how you planned to spend your evening."

"You keep things exciting," Will replied. "Has this ever happened before?"

"Kind of. My left knee subluxated a few times when I was younger, which is when the patella pops out but then goes back in on its own. But this is the first time I've had an issue with my right one. And I've never had a full dislocation before where it pops out and stays out."

"How did you know what to do?"

"I didn't. It was pure instinct."

They caught eyes in the rearview mirror. It felt sexually charged despite Emma's puffy face and disheveled appearance. Maybe that even added to it, like how couples always got hot and heavy in disaster movies despite all the dirt; forced proximity and coursing adrenaline was a hell of a combination.

"I'm impressed. I would have just lied there in shock."

"No, you wouldn't have. You would have tried to make the pain stop."

"I don't know. I think there's a large chance I would have just wailed like a little baby until an ambulance showed up. We can't all be brave like you, Emma Whatever-Your-Last-Name-Is."

"Uh-oh. Are you going to try to look at my medical forms to find it out?"

"No. I'll respect your strange no-last-name policy," he said as they locked eyes again. "But once you do tell me, I'm doing a *full* internet deep dive."

Emma tried not to convey her horror at the idea. It would probably be less painful to dislocate her knee again than have her entire internet footprint combed by someone she actually liked.

"Oh my god, are you okay?" Debbie nearly shrieked as she and Alan barged into one of the patient rooms at Beverly Hills Urgent Care. Both of Emma's parents were too distressed to notice Will seated by the door.

"Were you hit by a car?" Alan asked rather accusatorily.

"Dad, I already texted you what happened. My knee dislocated as we were walking down the street."

Upon hearing the word *we*, Alan and Debbie whipped around to take in a tired but friendly Will. He stood up to properly greet them.

"Mr. and Mrs....?" Will looked to Emma for guidance she didn't want to give.

"Nice try. You can just call them Alan and Debbie."

Will gave Emma a playfully annoyed look before reaching out to shake her parents' hands. "So nice to meet you, despite the circumstances. I'm Will. This is my second date with your daughter, but I swear I won't let her get hurt on the next one."

Emma was incredibly pleased to hear there was going to be another date. Apparently a major medical emergency followed by prematurely meeting her parents wasn't enough to scare him off—this boded well for their future.

After pleasantries were exchanged and Debbie sneaked Emma a thumbs-up, Alan turned his interrogation tactics on Will. "Was she doing anything that could have caused this? Because you don't want to lie to the doctor just to avoid a little embarrassment."

"Dad, we were just walking! Don't be gross." Emma covered her face with her hands as Will looked confused. It took him a moment to realize Alan was implying Emma might have been hurt in the bedroom. But instead of being embarrassed at the implication, Will laughed and caught her gaze. Emma was impressed with his ability to appear so confident in front of her father. Maybe parental approval wasn't important to him given his background.

"Emma's telling the truth. We were walking to my car from the restaurant and the next thing I knew she was on the ground screaming."

"That must have been terrifying," Debbie said as she perched on the table next to Emma and stroked her hair.

"I almost had a heart attack. But Emma was a hero. She whacked her kneecap right back into place."

"Emma, you're not supposed to do that! You should wait for a doctor if you dislocate."

"How was I supposed to know that? It'd never happened before," Emma argued before realizing she didn't want to revert to a petulant teenager in front of her potential future husband.

She wanted to wait at least another month or two before he saw that side of her. "I didn't even think about what I was doing."

"It was pure instinct," Will added for her benefit.

Emma's cheeks felt warm at the thought of their charged moment in the car.

"Where is the doctor?" Alan demanded.

"I don't know. They put us in here over twenty minutes ago."

"I'm going to go talk to someone."

"Dad, you can't—"

But he had already stormed off. Alan always preferred to take action over ruminating in his feelings. Between him and her overly private mother, Emma wasn't sure how she had ended up being so open with her emotions. She probably had her anxiety disorder to thank for being so comfortable crying in public.

"Just let him go. You know what he's like." Debbie sighed. "Will, I'm sure you're exhausted. We're happy to take it from here if you want to get home."

"Oh," Will said with an adorable touch of surprise.

Emma and Will exchanged glances, but they were too early in whatever was happening between them to know what the other person was trying to convey. Emma hoped her eyes said, *You can totally go if you want but I'd much prefer you to stay.*

"I guess I should probably get out of your hair," Will said politely as he walked over to Emma. Debbie did a pretty good job of pretending to give them privacy by turning to read a sign on the wall about the Heimlich maneuver. "Can I call you tomorrow?"

"Yes, please. Sorry about…" Emma gestured to the lower half of her body.

"Never apologize about that," he whispered in her ear before giving her a kiss on the cheek.

Emma fought off a full-body shiver so as not to embarrass herself.

"Great to meet you, Debbie."

"You too. Maybe we can take you out to dinner soon as a thank-you for all your help?"

"I'd love that. Assuming Alan doesn't get arrested for assaulting a doctor."

Both women giggled like schoolgirls as Will waved and walked away. As soon as enough time had passed for them not to be overheard, Debbie squeezed Emma's hand and declared, "Lock him down."

Emma was certainly going to try.

Thirteen

"IT ISN'T FAIR EVERYONE GOT TO MEET HIM EXCEPT ME," Jackie complained as she set up the ring light. Since their last recording, Jackie had also invested in new second-living-room wallpaper that went better with Emma's "ghostlike" skin tone. Emma probably should have been offended by the description but she knew the redesign was an act of love.

"It's not like I planned to dislocate my knee to orchestrate the meeting. I didn't even invite Mom and Dad to the urgent care. They just showed up."

This was technically true, but Emma knew as soon as she told them where she was headed they were going to come. They were "those parents" and based on all the other types she'd heard about over the years, Emma's gratitude outweighed her occasional annoyance.

"Mom is obsessed with him by the way. She keeps mentioning his striking blue eyes and asking me where to take him to dinner."

Emma smiled as she imagined the four of them at a nice restaurant together. No more tables for three and an empty chair to remind Emma she might be unlovable.

"I told her I'd only make a recommendation if Chris and I are allowed to come."

"Jackie! What are you trying to do, scare him off?"

"If a free dinner with your immediate family is enough to scare him off, good luck planning the wedding."

Emma tried to stop her face from betraying her feelings, but she wasn't quick enough and Jackie noticed.

"What?"

"It's just… I think I really like this guy. I know it's only been two dates and we haven't even kissed—"

"You haven't kissed yet? What if he's awful at it?"

"He won't be. Or maybe he will be and it will ruin everything."

"It won't ruin everything. Chris was a tongue darter when we first met and now he's fine."

"What is a tongue darter?"

"You know." Jackie quickly stuck her tongue in and out of her mouth a bunch of times. "But I told him to stop and he got better. Men need direction or they're completely useless."

Emma tried to vanquish the image of her hugely successful brother-in-law playing what sounded like tongue Whac-A-Mole in order to focus on the task at hand. "I'm just worried that if I bring up Operation: Save My Date I might sabotage something real. Or the potential for something real."

"Emma." Jackie squatted in front of her sister, which was a little awkward because Emma was currently sporting a cumbersome knee brace. She needed to wear it for the next two weeks before starting physical therapy. It wasn't an ideal time to have to dress with a brace in mind, but she figured if she didn't make a big deal about it, neither would her subscribers. "You can't give up just because you're scared. If Will doesn't get what you're trying to do, then he isn't the right guy for you in the first place."

"Is that true though? Because what I'm trying to do is pretty bananas."

"How many new YouTube subscribers have you gotten since you announced the plan?"

"I'm not sure."

"Fifty-two thousand." Jackie waved away Emma's surprised look. "I've been monitoring the stats. This thing you're doing is *huge*. People are invested. It's giving them hope for their own lives."

"Or they're watching to see me fail."

"Who cares why they're watching! You can't give up now. It wouldn't make any sense."

"You don't think fostering a healthy relationship without a ticking clock makes sense?"

"Not really. Because what happens if he turns out to be another Ryan? You'll have invested years of your life in another failed relationship *and* you won't be socially relevant or have a best-selling book. How is that the smarter choice?" Jackie was now standing above Emma with her arms crossed. Emma felt like she was in the principal's office. "Tell me. How is that the feminist option? You'd be putting a man's preference above your entire life and career."

Emma nodded as Jackie's words sunk deeper and deeper. "You're right. I'll tell him and see what he says. If he says no, it won't be the end of the world. I'll just keep looking."

"Exactly. And I'll help." Jackie smiled before returning to her position behind the tripod. "Now go check the mirror before we start recording. You have lipstick all over your teeth."

"Look at you," Will teased as he opened his front door to reveal Emma, her knee brace and a star-covered cane. She was glad his downtown apartment building had an elevator, even though she otherwise loathed the area. "I love the outfit."

"Thank you. I ordered these leggings special so they would

fit under my brace. They're already tearing," she announced
with a hair flip.

"Sexy," Will said seductively. Emma's brain knew he was
kidding, but her body...not so much. She resisted the impulse
to push him against the door and see if his tongue darted or
not. "Come on in."

Will led the way into his one-bedroom apartment. It was
on the eighth floor and had huge windows looking out over
the closest Los Angeles had to real city streets. The floors were
made of cement, but Will had managed to make the space feel
inviting with different colorful rugs. His walls were covered
with podcast art and framed photos of what Emma assumed
were his travels. She tried not to appear overly curious, but she
was happy to see everything looked clean.

"How are you feeling? I bought this sectional so you could
put your leg up." Will gestured to the inviting navy couch.

"Really?" Emma asked, completely shocked—until Will
started to laugh.

"No. That would have been super weird. But I do think it
might be your best option to get comfy."

"I think you're right." Emma hobbled over to the far end of
the couch. She carefully scooted her butt all the way back and
then put both her legs up. Will sat next to her. She felt herself
get nervous, which meant she was about to start talking a mile
a minute. "This couch is perfect. Where did you get it because
my parents are looking—"

Without any warning Will interrupted her word vomit with
his lips. They were soft and big and Emma immediately felt like
she wanted to crawl inside his mouth. She kissed back without
worrying if she was coming on too strong, and within seconds she moved to straddle him only to realize she couldn't
because of her knee. This left her in the uncomfortable position of hovering over him. After a moment of awkwardness,
they both laughed.

"Sorry. I forgot I can't bend my leg." Emma moved herself back into her original position even though she wanted their bodies to keep touching.

"I'm sorry I came at you like that. It was pure instinct."

Emma snorted at the callback. Then she had a second wave of delight as she realized they already had inside jokes. "Honestly, I'm glad you did. I hate the lead-up. It's much better to get the first kiss out of the way so we can relax."

"So why didn't you kiss me on the first date?"

"Oh, you know, patriarchal double standards. And I'm a coward."

Will laughed again as he tucked some hair behind her ear. "I've got two pitches for you right now. One: we order some food and put on a show. This option involves a lot of laughing and probably dessert. Two: I give you a tour of my apartment that ends in my bedroom. Totally up to you. Both options—"

"I'll take the tour," Emma replied as her heart raced.

"Great choice." Will reached out to help her up. "Over there is the kitchen. This is the living room." He put his hands on her waist, directing her from behind to walk down the narrow hallway. "To our left we have the one very small bathroom, but I assure you it gets the job done. And to our right—" Will veered Emma into his bedroom "—is where the magic happens."

"Oh no. You ruined it," Emma retorted without missing a beat.

"Damn it. How close was I to closing?"

"*So* close. But now I'll have to leave and never speak to you again."

"Wait! Give me a redo. Can I have a redo?"

"Fine."

"Whew. Okay, come with me." Will led Emma back out into the hallway to re-create the moment. He put his hands back on her waist and he once again navigated her into the room with the help of her cane. "And to our right," he paused for dramatic effect, "is my bedroom."

He looked at her expectantly, with his eyes wide and his head tilted to the side. She burst out laughing. "Much better."

"Oh, thank god." Will sighed before kissing her again.

Kissing standing up made it much easier for Emma to press her body against his. Her brain noted how much better it was to make out with someone closer to her own height—no neck craning or tiptoes involved.

As Will expertly moved them both toward the bed, Emma let her cane drop to the floor. It made a loud noise, breaking them apart, which offered a moment to check in with each other.

"Is this okay?" Will asked, breathing heavily, pausing on his way to take off her shirt.

Emma loved how obvious it was that he was into her. Ryan had always maintained his composure until right before he climaxed. It had made her feel self-conscious about fully giving in to the moment. But with Will she already felt like she could scream in ecstasy, and he would join her.

Emma reached her arms up to imply consent and make it easier for Will to undress her. She then leaned over and pulled his shirt off. His chest was covered in more dirty blond hair than one would expect from his boyish face. She immediately ran her hands through it.

"How should we...?" Will gestured to the brace on her leg.

"Maybe I should lie down first, so no risk of another collapse?"

"Great idea."

They both made the final few steps to the bed. Emma lay down on her back, while Will remained standing. She took in his body and realized it didn't feel weird or wrong that she was about to have sex with someone other than her ex-fiancé. For someone who was nervous ninety percent of the time, she felt in control and at ease.

Will gently took her right foot in his hand and slowly lifted her leg up. He expertly un-Velcroed each strap before sliding the entire brace off and placing it lovingly on the floor. It felt more intimate than getting her underwear stripped off. Emma shimmied out of her leggings and pulled him on top of her. His full weight on her body made her feel both safe and horny.

"I like you a lot," she confessed without thinking.

"I like you a lot too," Will replied immediately.

And then, for the first time since they had met, they stopped talking.

Fourteen

EMMA SAT ON THE TOILET WILLING HER BODY TO PEE. SHE knew she needed to to avoid one of her biggest fears—a UTI—but her brain and heart were still in overdrive, leaving very little energy for her pelvic floor. She just had sex with Will! And it had been *good* sex. The kind she was normally only able to achieve after a commitment of monogamy and at least one hit of weed (anxiety wasn't the sort of thing that simply went away when she took her clothes off). But now the approximately fifteen-minute reprieve from her normal self was over and she was back to panicking.

The moment they had finished Emma had sprung from the bed, thrown on her knee brace and declared she "had to take care of lady business." Will had laughed, apparently already knowing her well enough to not be offended by her abrupt departure. Her body had wanted to stay and cuddle with him, but her personality wouldn't allow it. She had to figure out how to explain Operation: Save My Date to him before it was too late and he felt overly manipulated. Her mind turned as she tried to relax her bladder.

A few embarrassingly long minutes later, Emma emerged

from the bathroom completely naked except for her right knee, which was safely secured in neoprene. She did her best to sexily saunter into Will's bedroom despite her limp. He immediately looked up and smiled.

"Success?"

"Eventually. The female body plays by its own rules."

Will chuckled and pulled back the covers so Emma could crawl in and snuggle up next to him. He put his arm around her and sneaked a kiss on the side of her head.

"That was really nice," he murmured, causing her insides to stir. In another version of her life, Emma would be climbing on top of him to initiate a second round, but in this version, she took a deep breath and braced herself for everything to be ruined.

"I have to tell you something."

"How bad? On a scale of one to ten?"

"That's going to completely depend on your reaction." Emma shifted herself into a seated position and Will, sensing this was actually important, did the same. They both leaned against his blue suede headboard. "I'm about to unload a lot of information on you. Is that okay? Or would you rather get dressed first and sit at the kitchen table?" Emma knew she was stalling but now that the moment of truth was finally here, she would rather be anywhere else.

"I actually prefer to have tough conversations in the nude," Will joked, although it was clear he was getting worried.

"Let me preface this by saying that none of this is inherently bad. You might actually find it unique and exciting."

"Are you about to sell me a time-share?"

"No. Although my parents do have quite a few." Emma breathed in through her nose and out through her mouth. "The reason I didn't want to tell you my last name is because about eight weeks ago my fiancé walked out on me."

"Oh, Emma. I'm so sorry—"

"Thank you but if you start to be nice, I will cry and then I won't be able to tell you all the things I need to tell you."

Will nodded and pretended to seal his lips but his eyes conveyed too much empathy for her to keep looking at him. She turned her head in the direction of his closed closet door. Even in her emotional state Emma found herself wondering if he hung up his clothes or kept them in piles. She guessed a mix of both.

"When Ryan—my ex-fiancé—left, I thought my entire life was over. And not just in the typical *I can't live without him* kind of way. It made me question my entire career and identity. I'm a couples therapist and I had no idea my own partner didn't love me anymore? How pathetic is that?"

"I don't think it's pathetic."

"I won't fight you on the logic of it, but it's how I felt. Like a huge freaking failure who was going to die alone after getting her book deal canceled."

"You have a book deal?" Will asked, equally shocked and impressed.

"I told you, it's going to be a lot of information all at once."

Emma took a risk and looked at him. Will's blue eyes were locked on her face and his (naked) body language exuded a calm she certainly didn't feel. Why was he not freaking out? Or faking an emergency before throwing her out of the apartment, never to be heard from again?

Instead of doing either of those highly understandable things, Will reached out and wiped away a tear that had escaped down her cheek. "It's okay. You don't have to tell me all of it if you're not ready."

"No. I have to tell you all of it now before I—" Emma realized she was about to say *before I fall in love with you.* She quickly cleared her throat and changed her approach. "Before things keep progressing between us."

"Can I say one thing first?"

"Okay, but it will probably make me cry more. I'm a big crier. You should know that."

"I'll add it to the list. No food sharing and order tissues in bulk." Will smiled. Despite her nerves, Emma felt one start to form on her own lips, which really proved the complexity of being alive.

"What I wanted to say," Will added with the most apprehension she'd seen from him thus far, "is that I think I know a little about how you're feeling. I've never been engaged, but I did live with my ex for four years until she left me for a fellowship in England. She didn't even ask if I wanted to come. She just packed up and left."

"That's terrible."

"Yeah, it was." For a moment Will looked like he was getting pulled back into the memory before he returned his gaze to Emma. "But it got easier. Sorry to hijack your big speech. I just didn't want you to think you were the only one in this bed who's been unceremoniously dumped."

Emma reached for his hand and gave it a squeeze. "I've been unceremoniously dumped *many* times. This one just stung the most." Will laughed and it gave Emma the courage to keep going. "Part of what made it so excruciating is that I have this YouTube channel…"

"Okay, now I understand why you didn't want me to know your last name. I'm going to have to watch everything."

"I had a feeling you'd say that, which is why we needed to have this conversation first." Emma realized she should have prepared for what was about to happen. Or at least done a role play with Imani to make sure she wouldn't sound completely bananas. "You see, my entire channel is meant to be a professional resource about therapy and relationships. But about a year ago, I started including Ryan in some of the videos to help demonstrate communication skills or review how we moved past a certain conflict. He became sort of a fan favorite, so I put him in more and more stuff."

"I get that. Audiences love authenticity, right?"

"Exactly! But when he left…" Emma trailed off, hoping that Will's emotional intelligence would help fill in some of the blanks.

"You thought you would lose them too."

Emma nodded, increasingly grateful for this man in front of her. "Then I had this idea. And at first, it's going to seem really bonkers and intense, but I think if you give me enough time to explain you'll see where I'm coming from and maybe even want to be a part of it."

"Oh my god. You want to murder Ryan and you need my help." Will shifted himself into a more upright position and flexed his biceps. "Where does that punk live?"

"Honestly, I have no idea," Emma replied with a laugh. "But that's not what I wanted to pitch you."

Emma took another one of her calming breaths and started to explain the strangest plan she had ever made.

"You haven't said anything in twelve and a half minutes," Emma announced. She and Will were now fully clothed and standing in his kitchen. As soon as she'd finished describing Operation: Save My Date, Will had jumped up from the bed and declared he needed coffee to properly process this new information.

"Pour-over coffee takes a lot of concentration. I don't want to mess up the ratios."

"Okay," Emma conceded. If she wanted any shot at keeping him, she knew she couldn't push too much. She went to sit at the dark wood kitchen table while he finished pouring his culinary masterpiece into two mugs. One was from *This American Life* and the other said, "Careful or you'll end up in my next podcast" in italicized font.

"Here you go." Will handed her the kitschy mug as he sat at the table.

"Thank you," Emma replied. "So, on a scale of one to ten how freaked out are you right now?"

"I'd say maybe an eleven or twelve. I guess I can't figure out why you think you need to do this."

"I don't *need* to do this. I want to. It's an opportunity for me to build the life I want and make a real difference."

"And the real difference would be proving that you can replace one guy with another guy whenever you want?"

"No. Of course not. The real difference would be showing that love isn't some magical thing you have to passively wait for. It's something you can choose to create with another person."

"Uh-huh," Will said, not at all sounding convinced.

"Look, I know how it sounds, but plenty of people get married after only knowing each other for a few months. Think about arranged marriages or soldiers about to go off to war."

"But those people weren't planning a wedding with someone else a month before."

"We can't know that for sure," Emma offered as a weak attempt at levity.

Will ignored this and used his right hand to massage his forehead. "It just sucks because I really liked you."

"I really like you, too," Emma replied—even though his use of the past tense tore through her heart like shrapnel.

"Then why are you doing this?" Will asked as he lifted his head up. "Why can't we just date and get to know each other at our own pace?"

It was a good question and one that Emma had certainly asked herself during his quiet period of contemplation. But she was already too far in. If she gave up now, she'd have no credibility and, more importantly, she might end up right back where she started: single and heartbroken. But older. Which, in an ageist society, was never ideal.

"What part is bumping for you the most? Do you not want to get married?"

"No, I do, eventually. Once I really know the person."

"Right, except that's the flawed part. We think a certain amount of time will protect us from making a mistake or getting hurt. But you were with your ex for how long?"

Will rolled his eyes, seeing where this was going. "Four years."

"Which is more than an acceptable amount of time to commit to someone. And yet..." Emma had the decency to trail off instead of stating the obvious: *she still left.*

"Look, I know relationships always come with risk. But let's be real, Emma. This isn't just about revolutionizing our approach to marriage or whatever you're telling yourself. This is about subbing in one human being for another one so you can still have a big party and look like a success."

Emma felt Will's words hit her like tiny glass shards. The sting was immediate, and the damage would be hard to extract.

She stood up from the table. "I should probably go."

"Yeah. You probably should." Will stood too, reaching for her mug as if to clear all evidence of their brief love affair. She hated herself for wishing he would change his mind and ask her to stay.

As he led her to the door, Emma turned to him one last time. "Are you sure you don't want to take a few days to think about it? I can send you one my videos where I probably do a better job of explaining everything."

"I'm not going to change my mind. So unless you are planning to change yours we should probably call this thing."

Emma nodded as she looked down at her watch. "Time of death: 8:52 p.m."

Fifteen

"LOVE IS A CHOICE. LOVE IS BUILT, NOT SPARKED. LOVE IS..."

Emma let out a groan and hit the delete key on her computer. Rewriting her book was turning into as frustrating a pursuit as finding a new husband.

"You okay?" Imani asked from across the table. They were having one of their legendary after-work work sessions at the coffee shop across from their office. Imani was finishing up client notes while Emma attempted to salvage her biggest career opportunity—and not obsessively think about Will. Or that thing he did with his tongue.

"I don't know how to write a book. Why did anyone think I could write a book?" Emma lamented as she let a wave of self-pity wash over her.

"Have you looked at the state of the publishing industry lately? It's not about who can *write* a book. It's about who can *sell* a book. They wouldn't have given you a contract if they didn't think you could deliver on that part."

"But what if the contents of the book are bad? Like, 'makes no sense, long rambling sentences followed by glimmers of a mental breakdown' bad?"

Imani shrugged. "Most people don't actually read self-help books after they buy them."

Emma had to admit this was somewhat comforting to hear— even if it wasn't a good sign for humanity. "If I pay you one million dollars, will you finish the book for me?"

Imani smirked. "Show me proof of funds and I'll consider it."

"What about five hundred dollars and I'll handle all your insurance billing for the next year?"

"Counter: ten thousand dollars and you handle all my insurance billing for the next *five* years."

"That's extortion and you know—" Emma's phone lit up with an incoming call and she forgot to finish her sentence. "Oh my god. Will is calling me."

It had been exactly six days since their disastrous encounter. Jackie had spent the entire time trying to get Emma back on the apps, but Emma was still too upset to banter with strangers. They'd finally agreed she was allowed one full week off from the operation before diving back into a sea of awkward messages and the occasional dick pic. The wedding was less than five months away after all; every swipe counted.

"Really?" Imani asked, rather surprised. "Maybe it's a butt dial."

"Why are you assuming it's a butt dial?"

"Why are you assuming that man wants to talk to you after your last interaction?"

Emma's phone faded to her lock screen. "Shit. I missed it."

"Maybe he'll leave a voicemail," Imani joked. No one left voicemails anymore, unless they forgot to hang up in time.

"I'm going to call him back," Emma declared, grabbing her phone and heading toward the door. "If I'm not back in five minutes, order me another scone. Actually, order me another scone either way."

As the surprisingly cool evening air hit Emma's face, she felt her heart rate quicken. Was it possible that Will had changed his mind? Was Emma finally going to receive good news for once? She prayed to whoever would listen as she hit the necessary buttons to call him back.

"Hey," Will answered after only two rings.

"Hi," Emma replied. A moment of complete silence followed that was as emotionally excruciating as the time her sixth-grade crush asked Emma to set him up with Jackie—even though Jackie was a high school junior. It was the first time Emma understood that most boys would rather swing for the fences than settle with her.

"You're probably wondering why I called."

"A little, yes," Emma lied. She wanted to know why more than anything in the world. But considering the massive amount of rejection she had faced in the last few months, she had to pretend to have *some* dignity.

"First, I want to apologize. I was probably too harsh on you the other day. If my job has taught me anything it's that just because I don't understand something doesn't mean it doesn't make sense to someone else."

Emma felt her entire body deflate. It didn't seem like he had suddenly come around to Operation: Save My Date. "Thank you. I know how it probably seems to you, but it isn't about replacing someone. It's about building the life I want for myself."

"Absolutely," Will agreed a little too eagerly. Emma didn't understand why he sounded so nervous. "I actually watched all your YouTube videos about it after you left. You've really hit a nerve with people. The comment sections are out of control."

Emma let a small laugh escape despite her best effort to keep her guard up. He was right. People were writing paragraphs back and forth on whether Operation: Save My Date was brilliantly revolutionary or, to quote one commenter, "a clear signal of humanity's active decline due to loneliness and depravity." She'd stopped reading after that one.

"It's definitely started a conversation." Emma wanted to say more. She wanted to share all the ways this experiment had already changed her—along with her doubts and fears around pulling it off. But Will hadn't earned that. He was no longer her potential future; he was just another guy who'd said no.

"How would you feel about continuing that conversation with me? For a new podcast?"

"Is that a joke?"

"Why would it be a joke?"

"Because of that mug you gave me the other day. 'Careful or you'll end up in my next podcast.'"

Will laughed, and then laughed a little more. "I guess our merch says that for a reason. It's a side effect of the job. Whenever we meet interesting people, we want to pick their brains and mine them for content."

"How lovely," Emma quipped. Even though she knew she was guilty of something similar on her channel and in her book.

"You don't have to decide anything now. But I threw the idea around to some of my bosses and they think it has legs. I'd basically follow your journey and interview you and the people in your life about Operation: Save My Date. It'd be good publicity for your channel and brand. And maybe it'll change some people's minds about Western dating culture."

Emma scoffed. "You don't mean that last part."

"Hey, I'm not opposed to any outcome that gets us listeners. But I'll admit that's not my main priority. I'm more interested in the human side of it all. What it means on an individual level for you to try to make this work and the impact it will have on your life."

"Mm-hmm."

"You know, you were much more receptive to my ideas when you didn't hate me."

"I don't hate you," Emma replied. She stopped herself from admitting that her main hesitation came from how much she *didn't* hate him. That she probably liked him too much to continue seeing him on a regular basis without being able to touch, kiss or grab him. "I just need to think about it."

"Fair enough. Let me send you some more info about what I'm envisioning. I'd want it to be something we're both excited about."

"You don't think it'll be weird? After we…" Emma refrained from giving the full play-by-play of what had happened between them in his bedroom. Even though it had been running on a loop in her head since she left his apartment. "You know."

"It will absolutely be weird. But I think that's part of the charm."

After Emma told him her email address and they hung up, she made her way back inside. She saw a pile of scones waiting for her and was glad they would soften the blow of Imani's reaction; her extremely rational best friend wasn't going to be pleased about this new development.

Her sister, however, would be thrilled.

"This is incredible!" Jackie squealed when Emma told her the news. The entire Moskowitz crew was having a barbecue in Jackie and Chris's enormous backyard—although Emma didn't know if it counted as a real barbecue if all the food was catered.

"I haven't agreed to anything yet." Emma's eyes flitted to her nieces playing on their custom handcrafted jungle gym as Alan and Debbie watched and occasionally applauded. A successful family life always looked deceptively easy to achieve from the outside. And maybe it was—for other people. "What if I'm being set up to look like a total idiot?"

Jackie waved Emma's concern away. "Who cares? You won't sound like an idiot, because you're you. And if they give you a bad edit, we can just sue."

"I don't think you can sue over a bad edit."

"Please, you can sue over anything. This is America."

"You really think I should do it? Even though I still have feelings for Will and have no actual prospects for a new groom?"

These were both points Imani had been quick to call out after Emma had shared the news of Will's pitch immediately following their phone call. Imani thought that Emma teaming up with her sort-of ex to mine the most vulnerable time in her romantic life for content was the total opposite of sound judgment; her exact words were, "Agreeing to do this podcast is the emotional equivalent of walking into a nuclear disaster site wearing a bikini."

But Jackie didn't seem the least bit concerned. "Absolutely. Just turn those feelings for Will off and get back on the apps."

"Jackie, you don't actually think people can turn their feelings off, do you?"

"Please. I do it all the time. Izzy has this one friend whose mom is a total nightmare. Always late for playdates, talks shit about all the other moms—which means she's also talking shit about me. But whenever I see her, I put on a smile and act like everything's fine and we're totally friends. She even invited me to her fortieth-birthday extravaganza in Turks and Caicos—not that I would ever go."

"I think what you're talking about is *suppressing* feelings, not turning them off."

"Same difference." Jackie's gaze suddenly flung toward her children. "Hey! Spit that grass out of your mouth."

Emma's youngest niece, Amelia, instantly complied and a green glob fell to the ground.

"You're not going to believe this," Chris shouted as he bounded over from inside the house. His laptop was dangling from his hand, and he wasn't wearing any shoes. "I found him."

"Found who? And why aren't you wearing your slides? I put them by the sliding doors for this exact—"

Chris cut his wife off, which was almost unheard-of in their dynamic. "I found Emma's new husband."

Sixteen

APPROXIMATELY ONE HOUR LATER, ONCE THE GIRLS HAD settled into their pajamas and designated screen time, Chris gathered the adult Moskowitzes around the ten-person Calacatta marble kitchen table. Emma and Jackie had unsuccessfully been trying to pry details from him, but he was insistent on not giving anything away before his "presentation."

"Thank you all for joining me," Chris said as he adjusted his laptop so everyone could see the screen.

"Are there going to be any snacks?" Alan asked.

"Officially, no," Chris replied. "But feel free to help yourself to anything. I have some Wagyu Beef Jerky in the pantry that'll blow your mind."

Alan's face lit up as he went to search for it.

"Can you tell us what's going on already?" Jackie complained. "I have to get ready for bed soon." Jackie notoriously went to bed around 9:00 p.m. It was probably why she looked so young and vibrant with only a minimal use of filler.

"Earlier today, I was on a Zoom meeting with some of my investment bankers and we were just shooting the shit, when Operation: Save My Date came up."

"It came up like someone else mentioned it or you brought it up?" Emma asked. If her plan had somehow made it to the finance bros circle, this thing was way bigger than she'd thought.

Chris's face mildly reddened. "I might have made a joke about it. But," Chris quickly added, "one of the guys, Matt, actually seemed interested so I told him more about it and..." Chris paused to click a few buttons on his laptop until the photo of an extremely well-groomed man appeared. "He wants to be your husband."

"Oh my god! That's amazing!" Jackie shrieked.

They all leaned in to get a better look as Alan returned with a handful of premium jerky. The photo was clearly a corporate headshot, but Matt still managed to appear friendly and likable. He had closely cropped dark hair, a chin dimple and the kind of muscular frame that looked great in a suit. Emma felt strangely hopeful.

"He's already agreed to marry Emma? Without even meeting her?" Debbie interjected, forever the unwanted voice of reason.

"I showed him some pictures first and he watched a couple of her videos. He wants to meet her first, but if it goes well, he's on board."

"An investment banker. Well done, honey." Alan put his hand out for a fist bump, but Debbie lowered his arm before he and Emma could connect.

"Let's not get ahead of ourselves. Maybe Emma won't like him."

"What's not to like? He's a nice, normal, successful guy who clearly wants to start a family," Jackie argued.

"How do you know that? Have you met him?" Emma asked.

"No. But you can just tell."

"I have more," Chris added. He clicked another key and a photo of Matt wearing a jersey on a soccer field popped up. It looked like he was celebrating a goal.

"Where did you get all of these photos?" Emma asked, rather impressed.

"It was super easy. Just dragged and dropped some images off his socials." Chris clicked again and an image of Matt holding a toddler at a children's birthday party appeared. "Don't worry, that's his nephew. But he is looking to have kids in the next two to three years."

"Is that in his Instagram bio?" Emma joked, only for Chris to take it seriously.

"No. After the Zoom we hopped on a call and went through some basics."

Another click and an image of a tuxedoed Matt with a gorgeous blonde in a wedding dress filled the screen.

"Let me guess," Emma ventured. "That's his sister."

"Nope. His wife." Chris realized his mistake as everyone collectively gasped.

"I'm sorry but I draw the line at polygamy," Debbie said defiantly, clearly assuming no one else did.

"Chris, why are you trying to set Emma up with a married man?" Jackie asked in disbelief. "What is wrong with you?"

"They're getting divorced. It should be finalized by July, making it totally legal for you to get married in August."

"See! And you all doubted him," Alan proclaimed in support of the one steady man in his life.

"Do you know why they're getting divorced?" Emma asked. She wasn't sure what answer she was hoping for but preferably something that wouldn't lead to lifelong damage.

"She cheated on him. But I told him Emma would never do anything like that because of her anxiety and stuff."

"That's true," Jackie agreed. "You'd probably tell on yourself immediately. Probably while you were actively cheating."

"My 'anxiety and stuff' is not the only reason I wouldn't cheat. I also have a strong moral code." She looked at her parents for backup.

"It's true. Emma once accidentally walked out of a CVS with a stuffed animal we didn't pay for and she cried out of guilt for over a week," Alan shared. "Remember that, Deb?"

"Oh, yes. But I'd argue that was at least partially fueled by anxie—"

"Okay, I have an anxiety disorder. We know that." Emma tried to parse through the rush of thoughts trying to clamor for attention in her brain. "Does everyone really think it's a good idea for me to marry someone who will have only been divorced for one month?"

"Emma," Jackie said as they locked eyes, "isn't that a rather judgmental take from someone who is trying to bash down societal dating norms, or whatever?"

Once again, her sister was right.

Emma stood in the fluorescent lights of the Santa Monica Nordstrom dressing room and examined herself in the mirror. She fought the instinct to compare her thirty-something body with her twenty-something body. Logically, she knew Matt had already seen her online and approved, but she wasn't used to dating men with six-packs. She ran her hands over one of the many formfitting dresses she'd tried on in the last half hour and thanked her sensory problems for making it impossible to wear shapewear. If she didn't have an extreme aversion to anything super tight on her body, she would probably be shoving herself into all sorts of body-modifying contraptions right now, which would only lead to more insecurity. Having to always show her body as it actually was had helped her come to love it.

Most of the time. Growth was a process.

As Emma reached for a promising high-waisted-skirt–cropped-top combo, her phone rang. This time she was less shocked to see Will's name on her screen.

"Hello, William," Emma said with a mid-Atlantic accent.

Now that they were no longer dating, she suddenly felt freer to say whatever came to mind. Funny how that worked.

Will immediately picked up on her energy and sent it right back. "Hello, Miss Moskowitz. I'm just following up on our email correspondence. Have you had a chance to peruse my offerings?"

The banter made her heart flutter a bit, which was not what she needed if they were about to embark on a professional endeavor together.

"Yes. I've just been taking some time to put together my thoughts and suggestions."

In reality, Emma had been rather impressed by the pitch deck Will sent over. His concept of the show had been far more balanced than she'd expected. He planned to interview other relationship experts to weigh in, as well as couples who'd found success with arranged marriages. She'd been expecting skepticism, but it seemed like Will was genuinely curious if Operation: Save My Date was a viable idea. Only for someone like Emma though—not him.

"Great. I want this to be collaborative."

"One question I have is if we are going to disclose how we met to our listeners." Emma knew that bringing up their failed relationship was slightly masochistic considering she hadn't wanted it to end. But she also didn't want to turn into a research specimen. She needed to make sure he remembered their initial connection—both for her own sanity and for the project. She also thought it would be interesting to dive into why he was so averse to the idea of taking the leap with her despite their obvious chemistry. Unless Will had chemistry with everyone and she'd completely misread the entire situation.

"I've gone back and forth on that. Maybe we can meet up tomorrow and talk it out?"

"I can't tomorrow. I have clients all day and a date at night."

"Oh." Will sounded surprised. And possibly a little thrown. "You've got a new target lined up already?"

Emma bristled at his word choice but didn't want to ruin the opportunity to make him jealous. "My brother-in-law found him. They work together and I guess when he learned what I was doing, he jumped at the chance to meet me."

Emma immediately cringed at her overexaggeration and not-so-humble brag. But talking to Will made her want to prove that he had let go of something good. She knew she'd need to get over his rejection for the podcast to work, but for right now she wanted to stick it to him a little.

"Sounds promising. Maybe we can meet this weekend to iron out the details and rehash how it went on mic. Sort of like a practice run, if you're open to it?"

"Sure. But I gotta run. I'm half-naked in a fitting room and I have to find something to wear before my next session."

"Don't tease me, Moskowitz. It's cruel," Will said flirtatiously. "Have fun on your date."

"I shall," Emma replied, hoping that if she willed into existence, it would become true.

The restaurant almost felt too nice for a first date. It was a well-known Italian spot on Washington Boulevard that Emma had only been to once before for a high school friend's birthday. She had spent the entire meal terrified that she would have to pay hundreds of dollars for her friend's drinking problem, but after dessert the birthday girl had slapped down her parents' credit card and Emma had let out a sigh of relief. She wondered if she would be expected to split this comically expensive meal with Matt, but sensed that tonight the patriarchy would work in her favor.

After a second round of shopping at Bloomingdale's after work, Emma had found a classy navy dress that showed off her cleavage without overdoing it. It also fell below her knees, effectively hiding the brace she still had to wear. She waited at their reserved table feeling confident and even a little bit cocky. Until she saw Matt breeze past the door.

Saying Matt was better-looking in person was in line with saying social media might be problematic for teenage girls—it was too much of an understatement to effectively capture the truth. Even across a crowded room, Matt exuded Roman-statue-level beauty. He was like a walking advertisement for masculinity and tailor-made suits.

Who the hell would cheat on this? Emma wondered. His personality must be insufferable.

"Emma?" Matt asked tentatively as he approached the table. His voice was softer than she expected, and it made her want to skip ahead to their wedding day—or maybe their wedding night.

"Yes, hi. You must be Matt," Emma replied as she tried to gracefully get up from the table despite her brace. He gestured for her not to bother and sat down. Their first skin-to-skin contact would have to wait.

"Sorry I'm a little late. Work is—" Matt seemed to catch himself midsentence "—not something I want to talk about on our first date." He smiled and Emma wondered if his glistening white teeth were veneers or simply good genetics. Either way, they highlighted his excellent bone structure.

"I appreciate that. Because I have to confess, I have no idea what investment bankers actually do."

Matt laughed and Emma felt herself relax a bit. She might not look like a Greek goddess, but she was good at conversation.

"It's pretty boring."

"Really?"

"No, I actually love it," Matt admitted. "But I'm worried admitting that will make me sound like a tool."

"Wow, I don't think I've heard the word *tool* used in that context for at least a decade."

"I never stopped using it. It's too good."

Emma nodded in agreement as they slipped into an easy back-and-forth. Matt shared he had grown up in Michigan but had gone to UCLA for college and decided to stay. He was the oldest of four kids and the only one, other than his rebellious youngest sister, to not already be a parent.

"How old's your sister?"

"Twenty-six. But in Michigan years that's nearing forty."

"Oof. I guess all the billboards advertising egg freezing in LA aren't so bad in comparison."

"Yeah, people are definitely on a different timeline here. My ex, Kelly, was also from the Midwest and she was constantly getting shit from her family that we weren't pregnant. Not that we hadn't tried..."

Matt's mind seemed to drift elsewhere, and Emma couldn't ignore the strained look on his face. She wondered if their fertility struggles had contributed to Kelly's infidelity. Infertility was a notorious couples killer. Its tentacles could find a way into every aspect of a relationship, causing once strong partnerships to tear at the seams.

"It must have been hard to hear people telling you to do something you were already trying so hard to do."

"It was awful. We didn't want to tell people we were trying because we weren't sure what was going on. And it felt unfair to get everyone's hopes up."

"I get that," Emma said gently. "But sometimes keeping things private makes it hard to get support because no one knows what's actually going on."

"That's...a great point," Matt said and for a moment Emma felt like she was in session. This often happened when having difficult conversations with the people in her life. It was a strange feeling because on the one hand, she was always happy to provide a new perspective that might bring some peace and healing. But on the other hand, she knew she wasn't supposed to give someone she knew—or was getting to know—therapy over dinner.

"Do you guys still talk at all?" Emma asked.

"Me and Kelly? No, not really. Except through our lawyers. For a while she kept trying to get back together but I just can't get past what happened." Matt suddenly looked like he had revealed too much. "I'm not sure what Chris told you."

"He mentioned there was some infidelity, but I don't know any details. You don't have to dive into it right now if you don't want to," Emma added even though her nosy nature was dying to know more.

"No, it's okay." Matt blinked a few times, the emotion around what happened clearly still raw for him. "Kel and I met back at my first job. She was only twenty-four, but already this badass office manager who everyone loved. I had gone right from undergrad to my MBA so even though I had an advanced degree I was just starting out as a lowly intern."

"A classic start to a love story."

"I guess it was." Matt chuckled. "Everyone in the office had this massive crush on her so I assumed she was out of my league."

Emma tried not to laugh at the idea that Matt—with his perfect face and charming personality—wasn't in everyone's league. His humility only made him more attractive.

"I never even attempted to flirt with her or anything. We just became friends. And then one night when we were both at the office working late, *she* asked *me* out. I couldn't believe it."

"Can I ask you a personal question?"

"Sure."

"Have you never looked in a mirror?"

Matt blushed and laughed simultaneously. "Let's just say I didn't have designer suits or a personal trainer at twenty-five.

I'd only had one serious girlfriend and she'd cheated on me while I was getting my MBA. I wasn't exactly confident with girls—I mean, women." Matt checked to see if Emma was offended. She wasn't, but it was nice to know he cared about offending people. Plenty of people didn't.

"That makes sense. And is maybe why what happened with Kelly is so hard to forgive."

"Exactly! She knew my history and swore she'd never hurt me like that. Cut to six years later and I find a bunch of texts on her phone to some guy claiming *it was a mistake* and *they can never do it again*." Matt was getting riled up at the memory and Emma noticed a vein starting to throb in his neck. "My entire life, my entire marriage, gone." He snapped his fingers for effect.

Emma felt both camaraderie and sadness for the similarities in their experiences. "I also had one of those earth-shattering, completely destabilizing moments when my fiancé walked out. It's like your entire conception of the world and how it works is flipped on its head."

"Yes! I love that you get that. I mean, I'm sorry you had to go through—"

"It's okay. I know what you mean. It's like there's a contingent of us who are living in an alternate reality of what our lives were supposed to be, but we're still expected to get up and walk around as if this reality is fine too. Even though it's not. At least not yet."

Emma felt tears form in the corners of her eyes. Since meeting Will, she'd been able to push down her visceral longing for Ryan and what was supposed to be her future. She'd told herself that in time this new path would be just as good as the old one, but sitting here with Matt, she didn't have the energy to toe the party line anymore. Even if she had been the one to come up with it.

Because the truth was, up until the night Ryan left, Emma had been living her happy ending. She'd gone home every day to someone she loved, trusted and felt lucky to be with. Sure, there'd been moments of disconnection and annoyance. Ryan had a habit of leaving his socks under the couch only for them to be discovered days later covered in dust. And he often didn't verbally respond when Emma was rambling about something insignificant. But none of that outweighed the joy she got from being his partner. Ryan was the guy that had bought every type of apple in the grocery store so they could meticulously figure out her favorite one, something she'd never once thought to do for herself.

And now he was gone.

Matt reached across the table and took her hand. Surprised, Emma willed her body to relax as his strong, long fingers wrapped themselves around her short, clammy ones. "You know, all my buddies told me I was crazy to meet you. They think I should be out hooking up and letting loose for once. But I'm really glad I'm here. Even if everyone else thinks we're nuts."

Emma squeezed his hand, stopped herself from calling out his harmful use of *crazy* and *nuts*. "I am too."

After a delicious dinner and a return to less emotionally charged topics, Emma and Matt made their way outside. He had not only insisted on paying but offered to cover her valet fee, which was both extremely courteous and unnecessary. Spending ten dollars plus tip to find a compassionate (and rich) potential husband was a steal in Emma's opinion.

As they waited for their cars to arrive, Matt shifted awkwardly from one foot to another. It was Emma's first glimmer of the guy who assumed the office manager was out of his league. "I had a really nice time. You're an amazing listener."

"I do do it for a living," Emma teased.

"I guess... I'm not totally sure how this all works."

"I'm not either," Emma admitted. "But maybe we can see each other again soon and try to figure it out?"

"I'd like that," Matt replied, and it looked like he meant it.

Emma's Honda CRV rolled up in front of them. "This is me." She turned toward Matt for a hug but instead he leaned down and gave her the softest, sweetest kiss on the cheek.

Emma was thrown by how much she liked it.

Seventeen

EMMA FELT FAINT AS SHE STOOD IN THE HALL OUTSIDE HER apartment. A large part of her hoped she would pass out so she could avoid what was about to happen. Emma hadn't been back to the home she'd shared with Ryan since the first week after the breakup—now more than a shocking two months behind her. Each previous visit had been a recovery mission where she'd tried to stuff as many things as possible into her parents' suitcases before fleeing. But now she was here to stay. At least for a few hours.

After some annoying back-and-forth with Will, Emma had offered her westside apartment as a space for their first production meeting. Emma had bristled at the thought of returning to Will's place so quickly after his rejection, and her parents' house wasn't viable on account of their personalities. She didn't need her mom and dad sporadically interrupting what was already going to be tricky conversation with her ex-fling-turned-podcasting-partner. So, without thinking, Emma offered up the unused two-bedroom apartment her father had so far failed to find a subletter for. At the time of her suggestion, her higher self thought the location might be good for the story and jog some important memories—but her current self knew it was a terrible idea.

As the lock turned and Emma opened the door to step onto the floating fake hardwood floor, she braced for a wave of emotional pain. While Emma had originally found the place with her old roommate—another classmate from her grad program who had already quit the field to start a juice business—she could barely remember that iteration of the space. In Emma's memory, this place belonged to her and Ryan, which was why it was so startling to realize all traces of him were gone.

A ball of dust sat where Ryan's armchair used to be, and the kitchen walls looked sparse without his baseball-themed artwork. Half the books were missing from the media center's shelves and the overhead light was struggling to make up for the absent floor lamp. She knew that if she looked in the kitchen drawers, anything other than the most basic necessities would be gone. Ryan was the chef in the relationship, and Emma was the picky eater. Maybe that was part of the problem.

Despite having to pee, Emma avoided going deeper into the space than absolutely necessary. Her heart wasn't ready to see the bedroom where they'd once tried to spice things up with a schoolgirl costume, only to fall all over themselves laughing instead. She didn't even want to go into the guest bathroom, where Ryan had held her hair back as she puked in the sink since the toilet grossed her out. Poor Ryan had had to scoop up the chunks that wouldn't go down the drain. It was completely disgusting but he did it with a smile.

Now, Emma wondered if Ryan had secretly added that moment to the con list while privately evaluating their relationship. Not knowing killed her. Was it possible to love someone enough to clean up their puke with a Solo cup, or did that level of intimacy slowly erode any chance at a lasting romance? She wished she knew before her acid reflux inevitably acted up again.

As Emma contemplated where to sit in a home that had once been as familiar to her as her own brain, there was a knock on the door. She took a deep breath and only slightly limped over to open it.

"I come bearing gifts," Will announced with a podcast mic in one hand and a bottle of wine in the other. He was dressed casually in jeans and a Henley shirt, but something about the way the fabric clung to him sprung Emma right back to the last time they'd been in the same physical space together. It angered her that she was no longer allowed to reach out and stroke him. Their window for stroking had been far too short.

"Do you try to get all your subjects drunk before you interview them, or am I special?"

"The wine is for after. As a celebration for baring your soul and giving up a Saturday."

"In that case, come on in." Emma moved to the side as Will entered the apartment. She watched him assess her once-shared living space and wondered if it was what he expected. Or if he noticed all the missing books and marks on the walls from artwork that no longer belonged to her. Allowing him inside felt like showing someone an open wound and giving them permission to poke around in it.

"Where do you want to set up?"

"Probably the dining room table." Emma gestured to the six-person oak table that was a hand-me-down from Jackie's starter house. It was by far the most expensive thing in the apartment even though Jackie had referred to it as "a piece of junk" because it had a single stain.

Will pulled out a seat in the middle and Emma joined him on the opposite side, immediately putting her elbows on the table as she anxiously rubbed her hands. She wondered if Will felt as calm as he looked or if he was just a premier professional.

"I brought the mics, but we don't have to start recording

today if you aren't up for it. We can just talk through the plan for the show and figure out some logistics."

"I'm okay to record. As long as I get to decide what we keep."

"Fair enough. Let me get us set up."

As Will went about connecting various wires to his laptop and what she assumed was some sort of fancy recording device, Emma felt herself growing more and more annoyed. Any intimacy they had built together appeared to have vanished. Emma knew she was supposed to be moving on, and she was genuinely excited about seeing Matt again, but realizing Will was so unaffected by her was bringing up old feelings she didn't want to confront—like how easy it had been for Ryan, her actual fiancé, to walk away from her without a second thought. As a therapist, she had seen countless clients do everything possible to hold onto their exes or unimpressive partners. But no one seemed to have any issue forgetting about Emma.

"I think we are almost good to go—"

"This doesn't feel weird to you?" Emma interjected. "Us immediately shifting from sleeping together to interviewing each other?"

"Actually, I was just planning on interviewing you," Will joked. When Emma didn't laugh, his mood became more somber. He let out a sigh. "Of course it's fucking weird. Two weeks ago, I was thinking about where to take you to dinner and now I'm writing episode outlines about you marrying someone else."

"Then why are you acting like everything is fine and you don't care about me at all?"

Emma felt a rush of embarrassment as the words left her mouth. She hadn't used that kind of language in a long time, after ruining one too many relationships with her insecurity. And the reality was, Will didn't have to care about her. They'd only been out a few times and she was clearly projecting her past hurt onto him. But that didn't make the emotion she was feeling any less real.

"I'm sorry. I think I'm just having a hard time being back here."

Will nodded with understanding. "I broke my lease after Simone left. It cost me thousands of dollars, but I couldn't live there anymore. I kept finding myself expecting her to come home. It felt like my body was trained to wait for her."

"Did it get better when you moved?"

"For the most part. There were still moments of hearing my phone ring and thinking it was her. But the change in scenery definitely helped—even if I had to cancel a trip to Machu Picchu to afford it."

"I'm paying for this place with my book advance. It's probably the worst financial decision of my life, considering I'm not even staying here, and I don't exactly have a ton of savings."

Will shrugged. "If there is a time for bad decisions, it's probably right after your fiancé walks out."

Emma laughed but it rang hollow. "That's probably what you think this whole thing is, right? An impulsive reaction to getting my heart broken? Instead of rebounding with a fuck boy like a normal person, I'm rushing into marriage with a stranger?"

"I honestly don't know what I think about it, which is why I want to do the show. The internet's trained us to have big, clear opinions about everything and if you don't know where you stand on an issue then you must stand for nothing, or whatever. I like that this operation isn't clear-cut. I like not knowing how to feel about it. It makes for great conversation, and it'll force our listeners think for themselves."

"You think ambivalence is a good thing? Because I hate not knowing how to feel about something. It makes my skin crawl."

"So there's no part of you that thinks going through with Operation: Save My Date might be a mistake?"

"There definitely is, I'm just powering through anyway. Exposure therapy and whatnot."

Will laughed and Emma's attraction to him bubbled up to the point of bursting. She realized how much she liked the timbre of his voice and how unapologetically he allowed himself to enjoy things. The thought made her remember how much he had seemed to enjoy exploring her. He'd taken his time soaking in each part of her body without making her feel self-conscious or overly exposed. She'd felt like something worth observing under his gaze, but Emma knew she needed to get back to focusing on the podcast before he caught on to her internal monologue or she flung herself at him.

"When do you think this will come out?"

"We'll want to bank a few episodes first, so maybe in a month? I figure we aim for a new episode once a week until the wedding and then we'll see if there's enough momentum to justify a second season."

"What happens if I don't make it to the wedding?" Emma asked, mostly to gauge his reaction.

"Then we pivot. And maybe go out to dinner," Will said with a smile. As if he hadn't just asked her out on a hypothetical date if her entire life plan failed.

She hated herself for knowing she would say yes.

"Should we start recording?" Emma asked, attempting to squash her growing desire for him by being productive.

"Sure." Will moved Emma's mic in front of her and explained that her mouth needed to be closer to it than felt natural to get quality sound. They did a few sound checks and then he hit the record button.

"We are rolling," Will announced as Emma fixed her hair, briefly forgetting that podcasts were an audio medium. "Don't worry about providing context or explaining who you are or anything. This is just going to be a conversation and I'll write proper scripts for the episodes later once we figure out what we have and how we want to present it."

"Okay," Emma said, feeling nervous and tongue-tied for once in her very vocal life.

"Great. Let's start off with a softball question. How was your date last night?"

Emma failed to hide her surprise. Was Will asking for the show or was he asking for himself? "That's where you want to start?"

"I'll admit I've been curious. Could he be the next Mr. Moskowitz?"

Emma felt torn between giving a truthful answer and trying to stir Will up. She decided on the latter. "Would that bother you?"

Will leaned back in his chair and smiled, bringing the mic with him. "This isn't about me."

"Don't you think it should be at least a *little* about you, considering how we met?"

Will looked at Emma and she was relieved that he seemed more impressed than annoyed. He opened his mouth, only to immediately close it again; it appeared he was seriously considering the question.

After another moment, he leaned toward her, and she felt the pull of his striking blue eyes. "If that's how you want to do it, that's how we'll do it."

"What do you mean?"

"I mean, let's tell it all. From my perspective and your perspective. I won't just be the host—I'll be part of the story. If that's what you want?"

"Yes, thank you. That's what I want."

Emma felt a rush of relief that she was no longer going to be the only person sliced open for the world to examine and judge. Will was going to have to open up too. They would be perfect foils to each other—Emma willing to take the biggest

risk of her life to find happiness and him willing to take no
risk at all. She wondered if the listeners would end up taking
sides, with the reasonable romantics proclaiming, "I'm such an
Emma," and the cocky skeptics declaring, "I'm a total Will."

"We're in agreement then. Now ask me again if your date
last night bothered me."

"Did my date last night bother you?" Emma asked, holding
her breath in anticipation.

"Only if you liked him more than me," Will replied.

It suddenly felt like they were walking toward each other on
a very thin tightrope, waiting to see who would fall off first.

"Don't you think it's a little too soon to mention Matt on the
channel? We've only been out once," Emma argued as Jackie
futzed with a new lens that attached to her iPhone.

Each time Emma came over to record a video, there was
more and more equipment. Jackie's second living room was
slowly becoming a full-fledged production studio, which was
definitely more useful than it simply being a second living
room.

"I don't think you should name names or anything. But your
audience will want to know you finally met someone who is
open to the plan." Jackie reached into the makeup belt she had
purchased off Amazon to "streamline the process" and "keep
things organized."

"Here, I got you a new powder. It's specifically designed to
reduce all the shine from the lights." Jackie handed Emma a
compact that looked like every other powder she had ever seen.

"I'm just worried I'll jinx it. Maybe I should wait until things
are more official."

"Emma, the whole point of including people on the journey is to *actually* include them on the journey. We want them
to be able to root for you, not just hear how it all worked out

afterward. Plus, sharing that there is a super hot, successful guy who wanted to meet you gives the whole operation credibility."

"You think Matt's super hot?"

"You don't? He's like a younger, fitter version of Chris with even thicker hair."

"Chris has very thick hair," Emma replied, feeling strangely defensive of her brother-in-law.

"I said thick-*er*," Jackie clarified. "I know I caught a good one. Even if he is totally useless around the house."

This was painfully true. The one time Chris had tried to fix something himself, he'd fallen off a step stool and sprained his ankle. Chris was an incredible athlete, but ask him to change a light fixture and all hell broke loose.

"I guess I can frame it as an exciting development instead of a clear-cut success," Emma conceded. "So much of dating is the push-and-pull of staying realistic *and* optimistic at the same time. Maybe I can lean into that."

Jackie nodded, even though she had dated a total of three guys in her life and had never once been rejected. "When are you seeing Matt again?" Before Emma could respond, Jackie's eyes lit up and she squealed. "Oh my god! We should double-date. That would be so fun."

The idea of Emma's second date with Matt being a conversational four-way filled Emma with dread. She didn't want to open the door for a Jackie comparison so early in their courtship. Right now, Emma's connection with Matt felt primarily built on a shared sense of loss. She needed it to build into something deeper before introducing him to her hot older sister.

"Why don't I kiss him first and then we can see about forcing him to meet my family."

"I'm not just family. He literally works with my husband. They could expense the whole thing."

"I know. I'm just…" Emma tried to put her feelings into words without disclosing how often she was still thinking about

Will. "Trying to find my footing. Once we have the kinks worked out, and we feel more like a proper couple, I'd love for us all to get together."

"Fine. I'll wait," Jackie agreed, before another brilliant idea came to her. "And then we should all go to the Hamptons for a weekend."

"Maybe," Emma fibbed. She wanted to make it to the wedding before committing to any group vacations. And she wanted to spend more time with Matt before committing to a wedding.

Eighteen

"I KNOW IT'S PROBABLY TOO EARLY FOR GIFTS," MATT SAID as they sat across from each other at a dimly lit cocktail bar that charged eight dollars for mineral-enhanced water. "But I passed by this store on my way here and I thought of you."

He carefully extracted a beautifully wrapped clear gift bag that held a glass container filled with what looked like fancy, light purple salt. Emma panicked that he had assumed she knew how to cook well enough to use artisanal seasoning.

"They're bath salts. One of my coworkers' wives is also a therapist and she once told me a warm bath helps her decompress after a hard session."

Emma felt a grin spread across her face. It was such a thoughtful gift, even if hot baths often gave her eczema. "Thank you. I love it."

"Really? I wasn't sure..."

"It's perfect," Emma assured him as she wondered if the salts would properly dissolve in lukewarm water so as not to anger her skin.

While other people thought honesty was always the best policy, Emma was a huge proponent of the white lie—why hurt someone's feelings if you didn't have to? Although this type of thinking had inadvertently led Ryan to believe Emma loved turquoise jewelry after he'd randomly gifted her a bright blue necklace early on in their relationship and she'd gushed over it. But if making Matt happy in this moment meant she would one day have a drawer full of unusable bath salts, so be it.

"I think gift giving might be one of my love languages," Matt admitted. "I love the moment when someone is unwrapping your gift in front of you. It's the good kind of suspense."

"My dad is the same way. He's always surprising my mom with random stuff. Sometimes we'll be out shopping, she'll casually mention she likes something and twenty minutes later my dad will reappear with it hidden in a shopping bag from another store just to throw her off. He'll act like he bought himself something, but we all know it's really a gift for her."

"Sounds like my kind of guy."

"He's the best. Even if my mom often responds by yelling at him for wasting money."

Matt laughed. "My mom yells at my dad all the time too. Growing up, I thought it meant they were going to get divorced, but now I realize that's just her way of communicating. It doesn't even faze him."

"Boomers are built differently than the rest of us," Emma said while holding back a laugh. Her mind had flashed to an earlier text exchange with Will where he had sent a video of him opening yet another box of his mom's jam. The video had included him trying to stuff the jars into an already full shelf of previously gifted jam. Emma had watched it at least seven times.

"What's your love language? Or languages?" Matt asked.

Emma didn't have the heart to tell him the entire love language concept was created by an unlicensed homophobe who wanted women to feel guilty for not sleeping with their "physical touch" husbands more. That lesson could wait for another day.

"I fluctuate. I love quality time and acts of service. But I probably rely the most on words of affirmation. Anxious minds love reassurance."

"Good to know," Matt said with a wink. It made Emma's stomach flip. How strange to be out with a man good-looking enough to pull off a nonironic wink.

"What about you? Other than gifts?"

"Probably physical touch. I'm a sucker for a head scratch or shoulder rub."

"Good thing I have long nails," Emma replied seductively, which made her realize she was on the cusp of slipping from tipsy to full-on drunk. Exorbitantly priced cocktails were apparently dangerous.

"I did notice that," he confessed as a slight blush hit his cheeks. "I love the color."

Matt reached out and let his fingers carefully run up and down one of Emma's dark purple, almond-shaped nails. Even though it was impossible to really feel his touch through the gel polish, her body responded as though she could. Sure, she didn't laugh with Matt the way she laughed with Will (or Ryan, or Tony). At least not yet. But they were still getting to know each other. Matt's gentle, caring nature was more important in the long run than the fact she had yet to snort in his presence.

As his fingers started to make their way up her hand, she instinctively flipped her palm over so it was facing up. This allowed him to gently run his own well-buffed nails up and down the sensitive skin of her forearm. She almost shivered at his touch.

"What does this mean?" Matt asked as he traced the delicate, single-needle, black-ink tattoo that sat directly in between her wrist and elbow. It was so small she often forgot she had it.

"It's a Hella Lacy flower," Emma murmured, as he continued to explore a part of her skin that had clearly been underutilized until now. "They're late-blooming flowers. It's a reminder that the best is yet to come."

Emma had gotten the tattoo in her early twenties after a particularly brutal breakup with the guy she dated before meeting Tony. Seth had gone to college with one of Emma's high school friends and after being introduced, they had spent six months nearly inseparable. It was the first time Emma met a boyfriend's family or had someone reciprocate her premature "I love you." For half of a year, Emma thought she'd done it—she'd found her future. But instead of appreciating what she had, she pushed and pushed and pushed for more. She wanted to move in together and start talking about wedding venues. At the time, it had felt like the natural and expected progression of things. In reality, they were twenty-three-year-old babies. They were supposed to be finding themselves, not settling down. Seth understood this. Emma...not so much.

After a month of public crying—Emma had always been somewhat of a sadness exhibitionist—she'd made an appointment at an acclaimed tattoo parlor on the Sunset Strip. A big burly guy covered in ink had taken her printed-out reference photo and sat down to delicately draw his beautiful interpretation of the flower. As the needle tortuously dipped in and out of her skin, Emma reminded herself that sometimes you have to go through pain to get to pleasure. She'd left that day genuinely excited about what was to come.

Now, nearly a decade later, maybe she'd *finally* found what she'd been looking for.

"I love it," Matt replied, looking up from her symbol of hope to stare directly into her eyes. It was the perfect opening for their first kiss and Emma thought she could actually feel her heart vibrating until she realized that it was actually just Matt's phone buzzing on the table.

"Sorry," he apologized, picking up his device and quickly scrolling through a barrage of messages. "One of my buddies is in town for the night and wants me to meet him at some club."

"Oh," Emma replied, trying to hide her disappointment at

both the moment being broken and the night potentially ending. "I don't mind if you need to go. Long-distance friendships deserve priority."

"That's so cool of you to say," Matt said. "Any chance you'd want to come?"

"To a club?"

He nodded.

A deluge of anxiety crashed through Emma's body.

The last time she'd been at a proper club, she'd wanted to rip her ringing ears off and move to the woods so she would never have to dance in public again. Every single one of her limited club experiences had ended in humiliation, overstimulation and a dangerously intense hangover.

But she was Emma 2.0 now. And Emma 2.0 could do anything.

The club was horrible. From the moment Emma followed Matt into the darkness, she felt like a fish who had been flung from the safety of its bowl into an MRI machine. The electronic music reverberated through her skull and the flashing lights illuminated a crowd of people who seemed to have no regard for personal space. Emma briefly contemplated fleeing until she felt Matt's hand give her three gentle squeezes. She owed it to him to try to stick around. Maybe she'd lose her hearing soon and it would become more manageable.

After navigating past the debaucherous dance floor, Matt flashed something at a security guard, and they were granted access to the VIP section. It was just as loud, but Emma was now able to walk without touching a stranger, further proving money could at least increase your happiness.

"MATTY MONROY," a booming voice shouted from a red velvet booth. A man with a popped collar and sunglasses waved them over with a level of excitement that was probably drug fueled. His table was packed with a combination of what appeared to be finance bros and Instagram models.

Emma looked down at what she had once considered to be her fashionable "going out" blazer and felt like a grandma crashing a frat party.

"That's him," Matt shouted in her ear, before leading Emma over. His preppy friend hopped down from his perch on the back of the booth and enveloped Matt in a bear hug.

When they finally broke apart, the Corey Hart wannabe screamed, "Who's this?"

"Kyle, this is Emma. Emma, this is Kyle."

"You look nothing like his wife," Kyle stated as though someone had asked him to weigh in on the subject. "Want a shot?" He leaned over and grabbed a bottle of tequila from the table.

"Oh…uh… I don't know—" Emma stammered as she sneaked a look at Matt. He swooped in to save her.

"We just came from drinks."

"Then let's keep the train rolling," Kyle declared as he took a swig from the bottle. "Don't worry, I use a lot of mouthwash, so my saliva is clean." He thrust the bottle back in Emma's face, daring her not to be a party pooper or challenge his flawed bacteria logic.

It struck Emma as remarkably unfair that at thirty-two years old, she was being peer pressured by a total stranger to take tequila shots straight from the bottle when what she really wanted was to be watching TV with a loving partner and a bowl of snacks. Emma wanted to be at home planning her wedding, not out on the town trying to seem like someone who wasn't about to cry from overstimulation. But sometimes what you want and what you have don't mix.

Emma contemplated the bottle that was now mere inches from her face and felt the familiar push and pull between staying true to herself and doing what would be easiest in a social situation. As an anxious child turned anxious teenager turned anxious therapist, she knew that for all the clamoring about the importance of "being yourself," there would be real repercussions if she didn't rise to the occasion and take a swig—both in the moment and later. She knew Kyle would loudly berate her and Matt might start to question if he could be happy with someone so uptight. Their unraveling wouldn't be immediate, but this moment could plant a destructive seed. It would be his first image of her as someone who said no instead of yes. After so many failed relationships, Emma had to wonder if avoiding the disgusting taste of Don Julio was worth losing another promising match.

But before she could reach for a brighter future, Matt grabbed the bottle, took a large gulp and managed to distract Kyle away from his mission to get Emma wasted.

"Have you heard from Collins lately?" Matt asked as he veered his friend back toward the group.

"Yep. He's having triplets. I told him he better get out of crypto if he wants to be able to send any of them to college."

As the old friends dissolved into gossip, which appeared to be a mashup of financial analysis and old drinking stories, Emma sat at the very end of the booth and tried not to fall over. Without missing a beat or breaking from the conversation, Matt instinctively put his arm around her to keep her from tilting. She let herself lean into his strong chest as if they were a proper couple and not two people who hadn't even kissed yet.

"I love your blazer," a pretty redhead shouted from across the table. "Where'd you get it?"

"Eileen Fisher," Emma replied, unsure if she was being made fun of or not.

"I think I follow her on TikTok!"

This was highly unlikely considering Eileen Fisher was a traditional and elegant clothing brand mostly utilized by older women and not fashion influencers. But Emma let it slide.

"How do you know, Kyle?"

"Who's Kyle?" the redhead replied. "Do you mean Kevin?" Before Emma could ask "Who's Kevin?" and get stuck in a Hollywood club edition of "Who's on First?" she recognized someone out of the corner of her eye.

"Oh my god," Emma exclaimed loud enough for Matt to hear her.

"You okay?"

"I'm… I… I have to pee." Emma shot up and took off in the direction of the neon restroom sign. After escaping the VIP section, she looked back to find Matt taking another round of shots as Kyle cheered everyone on. Feeling safe that he was no longer watching, Emma changed course and headed toward the club exit. She needed to make a phone call.

"Hello?" Jackie answered drowsily. At 11:43 p.m., it was far past her bedtime and Emma was a bit surprised she'd answered at all. Maybe she could sense that something was amiss. Some women had a six sense about these things. could do that. Unlike Emma, who had held on to the belief that she was being pranked until the moment Ryan left their apartment with her engagement ring in his pocket.

"Hey. Sorry to call you so late." Emma paced the littered sidewalk. She'd tried to find a spot that was far enough away from the club to hear her sister on the phone but not far enough away that she could be kidnapped without anyone noticing. "I'm out with Matt and…" Emma wondered if this was going to be one of those moments that changed both their lives forever. She wasn't sure if she wanted to carry that responsibility, but she also knew her sister deserved to know what she had just seen.

"We're at the club in Hollywood and I think I just saw Chris."

"Mm-hmm."

"He was…uh…dancing. With another woman." Emma braced

herself for the intensity of Jackie's reaction. Instead, she was met with silence. "Hello?"

"Sorry, was just checking my email now that I'm up. This one mom in Izzy's class keeps letting her kid bring a hamster to school and—"

"Did you not hear me? Chris is out in a club dancing with another woman," Emma cried out.

"Oh my god, Emma. Do you think Chris is cheating on me?" Jackie asked before bursting out laughing. "I know Chris is out. He goes out all the time."

Now it was Emma's turn not to respond. She'd known Chris had been a big partier when he was younger, but she'd always assumed that had stopped once he became a dad.

"You know he grinds with other women?" Emma finally asked, growing increasingly suspicious that her sister might be in some sort of open marriage. Not that there was anything wrong with that, but Jackie wasn't exactly the type to break social norms. She loved social norms.

"I don't know what he does. But I know he's not cheating." She let out a large yawn. "Deep down, Chris is a *family guy*. His mother would kill him if he had an affair."

Emma had never heard of this type of logic before, but she had met Chris's mom, who was quite formidable. "You really don't mind that he's out here, dancing with other people, without you?"

"Mind? It's great. He gets it out of his system, and I'm not expected to leave the house after nine."

As a couples therapist, Emma shouldn't have been so shocked to learn that her sister and brother-in-law had figured out a constructive compromise that allowed them both to have their needs met. This was exactly the type of negotiation she often encouraged in her clients even though it required a level of trust not everyone was capable of.

Yet, despite all her training, Emma was still finding it a bit difficult to believe that her sister was totally cool with this situation. Jackie had once stopped speaking to Chris for an entire week after he liked another mom's bikini photo on Instagram. But maybe that was because other people she knew could see it? And it was highly unlikely the PTA from McKinley Elementary School was out partying on a weeknight.

"They were very close together," Emma murmured into the phone, just to make sure she had covered all her bases.

"That's how people dance, Emma," Jackie replied with another yawn. "How's it going with Matt? Is he still as hot as last time?"

"Yes, he is still very hot," Emma said with a laugh. Jackie's obvious crush on Emma's maybe husband was perhaps the most unexpected twist in what had been a whirlwind of a few months. She wasn't used to her sister thinking much of her partners and it gave her a bit of a thrill to finally have something Jackie would want for herself.

"Take a photo for me."

"I'm not going to do that. I'm glad I called though because I was starting to worry that I couldn't marry someone who enjoys going to clubs if I hate them so much. But maybe we could work something out like you and—" Emma suddenly stopped her mindless pacing. "Let me call you back tomorrow." Emma hung up as a concerned Matt made his way toward her.

"Hey, I'm sorry if you were having a bad time. You could have told me and I would have—"

"No, no. It wasn't that. I mean I guess I was having a bad time because I don't do well with loud music or bright lights or tequila shots." Emma realized she was getting off track. "I only left because I saw Chris on the dance floor, and I panicked."

"Chris is here?"

"Yes. Apparently, he goes out all the time without Jackie and it's totally fine because his mom would kill him if he cheated? I don't know. They have a weird marriage."

Matt looked at her strangely, which felt justified. "I thought you'd left because I'd screwed up or something." He avoided her eyes as he looked sheepishly at the ground.

"Not at all," Emma assured him. "I screwed up by leaping to conclusions and waking my sister up in the middle of the night."

"It's not even twelve."

"Moskowitz girls have an unbalanced circadian rhythm."

Matt laughed and Emma reached out to take his hand. "I probably should have been more upfront about my inability to properly party. I just wasn't built for it."

"Never apologize for being yourself," he replied, continuing his streak of being wonderful. "I'm probably too old for places like this anyway."

"Hey, to quote a wise man I know, 'Never apologize for being yourself.' It's okay for us to like different stuff as long as…" Emma suddenly found herself too embarrassed to complete her thought.

"As long as what?"

"As long as we like each other," Emma whispered, forcing herself to look into his dark brown eyes. She felt a wave of relief as a smile emerged on his beautifully defined face.

"Then I guess we have nothing to worry about." Matt moved his head closer to hers, his eyes asking a question instead of his mouth. Emma gently nodded as an answer. He immediately closed the gap between them and suddenly they were kissing on a sidewalk like no one could see them.

Matt's lips were big and soft, and as soon as they were on Emma's, his whole body responded in kind. He used his right hand to pull her closer by the small of her back while his left one caressed her face. He kissed her like he hadn't kissed anyone in so long he needed to make up for lost time. She felt him start to make his way down her jeggings and was surprised when he grabbed her ass. He must have noticed her jolt because he pulled away, his face flushed.

"I'm sorry. I guess I got a little carried away," he murmured, clearly embarrassed.

"Me too," she admitted. "I don't normally make out in front of children." Emma gestured to the closed store behind him that featured child-size mannequins in the window.

Matt chuckled before leaning down and giving her another kiss that didn't last nearly long enough for her liking. "I should probably get you home."

Emma shook her head, placing a hand on his chest. She tried not to get too distracted by the firmness of his pecs. Were they genetic? Was he a superhero? "You should stay. Kyle's only here for the night and I can get an Uber."

"Are you sure?"

"Yes. As long as we can continue this again soon."

"How's tomorrow?"

"Tomorrow's perfect."

Minutes later, as Emma was driven home by a blissfully quiet stranger, she slowly traced her Hella Lacy tattoo and thought about the future without an ounce of despair.

Nineteen

"DISCONNECTION IS A NATURAL PART OF LONG-TERM RE-lationships," Emma said gently to the elderly couple in front of her. Frank and Connie Torres had been married for nearly sixty-five years. They had survived the loss of a child, three cancer diagnoses (two for him, one for her) and a criminal accountant who ate up a considerable amount of their hard-earned savings. But the thing that had finally brought them to therapy was Frank's iPhone.

"Believe me, I know that," Connie replied. "But how are we supposed to reconnect if he won't put his damn phone down?"

"It's down right now!" Frank bellowed. Emma was having a hard time discerning if his high decibel was due to emotion or hearing loss.

"I can see you gripping it through your pants right now," Connie countered.

Frank looked down at his lap and was surprised to see that he was in fact holding his phone through his pants pocket.

Emma braced herself for his response. Would he try to explain it away with some made-up excuse? Would he attempt to turn the tables and attack her for always being so critical of him? People were often their worst selves when caught.

But instead of doing any of those things, Frank merely shouted, "Whoops," and he and Connie erupted into laughter. Emma breathed a sigh of relief. They were going to be fine.

"For homework, why don't you both try to have at least one phone-free hour a day. And then we'll check in to see how it went next week," Emma said as she stood up to signal the end of their session.

"Fine, but I get to pick the hour," Frank insisted as Connie helped him up from the sofa.

"As long as it's one of the hours you're both normally awake, that works for me," Emma replied.

"She's on to you," Connie teased as they shuffled toward the exit. Emma opened the door and let out a slight gasp when she saw Will sitting in her waiting room.

"See you next week," Emma said in what she hoped was a normal voice. She waited until the Torreses were safely outside before turning to the annoyingly charismatic man sitting in front of her.

"Sorry, but I'm not accepting new clients at this time."

"That's too bad," Will replied as he stood up and walked himself into her office. "You have great Yelp reviews."

It was true. She hovered around a 4.5, which was higher than most.

"What are you doing here?" Emma asked, leaning against the doorframe. She watched as Will moved around the room, inspecting the details of her professional environment. Luckily, in the tradition of most therapists, they were rather sparse. Family photos revealed too much, and any artwork had to be nonoffensive and bordering on dull so as not to ignite too much of a reaction from her clients.

"I was in the neighborhood for a meeting and wanted to

share some good news. We've officially been greenlit for a full season of the podcast."

"Wait, we weren't greenlit before?"

Will shrugged as he sat down on the couch, flung his bag on the ground and spread his arms out. "It was basically a technicality. My bosses needed to hear a test episode to get a better sense of the show before committing to paying for it. I knew they'd go for it, which is why I didn't want to worry you."

"So instead you had me tell my friends and family that I was making a podcast before I was officially making a podcast?"

Will grinned. "Hey, if my tactics work out in the end I'm not allowed to be in trouble."

"I never agreed to those terms."

"Would you agree to them now?" He raised his eyebrows at her in what her heart could only interpret as a flirtatious manner. Emma let out a groan of frustration, both at his question and herself.

Only fourteen hours ago, Will had been the furthest thing from her mind as she'd melted into Matt. But now that they were in the same room again, she couldn't deny that Will still had a pull over her. She knew she had to ask him to leave even if she wanted him to stay.

"No deal. But thanks for the enticing offer." Emma moved back toward the door, hoping he'd get the hint. "And thank you for delivering the good news in person. It was quite a thrill to learn something I thought I already knew."

"Wait, before you kick me out..." Will leaned down and opened his bag, pulling out his laptop. "I thought we could record a bit. Get a feel for your workspace."

"Can't I just describe my office to you next time?"

"Not the same thing. I want to capture the ambient noise of this specific room. It will give the show more character."

Emma had no idea what he was talking about—her office didn't sound like anything other than the occasional struggle

of an overextended air-conditioning unit. But Will was looking at her with puppy dog eyes and...

No! She had to stand strong against his charm. This was her
place of work, where she was a professional with boundaries.
Even if his arms looked delightfully freckled in his formfitting T-shirt.

"Sorry, but now's not a good time. My sessions are over for
the day and my colleague is about to arrive."

As if on cue, Imani threw open the front door that led into
the waiting room and shouted, "I hate all of my clients."

"I knew it," Will declared, unseen from inside the office,
catching Imani off guard. "I knew you had to hate at least
some of them."

"Oh, fu— I didn't realize you were still in session..." Imani
stammered, checking her watch as Emma watched with amuse-
ment through the doorway. It was the most thrown Emma
had ever seen her and Emma couldn't resist having a little fun.

"We were just wrapping up."

"Of course, yes. Let me just go wait in the car." Imani started
to backtrack until Will revealed himself in the doorframe and
grinned. Imani stopped and considered his face, which was
instantly familiar from all the times Emma had shown her his
Hinge profile.

Emma burst out laughing.

"What the hell is going on?" Imani asked, instantly back to
her in-control self.

"Imani, this is Will, my troublesome podcast producer you've
heard so much about. Will, this is Imani, my coworker and favorite friend in the world," Emma said with flourish. "Will
stopped by unexpectedly and without permission to tell me our
podcast has officially been picked up by his network."

"It wasn't already picked up?" Imani asked, as confused as
Emma had been moments earlier.

"Consider it a technicality that is still worth celebrating," Will replied as he offered his hand to Imani.

Imani glared at him instead of shaking it. "You made me think I was about to lose my license."

"I'm sorry. I just always wondered if therapists actually liked their patients or not. And now I know. They hate them."

"I don't hate my clients," Imani clarified. "I was just frustrated because my four-o'clock canceled *again* and I know it's going to be a hassle to get them to pay for it anyway. Even though it explicitly states in our starting paperwork that—" Imani suddenly lost interest in what she was saying. "Never mind. I'll deal with it later."

"What just happened?" Will asked, bewildered by her sudden switch in tone and energy.

"Emotional regulation," Emma responded. "Now, let's get out of her way."

Will turned toward Imani. "Actually, if you suddenly have a free hour, I'd love to interview you for the show."

"You want to interview *me*? About what?"

"Your thoughts on the whole Save My Date thing—as both Emma's friend and a relationship expert."

Imani raised her perfectly shaped eyebrows and looked at Emma. "Are you okay with that?"

"Not even a little bit," Emma answered honestly. "But I don't want to be accused of avoiding criticism to push my own agenda."

Will clapped his hands together with excitement. "I'll take that as a yes."

After some maneuvering, the group decided it would be best for Imani to sit in the therapist chair while Emma and Will shared the couch. Will put a shotgun mic on the coffee table and aimed it away from himself because Imani's audio was the priority. He could always rerecord his questions later in the studio. Emma tried not to think about Will's leg being so dangerously close to hers.

"Want to start off by introducing yourself to the audience?" Will asked.

"Fine," Imani said as rolled her eyes. Despite the theatrics, Emma knew she was enjoying herself; once someone got her best friend talking it was hard to get her to stop. "My name is Imani Harris. I'm a marriage and family therapist from San Diego who now co-runs a private practice in Los Angeles with Emma Moskowitz. I combine an integrative approach with an emphasis on Emotional Focused Therapy, or EFT."

"And what exactly is EFT?"

"It's a modality that focuses on helping couples by exploring the root of their emotions and learning how to be emotionally vulnerable with each other."

"Sounds awful," Will joked.

Neither woman laughed.

"It's one of the most evidence-based treatments available to couples in need," Imani countered, completely stone-faced.

"I was just kidding. I'm sure—" Will noticed both therapists were now holding back smiles. "*And* you're fucking with me."

"Seemed only fair," Imani replied with a grin.

Will laughed, just as happy to be the target of a joke as the instigator. "How would you describe your relationship with Emma?"

"Cordial at best."

"Hey!" Emma protested. "I take you to all your doctor's appointments."

Imani had a huge fear of needles, so whenever she needed a blood test or vaccine, Emma had to tag along and attempt to distract her. It was one of the ways they'd gotten so close so fast. During their first class together, Imani needed to get a flu shot but kept putting it off until Emma insisted on going with her, and the tradition was born.

"My relationship with Emma Moskowitz is one filled with professional and personal respect, familial-level love and lots of cheap Mexican food. I feel lucky every day that she is such a huge part of my life." Imani said this completely deadpan, which was how she often expressed positive emotion. Therapists were works in progress, just like everyone else.

"I'm going to need multiple copies of that tape," Emma declared. "I want to listen to it every night as I fall asleep."

Imani groaned in what Emma suspected was fake annoyance.

"How would you describe Emma's relationship history since you've known her?" Will asked. Imani immediately looked at Emma for permission to speak openly.

"You can be honest." For all her flaws, Emma had never been someone to hide her failings. How could she hope to get better if she never admitted that she needed to?

"Whew, okay," Imani said, putting her feet up and getting comfortable. "When I first met this one in grad school, she was—how do I put this delicately?—a total disaster. She would go on one date and become convinced he was the love of her life. And if one of these losers didn't text her back right away, she'd have a full-blown spiral and leap to the conclusion that she was *totally unlovable* and *destined to die alone*. Absolutely no ability to self-soothe or think rationally when it came to dating."

"Do you dispute any of this?" Will asked, turning to Emma.

"Nope. One time a guy called me on the way to our third date to say I had been texting him too much that day, so he was turning around. It was kind of nice that he bothered to call."

"Was he the one who called you a stage-five clinger?" Imani asked, amused by the memory.

"No, that was the lawyer in Pasadena." Emma turned to Will. "In hindsight I can see how surprising someone at home is only romantic in the movies."

"I'm going to switch from my objective-journalist hat to

Emma's-short-term-fling hat for a second and say I didn't experience this type of behavior with you at all."

"I never really liked you that much," Emma teased. If Will had even an inkling of how much she had liked him—and maybe still did—he would also be running for the hills of Pasadena.

"Lie." Imani snorted, completely blowing Emma's cover. "Will, I bet I could quote your entire Hinge profile after how many times she showed it to me."

Emma felt her face turn warm and her heart speed up due to the all-too-familiar feeling of embarrassment. The last thing she needed was for Will to know she was obsessed with him.

"Really?" Will said with a grin and a nudge to Emma's right arm. "I had no idea. I felt like I was the one pursuing you."

"Until I brought up my plan and you fled," Emma countered with a touch of bitterness.

"That's not exactly how I remember it going down," Will replied before refocusing his attention on Imani and expertly avoiding an argument. "Did Emma's behavior change once she met Ryan?"

"It changed before they met. Emma knew she was pushing people away by being too intense, so she worked on herself and got better at dating."

"Better how?"

"More... I don't want to say chill because we are talking about Emma, but maybe that's the best way to describe it. Every date wasn't life-or-death anymore. And she did a better job of letting go of guys who weren't worth her time. Except for this guy Tony, but we all have an Achilles' heel. Mine is the legendary Holland Taylor and this one straight girl from my gym."

"She's not going to leave her husband," Emma interjected.

"You don't know that for sure," Imani countered before asking Will, "Who's your Achilles' heel?"

Not me, Emma thought with a dash of self-pity.

"I don't think I have one," he replied.

"Oh, come on," Emma prodded. "There isn't a single person living or dead who you wouldn't do anything to be with?"

"Living *or* dead?" Will asked. "No."

Imani nodded as though something was clicking together for her. "Let me guess. You're a pragmatist."

"Why are you saying that like it's a bad thing?"

"I'm not. I mostly am too. It just explains why you weren't open to Emma's plan, even though you clearly like her. You don't engage with things that haven't already been proven to work."

"Hmm," Will said as he leaned back and crossed his arms. He seemed to be considering Imani's point logically instead of emotionally, which was a major turn-on for Emma. "I see what you're saying but I wouldn't call my career choice pragmatic. Podcasting is a relatively new industry and shows get canceled all the time."

"Yeah, but for a creative career, being a producer is the most pragmatic choice. It's not like you're trying to be an actor or make it as a musician while waiting tables. You go into an office and have a steady salary with benefits."

"Not *good* benefits though," Will retorted cleverly.

Imani laughed and looked at Emma. "You were right. He is funny. Are you sure you can't convince him to marry you?"

Emma forced a laugh and an eye roll. Even though she had secretly been wondering the same thing.

Twenty

EMMA PULLED HER CAR INTO THE CONDO BUILDING'S CIR-
cular driveway and was startled to find a valet attendant already standing at her door. So much for having a moment to
collect herself.

"May I help you?" The young man in a handsome maroon
outfit asked with perfect enunciation.

"Yes, I'm here to see Matthew Monroy in unit 14C." Emma
gathered up her purse and tried to locate her keys. She always
felt flustered when giving her car to a valet, as if there was a
secret countdown happening and her clumsiness was going to
cause a major setback in everyone's day.

"Very good," the man replied. He couldn't have been more
than twenty-five and it felt a bit like he was cosplaying an old-
timey butler. "How long will you be staying?"

Emma had no idea how to answer. Matt had invited her over
for dinner and a movie, but Emma wasn't sure if he intended
for her to spend the night. She didn't think she was ready for
that level of intimacy although maybe after a few glasses of
wine she'd feel differently. There was also the possibility that
while she wouldn't sleep over, she might stay until rather late.

Or maybe she'd leave right after the movie, in which case it wouldn't even be nine o'clock–

"Miss?" The valet was now looking at her with concern.

"I… I'm not sure how long. Is that okay?"

"Absolutely. We are available 24/7," he replied as he climbed into her car and moved the seat back. "Just let the front desk know when you need to leave."

"Thank you," Emma said, wondering why he had bothered to ask the question in the first place if it didn't matter. Maybe he was as invested in Matt's dating life as she was.

As Emma entered the sleek lobby complete with a chandelier and two security guards, she tried to imagine what it would be like to live here as a married woman. Not having to find parking was definitely a plus, even if it meant having awkward encounters with the staff multiple times a day. Emma wasn't good at a casual hello; she always felt compelled to stop for a full conversation despite rarely having anything substantive to say.

"The second elevator will take you to Mr. Monroy's floor," the older security guard told her with the same level of formality as the valet. Emma offered her best smile to let him know she was a *cool* guest before walking over to hit the up button. The elevator smelled like it had been recently sprayed with a fruity home fragrance and was only slightly nauseating.

Unit 14C was at the end of the hallway, giving Emma just enough time to give in to her nerves. Before now, her dates with Matt had felt akin to playing pretend. Like they were two participants in a laboratory experiment being observed through a two-way mirror in order to test a love hypothesis. If it worked, great; if not, everyone went home. No harm, no foul. But now that Emma was about to enter Matt's apartment, the emotional stakes felt real for the first time. She wanted things to work out with Matt so badly she wasn't sure if she could trust her opinion of him. Could he really be as wonderful (and ripped) as he seemed?

"Hi," Matt's voice rang out from a few feet away. He'd opened his door and was waiting for her. She was glad to see that he wasn't wearing any sort of novelty apron.

"Hi," Emma replied with a smile as she came to a stop in front of him. He reached down and lightly brushed his lips against hers in greeting.

"You look great," he announced, and it hurt to realize she didn't believe him.

As much as Emma had worked on her self-esteem the last few years, she still found herself lacking in his presence. Part of her was having a hard time believing that he would have approached her in any scenario other than Operation: Save My Date.

"I'm officially brace free." Emma stuck out her right leg as proof. She'd been cleared by her physical therapist that morning to resume normal outfits—or normal for Emma, which exclusively meant pants with an elastic waistband.

"Congratulations," Matt said with genuine delight. "Come on in."

Emma entered his large, two-floor condo and was shocked to find it mostly empty. It was an open floor layout, with a giant stainless-steel kitchen and barely any furniture. Aside from one of the biggest TVs Emma had ever seen, there was nothing on the white walls.

"This…feels like a serial killer's apartment," Emma joked.

"I know," Matt replied in a sad voice. "I let Kelly keep the house and I guess decorating isn't one of my strong suits."

Emma's heart sank. She'd just arrived and already put her foot in her mouth. Hurting Matt, intentional or otherwise, was like stealing candy from a generous baby who would have given it to you if you'd just asked. She tried to salvage the moment.

"No, no. I was just kidding. It's a great space. Really. I love it. You just need a couple more things to fill it out."

"Maybe we could go shopping for stuff together. I bet you have great taste."

Emma smiled, relieved that he wasn't still upset even though he had her pegged all wrong; Emma did not have great taste. In fact, Jackie had gotten all of the design sense in the family and Emma often found herself gravitating toward things her sister would consider tacky. After moving in together, Ryan had put a limit on how many new animal statues Emma was allowed to get in a given year—only three, which seemed criminal. She had tried to get around this by buying functional pieces, like lamps or plates, that were also animal shaped. A great loophole, in her opinion, until the night Ryan broke up with her and she was left wondering if her fox-shaped coffee table had been the final straw.

"I can certainly come, but I don't know if I'll be much help."

"Just making me actually go would be a win."

"That I can do," Emma replied, her confidence slowly returning to her body as she noticed Matt sneaking a peek at her chest.

After deciding to order Greek food, Matt turned on his massive flat-screen and asked Emma what she wanted to watch. She racked her brain for a good reply, trying not to get distracted by how close they were on the couch. His thigh muscles were practically bulging out of his designer jeans.

"Have you seen the new Coen brothers' movie?" she asked. Will had watched it earlier that week and told her she needed to see it soon since he planned to quote it a lot moving forward. Emma had agreed because she hated missing a good reference.

"Nope. I don't watch a lot of movies," Matt admitted.

"Are you more of a TV guy?"

"I'd say I'm a sports guy who occasionally gets wrapped up in *The Bachelor* when it's on in my living room. Kelly loves that show."

"It is pretty captivating," Emma agreed. "I've always found it fascinating that middle America is totally fine with polyamory so long as it ends in a monogamous engagement."

"Huh, I never thought of it that way."

"Sometimes the presentation of something has more impact on people than the thing itself. That's why I've thought a lot about how to explain Operation: Save My Date in a way that's appealing and not off-putting."

"How do you explain it? I mean I've seen your videos but it's different to talk to you in person about it."

"Totally," Emma agreed as she collected her complicated thoughts on the subject. "I guess one of the best ways to explain what I am trying to do is to start by explaining what I'm *not* trying to do. To me, this isn't about swapping in one guy for another guy so I can still have a big wedding." She felt the need to clarify that point, because Will's accusation still stung. "And it's not about avoiding my grief by immediately jumping into something new. If I had discovered a way to successfully avoid grief, I'd be a millionaire."

"More like a billionaire," Matt added.

"Exactly. I haven't solved how to get over a broken heart—and I don't think that's something we need to solve. But I do think I'm in a unique situation with the opportunity to try something new. Our society has basically fallen into a soulmate trap, where if you aren't sure someone is The One, you have to keep looking. Except if my job has taught me anything it's that love and attraction only get you so far."

"That part I know," Matt replied with sad laugh.

"It's a weird thing to learn though, right? I feel like growing up is realizing that most people don't stay married because of passion, they stay married because of mutual respect and commitment. So if you change your mindset from looking for your *one true soulmate* to looking for a lovely life partner who wants the same things as you, you suddenly have a lot more options. And you don't have as much doubt that you picked the wrong person because you aren't on a quest for someone perfect. You're just looking for someone you enjoy who will care enough to try."

Emma had gotten herself so worked up she hadn't realized how intensely Matt was listening to her. But now that she was done with her impassioned speech, she looked over and saw him vigorously nodding.

"That's what killed me the most about Kelly cheating. It felt like she was throwing in the towel when I wanted to keep fighting."

"I thought she tried to get back together?"

Matt rolled his eyes and Emma got the sense she wasn't the first one to point this out. "Cheating was my *one* deal-breaker. From the very beginning. She knew what she was doing when she crossed that line."

"Maybe. Or maybe there was a lot going on with the stress of you guys trying so hard to get pregnant and she's just a human who made a mistake." Emma didn't know why she was defending her new love interest's ex-wife so vehemently. Her professional ability to see both sides wasn't always a blessing for her personal life. "Or maybe you're right and it was her way of blowing everything up so there was no going back. Subconsciously or consciously."

Matt reached out and tucked some hair behind her ear. "I don't want to talk about Kelly anymore. Not when we should be focusing on us." Emma knew they were about to transition into the physical part of the evening, but she couldn't ignore a question that had been gnawing at her.

"Can I ask you something?"

"Of course." Matt's hand had now moved down to her significantly less muscular thigh.

"Why are you doing this with me? I know you liked being married, but I can't imagine it would be that hard for you to find another wife in a more traditional way. I'm sure half of Bumble would want to marry you if they could."

Matt laughed as if Emma was joking or exaggerating. "I think you're overestimating my success rate with women."

"When was the last time you were single? Eight years ago? You don't have any current data. I guarantee you would crush the twenty-eight-to-thirty-five-year-old demographic."

"But why would I want to when I've already met you?" Matt asked sincerely. "I believe all the same things you just said. My parents aren't a perfect love story—they're just two people who have worked hard to raise a family and support each other. If my divorce taught me anything, it's that I need someone who won't disappear when things get tough. And from everything I've learned about you these past couple of weeks, you seem like that kind of person. I feel like I can trust you with my heart. Before we met, I wasn't sure if I'd be able to do that again."

"So you *really* want to do this? You want to go all the way?" Matt raised his eyes suggestively and Emma blushed.

"I mean with the wedding."

"Emma Moskowitz, I want to go all the different ways with you."

And with that declaration of something bordering on love, he kissed her.

Emma waited for the valet under the building's awning, hoping the dim light wouldn't reveal the full extent of her splotchy, red face. She had just spent the past forty minutes making out and it showed. Even though they were now pretty much engaged, she and Matt had mutually decided to take the physical aspect of their relationship slow. Part of Emma worried that Matt must not be that attracted to her if he wasn't trying to get her naked, but a more mature part understood where he was coming from. Just because they had a wedding date didn't mean they had to rush their courtship. They had plenty of time to sleep together—hopefully a whole lifetime.

There was something special about this phase of their relationship, before they knew what it was like to be with each other physically. It made everything more charged, more exciting. Emma had felt like a teenager again as she straddled Matt on the couch with all her clothes on. Just because they knew where the relationship was going, it didn't mean they had to rush through the journey.

Feeling more at peace than she'd felt in months, Emma smiled eagerly at the valet when he handed over her keys. She then smiled the whole way home. Her smile even managed to stay in place as she drifted off to sleep because she was stubbornly ignoring the one nagging question in the back of her mind: *Am I really willing to get hurt again?*

Twenty-One

"DO YOU THINK THIS WILL LOOK GOOD?" EMMA ASKED her mother and sister as they sat side by side by side in pedicure chairs. Both women leaned over to inspect the bright blue Essie polish Emma was considering for her toes.

"No," Jackie replied.

"Really? I think it would be fun," Debbie countered.

"Why would you want your feet to look like a *Sesame Street* character? Go with something more natural." Jackie held up a bottle of Mademoiselle, the same shade of light pink she had been using for decades; nail salons were an important part of their affluent childhood.

"Pink nails aren't exactly natural either," Emma argued even though she knew exactly what Jackie meant. Sometimes annoying younger-sibling instincts were hard to shake.

"How about this?" Debbie showed them her selected color, a brighter pink that was more fun than Jackie's shade but not quite as daring as what Emma had proposed.

"That'll work," Emma agreed, not at all embarrassed that she was going to match her mom. There was already quite a bit of crossover in their wardrobes.

"Your phone is buzzing," Jackie said with a nod toward Emma's purse. "Is it Matt?"

Emma checked her screen and saw a message from Will asking if she would be down to do another recording session soon and if she was willing to share bagels with other people. It was a playful tease about her strange eating habits, and she grinned as she texted back her reply: Yes and yes (but only if I get a full bagel to myself).

He quickly wrote back: That's not exactly sharing.

No one shares bagels! That's why they're so wonderful! Emma replied.

"It's totally Matt," Jackie declared. "Look at that smile."

Feeling caught, Emma put her phone back in her bag. "Actually, it was Will. We're trying to figure out when to record again."

"I like Will," Debbie said. "I can tell he really gets you."

"What do you mean? You barely met him."

"I know, but you two seem to have the same kind of energy. Super playful but smart. Call it a mother's instinct," Debbie said with a shrug.

"Well, Will didn't want to marry her," Jackie replied. "So we leveled up and found someone better."

"Did Ryan and I have the same energy?" Emma asked, not ready to move on.

It was rare for her mom to make bold observations like this, even though Debbie had an uncanny habit for being right. Like when Emma had briefly considered getting a PhD after her master's to become a psychologist. Debbie had deftly asked if Emma actually *wanted* to go that route or if she just felt compelled to because of other people's opinions. Psychologists tended to be more highly regarded in the field than marriage and family therapists. Emma hadn't even realized she was caving to professional peer pressure until her mother brought it up. Now she loved her job and was delighted to not have spent an extra four years in school for no real reason.

"That's a good question," Debbie said as she considered her daughter's ex-fiancé. Ryan had become a fixture in all their lives before his abrupt exit, so she knew him well. "I know you two had a lot of fun together. But I always got the sense that Ryan was too conventional for you."

"Conventional? In what way?" Emma prodded.

"You've always been a bit…unorthodox. Even when you were a kid. I remember I had to take you to a speech therapist because you were using your tongue wrong. She asked you all these questions as part of the assessment and you told her that your favorite color was black, and your favorite food was artichokes. You were four."

"I stand by both those choices," Emma said as she gestured to her entirely black outfit.

"Exactly. You've never had any problem going outside the box or not following a crowd. I mean look at what you are doing right now. Operation: Save My Date couldn't be more unconventional," Debbie explained. "And Ryan… Ryan was vanilla."

"Ew, Mom," Jackie complained.

"I don't mean sexually. And I don't even mean it in a bad way. There's nothing wrong with liking what most people like or following a more traditional path. But that has never been you, Emma. You forge your own way."

Emma could feel the prickle of new tears. For her entire life, Emma had wanted nothing more than to fit in. But growing up, her anxiety had made social situations difficult, and her personality quirks had always gotten in the way of presenting as *totally normal*. She'd always viewed her inability to fit in as a bad thing. As something that needed to be corrected through a lot of therapy and self-restraint. It was shocking to hear her mother describe it as a strength.

"Ryan was a good guy—or at least seemed like a good guy. But he wanted a predictable life. I could tell he wasn't super comfortable with you getting so big on YouTube or selling your book. Not that he wasn't proud or impressed—I just got the sense that he was worried your career might knock his plan for himself off course."

Emma nodded as a tear escaped from her eye. She had only ever allowed herself to hope that she could find someone *as good* as Ryan. She had never imagined that there might be someone even better.

"Why didn't you tell me all this when we were still together?"

"Why would I? You seemed happy and certain about him. I had no reason to think I knew better than you as just an outsider looking in."

"If either of my girls date someone I don't like I'm going to tell them," Jackie declared.

"I *liked* Ryan. I just wasn't sure if I liked him for Emma."

"Same difference. I'm not going to let them waste their time with losers."

"Good luck with that," Debbie said with a laugh. "Do you not remember your high school boyfriend?"

"Drew was very cool. And on the football team," Jackie said defensively.

"Didn't he get kicked out of UConn for trying to fill a pool with alcohol?" Emma asked.

"I don't know. I'd already dumped him by then," Jackie replied. "None of this really matters anyway because Emma has Matt now and he is the real deal."

"Wait, did you meet him?" Debbie asked. "I want to meet him!"

"I haven't met him in person, but I can tell. Like how I knew Chris was going to be my husband before I even talked to him."

Emma bit her tongue like she did every time her sister

brought up her relationship origin story. Jackie was clearly proud of her ability to locate, target and procure Chris, but it had always felt a little to Emma like Jackie had trapped a wild animal rather than found a willing and ready partner. Chris hadn't been looking to settle down when they first met in college, and he certainly hadn't been planning to get married so young. But Jackie had made her intentions clear: either get in or get lost. Clearly Chris had gotten on board. Meanwhile, each time Emma had tried a similar tactic, her boyfriends had had no issue getting lost—Will included.

"How are *you* feeling about Matt, honey? Do you like him as much as your married sister seems to?"

Emma laughed at her mother's gentle dig. "I definitely like him. He's not my normal type and I feel a little insecure around him sometimes because he is so tall and beautiful. But overall, I feel super lucky that he's open to trying this with me."

"In that case, I'm excited to meet him. Whenever you two feel ready," Debbie said.

"I'm ready now," Jackie added.

"I'll introduce you all soon. I just want us to get to know each other a bit better first."

"I understand," Debbie said. "I waited three months to tell our friends that your father and I were dating. He's still touchy about it."

Debbie's relationship origin story was eerily similar to Jackie's, but in reverse. After being in the same college friend group for a few years, Alan had suddenly decided over a Christmas break that he wanted to date Debbie. Like Chris, Debbie had taken some convincing before ultimately falling for Emma's charmingly awkward and persistent father. Emma was the only one in her family who had to date as a college graduate. It was immensely frustrating that it was taking her so long to find someone.

"When you do meet Matt, are you going to give me your real opinion of him?" Emma asked.

"Only if you really want me to," Debbie replied, which they both knew probably meant no.

"You found it," Will announced as he held the door open for a slightly wet Emma. It rarely rained in LA, but when it did everyone was completely unprepared.

"The sign helped." Emma gestured to a sizable orange neon light in the shape of headphones with the podcast network's name, Pretty Sound, underneath. Their studio took up half a floor in an office building designed more like a motel than a skyscraper.

Emma followed Will into the lobby, relieved that he had been too focused on letting her in to initiate a hug. His hugs always set her heart back a beat.

"Can I get you anything?" Will asked as he led her into the kitchen area. "We have twelve different flavors of LaCroix, four different seaweed snacks and a bunch of samples from products that used to advertise with us until they went out of business."

Emma surveyed the crowded countertop filled with a variety of energy bars, fruit snacks and chips made out of pretty much anything other than potatoes. She immediately felt overwhelmed.

"I'm okay for now."

"Will! Just heard the *Gunpowder* edit," a man in a tie-dye sweatshirt and wide corduroy pants declared as he walked by. "Loving it. Keep up the good work."

"Thanks, Neil. Excited to get it out soon."

Neil gave a thumbs-up over his right shoulder as he headed down a carpeted hallway.

"That's my boss," Will explained as he unpeeled and bit into a banana. "I'm producing a series on the Gunpowder Plot of 1605, where a group of Catholics tried and failed to blow up the

House of Lords. It's a wild story. Requires a lot of research and time set aside for explaining Zoom recordings to historians."

"Seems pretty different from what we're doing."

"That's why I love working in podcasts—no one gets pigeon-holed. If it's a good story, you get to tell it. Or help tell it." He threw his banana peel in the trash. "Come with me."

Emma followed Will down the carpeted hallway as he led her to a room marked Studio C. Inside was a square wooden table and four chairs, each set up with its own microphone and headset. One of the walls was made of glass and showed a small room next door filled with what Emma assumed to be audio equipment. A short woman with curly hair and bright red lip-stick waved at Emma through the glass.

"That's Anika. She's our audio engineer."

"This is all becoming so official."

"I'm an official sort of guy," Will replied as he plopped him-self down in one of the rolling chairs and smoothly put on his headphones.

Emma scoffed because that's the appropriate social reaction to arrogance. But internally, she could feel her annoying at-traction to Will growing now that she was seeing him in his professional setting. She had always been attracted to people excelling at things, whether it was the impressive magician in her sixth-grade talent show or her months-long obsession with a random business major from college who was really skilled on a Razor scooter. Something about people being in their ele-ment superseded all normal barriers for her arousal like people's physical appearance or overall personality. That's why Emma didn't let herself watch the Olympics; it was too alluring.

"Do I need to put mine on too?" Emma asked as she picked up a pair of headphones and sat down across the table.

"Not today. I just need them to hear Anika."

Emma nodded, happy to not have to worry about her ears getting crushed. Sensory sensitivity didn't only apply to clothes.

"Are you good to go?" Will asked into his mic. Anika replied with a thumbs-up. Emma was officially on the record, which meant her palms were starting to sweat.

"Let's dive in. How did your parents fuck you up?" Will asked far too casually given the intensity of his opening question. "I've been doing some research on romantic relationships, and it seems like a lot of our dating habits can be traced back to our—" Will looked at a sheet of notes in front of him "—primary care givers."

"What makes you assume I'm fucked up?" Emma replied with mock indignation. In her experience, everyone was fucked up in some way or another.

"You're right, publicly trying to find a new husband in time for your original wedding to someone else screams well-adjusted."

"It screams *innovative*," Emma joked before taking his question seriously. "In all honesty, I think they fucked me up by making it all seem too easy. I grew up assuming that if I was a good person I would meet another good person, most likely in college, and then we would get married before I turned thirty. So when that didn't happen, I started to assume *I* was the problem instead of realizing that my parents, and my sister, had just been pretty lucky."

"Makes sense."

"Not to say that I wasn't also the problem," Emma admitted with a grin. "I can't exactly blame my stage-five-clinger behavior solely on my parents' happy marriage. I also had a lot of personal healing to do tied to my anxiety and total lack of self-esteem."

"Are you healed now?"

"I thought I was," Emma admitted. "But then my fiancé left me, and all of my greatest fears came true. That caused a bit of a backslide."

"I think that's understandable."

"Or maybe it was silly to think we can ever be fully healed. Life is probably too complicated for that."

Will looked at her and shook his head, like she was a puzzle he couldn't figure out.

"What?"

"I just don't know how you can be so reasonable and thoughtful about the world and still want to marry a guy you barely know."

"Maybe Operation: Save My Date is also reasonable and thoughtful when you really break it down and remove societal bias."

Will seemed to consider this option for a moment before replying. "No. I still think it's pretty nuts."

"Don't say *nuts*," Emma corrected.

"Sorry. I meant completely bananas."

"Better. But I thought you were going to try to be objective."

"We both knew that was never going to work," Will said. "Especially when it comes to you."

As those words hit her ears, Emma's heart wanted to leap out of her chest, burrow into Will's body and fuse with his heart so they could be together forever. Had he really just admitted that Emma was his weakness? That was the exact kind of *you are incredibly special to me* sentiment Emma had searched for her whole life. But she knew better than to admit all that out loud. Will probably didn't even realize how it sounded.

"How did your parents fuck *you* up?" Emma countered instead of leaping over the table to kiss him. Maybe if she could expose more of his issues, she wouldn't be so goddamn attracted to him all the time.

"I don't know if I've had enough therapy to properly answer that question," Will admitted. "Although one of my exes did once refer to me as 'a classic Cancer' if that gives you any insight."

"It doesn't." Emma had never gotten into astrology mainly

because she thought it was completely made up. "Let's try another route. Are your parents happy together?"

Will let out a long whistle that would make for good audio. "Now that is a great question."

Emma smiled. Asking good questions was kind of her whole thing.

"I think if you asked my parents if they were happily married, they would say yes. Well, my mom would say yes, and my dad would grunt. But I don't really understand how that's possible. I would never want their version of marriage."

This wasn't surprising. Most people seemed to either want to re-create what their parents had, like Emma, or run in the opposite direction, like Will.

"What's their version like?"

Will suddenly seemed aware that their conversation was being recorded. He sneaked a glance at Anika, who raised her eyebrows. It was either a challenge or a warning; Emma didn't know her enough to tell.

"Fuck it, they never listen to my shows anyway," Will declared as he readjusted himself in his chair. "My parents' marriage isn't really a marriage. It's more like a cult of one where my dad is the leader, and my mother is his loyal follower. She does whatever he wants, and he rewards her by…continuing to dictate her entire life."

Emma nodded. It was an unfortunately common dynamic and not one that created a peaceful home for children.

"For a long time, I only blamed my dad. But part of me thinks my mom likes it this way. If my dad is in total control, she doesn't have to think for herself or take responsibility when he blows up at a waitress or yells at her son for not being a varsity athlete. She can just coast and make mediocre jam."

"I'm not sure if it's ever that black-and-white, but I can definitely see why you would think that," Emma replied, shifting comfortably back into her role as a neutral third party.

Will put his hand up to cover his mic. "Don't do that."

"Don't do what?"

"Don't become Therapist Emma. This is supposed to be a conversation. Give me your real reactions as a person not a professional." He took his hand off the mic, signaling they were back on the record. She both hated and loved that he had called her on her shit so efficiently. Most people took far longer to figure out when she was hiding behind her credentials.

"Okay. Fine. My *real* reaction hearing all that is sadness. It sucks that their dysfunctional relationship is your main reference for marriage. And, if I'm being totally honest, I also feel slightly better because I just realized your *mom* is the reason you didn't agree to my operation. Not me."

Will looked at her baffled. "Um... I don't want to marry my mom, Emma. She's pretty good-looking for her age, but she's also my mom."

Emma laughed. "I don't mean you love your mom more than you could ever love a wife. Although those people do exist." She shuddered as the memory of one high school boyfriend came to mind. He'd tried to get Emma to wear his mommy's hand-me-downs because they were "nicer than anything she owned." Last Emma checked, he still lived at home.

"What I meant is that you weren't at all open to my idea because you don't want to end up *like* your mom," Emma explained. "Trapped in a relationship with no autonomy or control."

"Oh. Yeah. I don't want that at all."

Emma laughed again—this time at his visceral disgust. "What I'm wondering is why you think marrying someone after only a few months implies that you'll end up trapped in a relationship with no autonomy or control?"

"Because..." Will thought for a moment. "Because I'm not the kind of person who would want to get married that quickly so if I did it would mean I am fundamentally changing who I am to make someone else happy. And that feels like a slippery slope, Moskowitz."

"I'm going to take a wild swing here and say you aren't very good at compromise in relationships."

Will glared at her. It was clear she wasn't the first person in his life to suggest such a thing. She probably wasn't even the second.

"Let's move on to our next topic," Will replied as he referred to his notes. "What are your thoughts on the wedding industrial complex and what role, if any, has that played in your decision-making?"

She'd gotten under his skin. And she liked it.

Twenty-Two

AS EMMA ATTEMPTED TO PARK HER SUV IN A SPOT CLEARLY
labeled Compact, she found herself returning to Will's comment from earlier in the week. *Especially when it comes to you* had
pretty much been running on a loop inside her head since their
conversation. The rest of their recording session had been relatively tame once Will steered them to less personal topics, but
there remained a charged undercurrent under everything they
said to each other. She could almost still feel the vibrations—

Stop it, Emma admonished herself. It was not appropriate to
waste any more mental energy on a man who she wasn't dating. Especially when she was dating someone else.

As she got out of the car, Emma noticed her front right tire
jutting over the painted line, but she didn't want to correct it
and be late. She was meeting Matt at the two-story Crate &
Barrel in Beverly Hills to help zhuzh up his condo. It felt like
the most established couple activity they'd done so far, and she
wanted to be fully present with him, not secretly trying to dissect the inner workings of Will's mind.

When Emma spotted Matt perusing the kitchen appliances,
she considered sneaking up on him as a goof. It was an old bit

she'd picked up from Alan, who was always popping out of nowhere to surprise Debbie. But something told her Matt wasn't the kind of person who was looking to shriek in surprise at a furniture store. She approached him normally instead.

"See anything you like?" Emma asked by way of greeting.

"Now I do," Matt replied before reaching down to kiss Emma hello. She stretched up on her tiptoes to help him out.

"Do you have any idea what this is?" Matt held up an oblong green-and-black culinary object that appeared to have no obvious use.

"Not a clue."

"Me neither. That's probably why Kelly wouldn't let me near the kitchen. I don't know if I told you, but she was quite the chef. She even did a summer program at the Culinary Institute."

Emma tried not to flinch at yet another mention of his ex-wife. It was starting to feel like Kelly was haunting their every exchange. No matter what topic came up through text or conversation it somehow circled back to the woman who broke Matt's heart. For having never met her, Emma already knew far too much about Kelly. Like how she always wore heels to work and her favorite place to run was Griffith Park and *not* Runyon Canyon, like you'd expect—two personal details Emma couldn't find less relatable.

"Do you want to check out the lamps first? I know you think your bedroom is too dark."

A familiar voice rang out. "Oh my god, Emma? What are you doing here?"

Emma turned to find Jackie and Chris pretending to be shocked at this clearly planned encounter. Chris even had his mouth open; he was a good and loyal husband.

"Helping Matt shop for his condo," Emma replied. "Like I told you on the phone earlier today."

"I thought you said you were meeting him *tomorrow*," Jackie lied as she made her way toward her real target, Matt, who was already hugging and slapping backs with Chris.

"So great to see you, man," Chris said, turning to introduce Jackie. "This is my wife, Jackie."

"Hi!" Jackie nearly shrieked as she threw her arms around Matt. "It's so nice to finally meet you."

"Same here," Matt replied genuinely as he looked between Jackie and Emma. "I can definitely see the resemblance."

"Really?" Emma asked skeptically. Most people were thrown when they found out Emma and Jackie were sisters. One notable waiter had even said, "You mean *stepsisters*?" because her brain could not compute their shared DNA. But maybe Matt saw something most people didn't. Or maybe he was just being polite.

"What exactly are you looking for?" Jackie asked Matt. "Not to butt in, but I took a few interior design classes before Izzy was born."

"Oh really? That's awesome." Matt turned to Emma. "What was it we needed again?"

Emma was both surprised and flattered that Matt had said "we"; he seemed to be adapting to their partnership much faster than she was. Probably because her brain was too focused on a certain podcast producer with a penchant for matching his shirts with his eye color.

"I think we said some lamps, a bunch of artwork and a new coffee table?"

"I'm not going to let you buy artwork at Crate & Barrel, but I bet we can find a nice coffee table," Jackie declared as she headed toward the stairs. The other three obediently followed.

"Your sister seems really nice," Matt whispered as Jackie surveyed the store's offerings with military-grade precision.

"I'm sorry she bombarded us. I told her it was too soon, but Jackie has selective hearing."

"You don't need to apologize. I've been wanting to meet your family," Matt assured her.

"In that case, let me see if my parents are free right now," Emma joked. "My father loves a store with fluorescent lighting and comfortable chairs."

"You're hilarious," Matt said, plopping a kiss on her head.

Emma let herself lean into him as Jackie watched, delighted, from across the store. It felt good to make her sister happy after all the time Jackie had spent trying to help Emma not be so sad.

Three hours and five home decor stores later, Jackie had successfully redesigned Matt's condo without ever having stepped inside it. She had worked solely off of a few iPhone photos and pure instinct. But Matt was thrilled and that was all that mattered—even if Emma felt a little steamrollered and useless. She was beginning to suspect Jackie had chosen to crash this particular outing because she didn't want Emma's lack of design sense to ruin their whole operation.

"I really can't thank you enough," Matt gushed as he hugged Jackie and Chris goodbye in front of their Lexus SUV.

"It was our pleasure," Jackie replied, holding on to him for a bit too long. Emma was surprised Jackie hadn't reached out and felt his bicep.

"We've got to do this again soon. But maybe at our house with a game on instead," Chris said. Emma suspected his shopping limit had been reached for the year. Maybe the decade.

"Actually, I was going to see if you and Mr. and Mrs. Moskowitz wanted to come over for dinner next week," Matt asked. "My family always has a big Sunday dinner together and I'd love to continue the tradition." Matt looked at Emma, who was hearing about this plan *and* tradition for the first time. "If that's okay—"

"Of course that's okay," Jackie interjected. "We'll get a sitter for the girls. Just let us know what to bring."

"You don't need to bring anything," Matt insisted.

"We're Jews," Emma explained. "Not bringing anything isn't allowed."

"In that case, bring whatever you want," Matt replied, squeezing Emma's hand.

She squeezed it back, trying not to overthink what was quickly becoming her family's biggest event since her cousin hosted a bris at the Four Seasons.

Good luck tonight. I hope everyone behaves.

Emma read Will's text with a grin as she sat in the back of her parents' car on the way to Matt's condo. She was trying to decide if she should respond sincerely or with a joke when Debbie interrupted her concentration.

"Did you hear your father?"

"No, sorry," Emma said as she put her phone back in her bag. She could reply to Will later, even if an unanswered text message was in complete opposition of her anxiety's rules and regulations. "What did you say, Dad?"

"I asked if Matt is a baseball guy."

"He's definitely a sports guy. But I don't know about baseball specifically."

Alan hmphed in response. He had a chip on his shoulder about the contingent of fans who loved every major American sport except baseball because it was "too slow." As a lifelong Dodgers fanatic, he took it as a personal attack.

"I didn't say he doesn't like it. I said I didn't know," Emma clarified.

"Okay, I'll ask him about it. Try to figure out his team."

"Please don't turn tonight into an interrogation. You don't need to learn everything about him all at once," Emma pleaded.

That was the approach she had been trying to take as well. Now that things were moving forward, Emma was starting to feel a bit freaked out about how little she knew about Matt. She hadn't even met his friends or FaceTimed with his family. Did his parents know about her? Did they think she was bananas?

"I need to know his stance on reproductive rights and the electoral college," Debbie said. "But I'll wait to ask until dessert."

Emma laughed, hoping that her mom was kidding. Her parents tended to be on good behavior when meeting a new boyfriend, but this was an unusual situation. The stakes were significantly higher than when they took one of Emma's flings to Dave & Buster's three days before he broke up with her.

"Will you look at this," Alan said with his signature whistle as they pulled up to the valet stand at Matt's building. "I no longer care if he watches baseball."

"Wait until you see the apartment." Emma gathered her bag, trying her best not to think about the unanswered message on her phone. She then did her best to lead the way into the lobby, up the elevator and down the hall as if she belonged there and wasn't just some random guest—which was how she felt.

Emma knocked twice to no response.

"Do we have the wrong time?" Debbie asked.

"Let me try to call him," Emma offered as Chris and Jackie got off the elevator. At least Emma assumed it was Chris since his head was being blocked by one of the biggest gift baskets Emma had ever seen.

"What's going on?" Jackie asked.

"We're being stood up," Alan announced before turning his attention to Chris. "What's in there?"

"I have no idea. But it cost four hundred dollars so it better be good."

"Chris, don't tell people what we spent. It's tacky."

"It's not *people*. It's your family. And if I'm going to spend this much on a gift basket, I want people to know about it."

"He's not answering," Emma said as worry started to take hold. Was she really about to be stood up in front of her entire family? How much humiliation could one heart take? Maybe Jackie would let her keep the gift basket to soften the blow.

"You probably didn't knock loud enough," Jackie offered, leaning in to pound on the door. They all straightened up as they heard the distinct click of the door being unlocked. But when it didn't open, they looked at each other in confusion.

"Try the doorknob," Chris suggested as he struggled to re-adjust the basket.

"We can't just barge into his home," Debbie replied.

"He unlocked it. And this thing weighs a ton."

"I'm opening it," Alan interrupted as he leaned over and flung the door open. A collective gasp rang out as they took in the scene.

Matt's apartment was aglow with a reddish light and dozens of candles. There were rose petals all over the custom hard-wood floors.

"Oh my god. Oh my god," Jackie squealed as she shoved Emma inside. The rest of the family followed.

"What is going on?" Emma whispered even though she had a strong inkling.

Her mind flashed to the last time she realized she was about to be proposed to. It had been a random Thursday night and she'd just gotten back from a long day of back-to-back sessions. She was so tired and distracted she almost missed the Post-it note on the door.

Ryan had written on it the first of ten instructions for an elaborate scavenger hunt he had set up throughout their home. Emma grabbed it gleefully as she darted into the apartment to begin her mission. She immediately found Ryan waiting for her in the kitchen.

"You have ten minutes to find what you are searching for," he announced in a deep voice. She wanted to jump all over him in excitement and demand to see the ring, but knew she had to let his thoughtful plan play out first.

"What happens if I don't find it in time?"

"Stop asking questions and get to work."

Emma listened, diving into the various clues that were hidden throughout their apartment, all of which were extremely specific to Emma and their relationship. She found a Post-it on "The Best Gift Ever Given," which was a screen-printed T-shirt she had made for Ryan's birthday with a picture of Emma's head on Emily Ratajkowski's body. She found another one on "Your Greatest Fear," which was a bottle of Raid underneath the kitchen sink. And exactly nine minutes and forty-two seconds into her hunt, she found the final Post-it note on a ring box in her nightstand drawer that simply said, "Will you marry me?"

Emma had turned around to see Ryan kneeling on the ground with a diamond ring in his hand. He proceeded to give a speech that Emma couldn't remember because she was so excited, she pretty much blacked out. It had been the happiest day of her life so far.

Now, less than a year later, Ryan was just a painful memory, and Emma was about to get engaged to someone who wasn't even aware of her debilitating fear of bugs. Part of her felt compelled to flee, which was a stark contrast to how she'd felt about Ryan. She hadn't had an ounce of uncertainty as she accepted his ring and attempted to jump into his arms, causing both of them to tumble onto the bed, hysterical with tears and laughter. But her certainty about their relationship hadn't protected her; if anything, it had only made it more shocking and disorienting when he ripped it all away.

So maybe the anxiety she felt right now as she waited for Matt to appear wasn't a bad thing. Maybe it was a sign that she was growing up. It was unrealistic to feel completely certain about any major life decision. Certainty was naivety in disguise and she wasn't going to be naive anymore.

"Emma," Matt said as he finally appeared on the stairs wearing a suit and a nervous smile. "I know we haven't known each other very long. And I haven't even met your parents before tonight." He turned to look at Alan and Debbie and gave them a wave. They immediately waved back. "But I can already tell that we want the same things. We both want a long and happy partnership filled with children and family and complete trust in one another."

Having gracefully made his way downstairs during his speech, Matt was now standing right in front of Emma. He looked even more handsome than he had in Chris's PowerPoint presentation. Emma watched as he pulled a ring box from his jacket pocket and went down on one knee.

"I know we've each been hurt, and I know this isn't either one of our first proposals. But, if you agree, I can promise it will be our last."

Assuming neither one of us dies early and the other one wants to get remarried, Emma thought before admonishing herself for thinking about that sort of thing at a time like this. What was wrong with her?

"Emma Moskowitz," Matt said with a tremble in his voice as he opened the ring box and revealed an engagement ring that was so big it looked fake, "will you marry me?"

"Yes!" Jackie screamed, before catching herself. "Sorry. Sorry. Forget I'm here." She hid herself under Chris's arm as everyone laughed.

"Should we try again?" Emma whispered to Matt, who grinned and nodded.

"Emma Moskowitz—and just Emma Moskowitz," he said with a playful look at Jackie, "will you marry me?"

"Yes," Emma declared as Matt whooped and wrapped her in a hug. Her whole family cheered and the anxiety Emma had been feeling dissipated. She was taking a risk, but she was taking it with a great guy.

"This is for you," Matt said, putting the huge round solitaire with a platinum setting on her ring finger. It immediately slid off. "I didn't know your size."

"That's okay. I have unusually small fingers."

Matt took her left hand and kissed where the ring would go. "I think they're perfect."

"Let me get a video of you putting the ring on," Jackie declared as she came over with her iPhone. "I totally blanked and forgot to film the proposal. Maybe we can do it again? Emma, show me your shocked face."

"That won't be necessary." Matt gestured to a dark corner of the apartment. "I hired someone to record everything."

An artsy-looking man and a video camera suddenly appeared as Debbie yelped in surprise.

"He was here the whole time?" Debbie asked with a hand on her chest.

"Yes. Sorry. This is Nicolas," Matt explained. "A buddy recommended him."

The videographer waved. "Great proposal. Got a lot of good stuff." He pointed at Jackie. "You really pop on camera."

"I always thought that I would," Jackie replied, beaming as she turned to Chris. "Don't I always say that?" Chris nodded.

"I'm sorry for scaring you," Matt apologized. "I just figured it'd be nice to have the proposal on video for the future and to show my parents. And maybe you can use it for the You-Tube channel?"

"That is freaking brilliant, Matt," Jackie exclaimed. "The fans are going to lose their minds."

Matt grinned at Emma. "I hope they like me."

"They're going to love you," Emma said, realizing with a bit of alarm that even though they were now officially engaged, they had yet to say that word to each other.

Twenty-Three

"SHOW ME THE RING AGAIN," MATT'S MOM SAID OVER FaceTime.

After a celebratory dinner, Emma's family had departed for the night, leaving both Emma and a half-eaten gift basket behind. As soon as they were gone, Emma suggested calling Matt's parents and he lit up at the idea.

They had now been on a group call with his entire family, nieces and nephews included, for over an hour. Emma's cheeks hurt from trying to maintain a smile. Apparently, Matt's family wasn't just aware of her; they were impressed by her traditional family-based values—something Emma never realized she had, as a progressive Jewish therapist from LA.

"It is stunning," Matt's mother cooed as Emma displayed the ill-fitting ring for the fifth time.

"I'm so happy for you two," Matt's youngest sister, Katie, said. She was the only sibling not having to split focus with a demanding toddler or newborn. "We should probably let you guys celebrate."

"But I have more questions," Matt's other sister, Mary, whined as her husband, Shane, completely zoned out next to her. Mary's dour facial expressions had made it known from the beginning of the call that she was the most skeptical of the bunch. "She's going to be my sister-in-law even though I don't know her *at all*."

"There'll be plenty of time to get to know each other when we fly out for the wedding," Matt's father replied. "Your mother is already looking into flights."

"What airline?" Matt's brother, Dave, asked with the kind of energy that suggested this was a contentious topic in their family—much like the 405 freeway was in Emma's.

After another five minutes of airline debate, goodbyes and one more close up of what Emma had to assume was at least a two-carat diamond, they finally hung up.

It was Emma's and Matt's first time alone as an engaged couple.

"Your family is great," Emma said, meaning it. It was obvious the Monroys cared deeply about each other even if their decidedly Midwestern vibe was a bit of a culture shock. Emma could already tell that twenty-six-year-old Katie was likely to be her closest ally because she hadn't once said the words *blessed* or *god willing*.

"They can be a little much," Matt offered politely. "But I can tell they really like you."

"Even Mary?" Emma asked as Matt laughed.

"She's just protective. The first time I took Kelly home to meet them, Mary cornered her for the entire night grilling her with question after question. But by the time we left two days later, they were best friends."

"Do they still talk?"

"No," Matt replied before fully considering the question. A look of concern crossed his face. "At least I don't think so."

Emma nodded, not knowing what to say next. As much as she liked Matt, they didn't have the level of repartee she was used to in her relationships. She suspected Matt might still be carrying around too much grief over the end of his marriage for him to be fully present with her. It was like looking at a work of art covered in a layer of grime and dust. She could see the beauty underneath but wasn't sure how to access it without doing more damage.

"Is there anyone else you want to call?" Matt asked.

"I don't think so. You?"

"Nope."

They locked eyes and Matt shifted slightly closer to Emma on the couch. He reached his hand out and slowly caressed her face. Emma tried not to breathe too loudly despite her nerves and surgically constructed small nasal passages. He leaned in and suddenly they were kissing with more intensity than Emma expected. He was one of the best kissers she'd experienced in her rather eventful dating history, and something about the way Matt touched her helped wash her nervousness away. She was able to zone in and focus on her body in a way that normally eluded her.

"Did you want to go to the bedroom?" Matt asked, his voice husky and a bit ragged.

"Yes, please," Emma replied even though the break in physical contact had caused her brain to reengage. She suddenly felt unsure if she was ready to go all the way. But Matt was already holding his hand out to help her. She followed him up the stairs to the primary bedroom, the whole time focusing on putting one foot in front of the other. Her knee injury had required her to relearn how to go up and down stairs without second-guessing herself. It was similar to how her broken heart was making it difficult to effortlessly fall into bed with her new fiancé, even if her lower half really wanted to.

Matt sat down on his all-white bed. Emma wasn't sure if this clean look was his preference or a holdover from life with Kelly. She'd always found all-white bedding devoid of personality. But then again, Emma wasn't known for her taste.

"Come here," Matt said with a level of authority Emma could get behind. She stood between his legs as he wrapped his arms around her waist. He was so tall they were almost the same height with him seated. Emma leaned down slightly and kissed him. He then masterfully picked her up and flipped her onto the bed. Suddenly she was on her back, and he was on top of her, kissing her neck and her chest and—

A loud jingle suddenly rang throughout the apartment, jolting them apart.

"What is that?" Emma asked, her heart racing from a mix of sexual arousal and primal fear.

"The doorbell," Matt replied as he got up and adjusted himself.

"You have a doorbell?" Emma's mind flashed back to her entire family standing uselessly in the hallway.

"Yeah, it's a little off to the side. Let me go check who it is."

"What if it's a murderer?"

"Then the security guard is in a lot of trouble for letting them up here."

Matt made his way to the front door as Emma tried to fix her bangs behind him. If an intruder was going to take Matt down, they would go down together.

"Oh, hey man," Matt said as he opened the door.

Emma instantly breathed a sigh of relief that Matt recognized their mystery visitor. Because despite her best intentions, she was a coward at heart.

"Sorry to barge in but Emma wasn't answering her phone," a familiar voice said. She joined Matt at the door and saw her brother-in-law now dressed in sweatpants and an old high school T-shirt. Emma's first thought was surprise that Jackie had let him leave the house like that. Her second thought was panic.

"Is everyone okay?"

"Yeah, yeah," Chris assured her. "Jackie just left her phone here. I told her we could get it tomorrow and she reacted as though I had stabbed her."

"Understandable," Matt said graciously. "Come on in."

"Sorry to interrupt your big night," Chris said, sending a knowing look in Emma's direction, making her want to vomit. The idea that Chris knew she had sex sometimes was revolting, which proved she viewed him like a brother and not just a brother-in-law. So that was nice.

"Found it," Chris announced as he held up Jackie's iPhone in a quilted Chanel case. As he headed back out of the condo he waved goodbye over his shoulder. "Pretend I was never here."

"We'll try," Matt replied as he closed the door. But when he turned to face Emma, it was clear to both of them that mood had changed. After a moment of trying to figure out what to say next and not succeeding, they both laughed, which was a good sign. Humor was kryptonite for awkward situations.

"Should we get something to drink?" Matt asked.

"Absolutely we should."

As he poured them each a glass of red wine, Emma could tell there was something on his mind. She gently nudged him with her hip. "What's up?"

"I…" Matt started before shaking his head. "Never mind. It's stupid."

"Now I have to know. Because you have yet to say a single stupid thing and it's been getting on my nerves."

Matt laughed again and took a rather large gulp of wine. "I've just been thinking about the wedding and how we've been doing so many things out of order."

Emma nodded as a knot formed in her chest. Was he having second thoughts already? Was she about to have to give a *second* ring back?

"And I was just wondering what you would think about us not sleeping together until our wedding night?" He looked at her bashfully as every insecurity Emma had ever felt about

her desirability or lack thereof came crashing into her brain.
He must have seen the look of horror on her face because he
quickly clarified, "It's not that I don't want to sleep with you.
Obviously, I do. I've just always wondered if couples who wait
for marriage have a kind of advantage. Like, they understand
how sacred it all is or something." Matt shook his head with
embarrassment. "It's stupid. Forget I said anything."

"I don't think it's stupid," Emma replied delicately. "But I
guess I am curious about your reasoning. Do you have like a
moral or religious issue with premarital sex?"

"Not at all," Matt protested. "And I normally never would
have considered something like this before we met. But…how
do I say this? It's like we're already trying a new thing by committing to each other so quickly, so why not try this too? I think
there's something kind of beautiful about waiting until right
after the wedding. And I mean *right* after."

Emma laughed as she started to realize he had a point. If
they were already trying a new approach to their marriage,
why not try this too? Plus, Matt's relationship to sex was probably complicated now that he'd been cheated on by his ex-wife.
Maybe waiting until marriage was a way for him to feel safer
being intimate again. Not every guy could pump and dump
without emotional risk, despite what the media would have
everyone believe.

"You aren't worried that if we wait, you might end up feeling disappointed or something?"

"Emma, no." Matt took her hands in his. "I'm not worried
about that at all. I can already tell we have incredible chemistry. If Chris hadn't interrupted us, I have no doubt we would
have been up all night."

Emma smiled at the thought, even if it now seemed off the
table.

"It was just an idea. Probably a bad one. We don't need to do it."

"I don't think it's a bad idea. I just have to adjust to it." *And figure out how to not take it personally*, Emma added silently in her head. "I'm the one who came up with this whole plan to begin with. It seems only fair to incorporate one of your ideas."

"Really?" Matt looked at her so earnestly she felt compelled to protect him and his heart at any cost.

"Really," Emma replied as she held out her hand for an official shake. "No sex until marriage."

Matt put his hand in hers and shook.

"No sex until marriage."

And with that, they went to bed. Or, more accurately, to sleep.

Twenty-Four

"MAYBE WE SHOULD HIRE A REAL EDITOR?" JACKIE ASKED as she and Imani crowded around Emma's laptop. Jackie had laid out a spread of snacks and champagne to celebrate Emma's engagement and make the most of her proposal video. They had just spent the last half hour attempting to coherently intercut Nicolas's footage with a video of Emma explaining what it felt like to get engaged for the second time. It wasn't going well.

"I think it's fine. YouTube is chaotic anyway," Imani countered. "No one expects it to be perfect."

"I just need to figure out how to blend the two audio tracks," Emma lamented as she tried to be precise on iMovie, which required a level of fine motor skills she did not possess.

"This is so dumb. Let me just hire a professional. We don't want to blow a chance to go viral just to save a few bucks." Jackie was already reaching for her phone, so Emma closed her laptop and gave in.

"Fine, but I want final approval."

"I personally think you should do the whole thing in black and white with a kind of ominous space opera feel," Imani suggested as Jackie looked at her in total confusion.

"She's kidding," Emma clarified. "Imani thinks this whole idea is a disaster waiting to happen."

"What? Why?"

"Why do I think Emma marrying some random finance guy to prove a point is a bad idea?" Imani asked sarcastically. "Hard to say."

"Have you met Matt yet?" Jackie asked. "Because once you meet him you won't be worried. He's a gem."

"Jackie's in love with my fiancé," Emma joked before realizing how strange it felt to refer to someone other than Ryan as her fiancé. She made a note of the sensation on her phone so she'd remember to bring it up on the podcast. Will had told her to jot down her thoughts as they came up so she'd remember what each stage of the operation felt like. She'd taken his advice but had failed to inform him that she'd been officially engaged for almost a week now. Even though they were basically texting each other all day, every day. The podcast was about to launch and all the work that required had forced them to shift into what was finally starting to feel like a friendship. A friendship with a romantic history, but a friendship nonetheless.

Emma rationalized her reluctance to share the big news with Will by convincing herself it would be better to do it in person and on mic. But part of her acknowledged that once Will knew about the ring that was currently being resized by Matt's jeweler, things could change between them. Will might pull back just as Emma was starting to become more and more reliant on his emotional support and witty retorts. She could tell Will was expecting her plan to fail and wasn't sure how he would react to learning it was going better than she had ever imagined.

"How could I not love Matt?" Jackie replied to Emma's jab. "He's going to be my brother-in-law and he has excellent taste in diamond rings."

Emma didn't have the heart to tell Jackie that while the ring was beautiful, it didn't feel like *her*. She'd preferred the three-stone arrangement with a yellow gold band that Ryan had found after Emma sent him a series of inspo photos. Her new ring felt rather ostentatious for a therapist who rented an office space next to an El Pollo Loco. But maybe her clients would see it as proof that she knew what she was talking about.

"Do *you* love Matt, Emma?" Imani asked as she popped a pita chip in her mouth.

"Oh, you know, what even is love? Is it a feeling? Is it a moment in time?" Emma mused in an attempt to evade the question. Based on Imani's and Jackie's faces, it hadn't worked.

"Have you said 'I love you' to each other yet?" Imani probed.

"No. But I think that's okay. We had a big discussion the other night about doing things on our own timeline and not having to follow the standard order of a relationship."

"I love that," Jackie said with a vigorous head nod. "He seems so understanding."

"Yeah, it took a lot of the pressure off," Emma admitted as she tried to determine whether to share the next part. She was afraid of Imani's reaction, but talking things out with trusted confidantes wasn't something she could only recommend for other people without doing it herself. "He even suggested that we wait until the wedding to…you know."

The silence that followed felt like the worst drop in a roller-coaster ride. It instantly filled Emma with regret and a wave of nausea.

"You aren't going to sleep with him before you get married?" Imani finally asked, rather diplomatically. That's how Emma knew it was bad; Imani saved diplomacy for dire situations.

"Nope. He thinks—*we* think—that waiting might help set us up for a more successful marriage."

"How?"

When Matt had pitched the idea, it had made sense to Emma, but now that she was trying to replay his argument, the logic was foggier. "It will…make it more sacred."

Imani snorted in disdain. "Since when does sex have to be sacred?"

"It doesn't," Emma clarified. "I think he just wants to try something different after what happened in his last marriage. He's still recovering, and I don't want him to do anything he isn't ready to do yet."

"Wait," Jackie interjected. "*He's* the one who asked to wait? I didn't know men did that. Do you think there's something wrong with his…" Jackie gestured down below.

"Not that I know of. And even if there was, it wouldn't be the end of the world. There are plenty of workarounds." Emma thought about the weeklong, incredibly informative seminar she'd attended on sexual dysfunction the previous year. "I just think he needs to trust me more or something. And once we're married, we'll have built that trust."

Imani snorted again.

Emma turned to her, annoyed. "You don't buy it?"

"I think you're both putting too much emphasis on a piece of paper. Things aren't going to change the moment you get married. He's not immediately going to get over his trust issues and you're not suddenly going to fall in love."

"I know that. But I do think there can be power in ceremony and ritual. They mean something to people for a reason."

"You're right," Imani agreed. She had been the one to convince Emma that spirituality and psychology could mix after all. "I just don't want you to ignore any issues that might come up in the next few months because you assume they'll work themselves out once you're married. We both know it never works like that."

"My relationship got better once we were married," Jackie countered. "Mostly because I was no longer constantly bugging Chris about when we'd get married. But I do think it can be smart to test the car before you buy it."

"I think she's talking about sex," Imani stage-whispered to Emma.

"I don't know, she could also be talking about his Porsche."

"Matt has a Porsche? Never mind, just risk it," Jackie replied. "Sex is overrated anyway."

"This should only take a few hours." Emma leaned over Matt's fancy sports car's console to kiss him goodbye. "I can grab an Uber home."

"Nope. No rideshares for my fiancée. Just text me when you're done and I'll come pick you up. There's a new taco place—"

A loud knock on the window interrupted their conversation. Emma turned to find Will staring into the car with a grin. She rolled her eyes at him while trying to calm her accelerated heart rate. She was not planning on this interaction.

"That's my producer, Will," Emma explained as she opened the car door. Will backed away from the Porsche to give Emma room to get out before reclaiming his spot at the now-open door.

"Hey, man." Will leaned into the car for a handshake. "Nice to finally meet you."

"You, too," Matt replied, even though Emma barely talked to Matt about Will. It seemed safer that way. Less opportunity for potentially troubling information about her complicated feelings to slip out.

Once the handshake was complete, Emma intervened before Will could say something embarrassing—or life ruining. She also didn't want Matt to mention their engagement before she could tell Will privately. She knew owed him that courtesy out of respect for their peculiar relationship. Now that that disclosure was imminent, Emma was increasingly nervous about his response. What if Will was annoyed the podcast had been cut out of the proposal? Or worse, what if Will was happy for her, relieved, even? The fact that this concern existed at all was proof that Emma liked jealous Will a little too much.

But, Emma reminded herself for the umpteenth time, Will had made his choice. And now he had to live with the fallout. Which might include a lot more time with Matt now that he was officially her fiancé and a likely future guest of the podcast.

As the thought of Will interviewing Matt threatened to induce a panic attack, Emma took a few calming breaths to place herself back into the present moment. A moment in which she very much wanted Matt to drive away before things got even more awkward.

"I'll see you soon," Emma sputtered as she nudged Will toward her apartment building, where they were planning to record.

"Bye," Will sang out in a pitch that felt like he was poking fun at her. "Wow." He whistled. "That's a good-looking man."

"Are you surprised?"

"No, but it is a good reminder to renew my gym membership," Will joked as she punched in the building code to open the front door. Emma tried to push away the guilt she was feeling for unintentionally shoving Matt's perfect hairline in Will's face. Matt wouldn't be chauffeuring her around if Will hadn't rejected her first, so any discomfort he was feeling was really his own fault.

Emma loved when a reframe absolved her of all responsibility.

"Thank you for helping me with this," Emma said a few minutes later as she not so carefully put her West Elm dishes in a packing box. They were four years old and purchased at a big discount. It didn't feel worth the time to individually wrap each one. Especially if she was going to be moving in with Matt soon.

"I'm not here to help. I'm here to document," Will replied as he unpacked a new kind of mic that he could attach to her body as she moved around.

Alan had finally found a subletter for Emma's apartment, some son of a friend of one of his tennis buddies. Emma had the weekend to get all her stuff out once and for all. It was the end of an era that had already been on life support.

"If you do help, you get to go through my stuff."

"Now you're talking. I call the nightstand drawers."

Emma laughed, pleased that she had already removed her vibrators during an earlier sweep. Will was more than welcome to pack up her emergency flashlight and overnight moisturizing gloves.

"Have we moved up at all?" Emma asked as calmly as she could. The first episode of the podcast had officially launched yesterday, and the last Emma had obsessively checked they were number seventy-six in Apple Podcast's top one hundred shows under Society & Culture.

Will looked at this phone and grinned. "We're up to number fifty-eight."

"Oh my god, really?" Emma squealed. It blew her mind that their show was now more popular than *The Happiness Lab* with Dr. Laurie Santos, which was in her own regular listening rotation. It was both good and bad to know that one of the quickest ways to feel happy was to have a successful podcast.

"And Anika just sent me a link. Apparently, we already have our own subreddit. People are popping off in the comments."

"Let me see," Emma replied as Will walked into the kitchen with the lavalier mic in his hand. She tried to grab his phone but he put it back in his pocket.

"No way. I'm not letting you get lost down a Reddit rabbit hole."

"Why, does everyone hate me? I knew my voice was too high-pitched for audio."

"You have a great voice," Will replied as he untangled the mic's long cord. "It's just not going to be productive for you to read random people arguing with each other right now. Let's build the show *we* want to make before paying too much attention to other people's opinions."

"I hate it when you're reasonable."

"That does seem to be our central conflict." Will held up the lav. "Do you know how to put this on?"

"Not a clue."

"We need to clip this part to your pants and snake this part up your shirt and clip it to your collar." Will had a battery pack in one hand and a small mic in the other.

"Okay."

"Do you want to do it, or do you want me to do it?"

"You're the expert."

Will nodded and took a step forward. He seemed unusually bashful and Emma realized he was worried about having to touch her. But why was he worried? Did he think he was crossing a professional line? Or was he concerned that once he started, he wouldn't want to stop?

"I just need you to lift up your shirt."

Emma did as she was told and stood completely still as Will slipped the silver clip over her jeggings. He then slightly tugged at the battery pack to make sure it was secure, revealing even more skin. "That part's good."

Emma nodded, trying to appear nonchalant even as her heart sped up. It was the closest they'd physically been to each other since... *No.* Thinking about that wasn't a smart idea. They were finally getting good at being friends.

"And then we normally put this part under the shirt to conceal it but since we aren't recording video I can just clip it over your shirt." Will was now standing directly in front of Emma, their faces only inches apart. She was wearing one of her go-to black tank tops, which meant he was contemplating how to clip on the mic without touching her cleavage.

"Is it okay if I...?" Will gestured to the area in question.

"Go for it," Emma replied, delighting in her ability to fluster him. She'd never been someone who felt irresistible before. She knew her various partners and hookups were attracted to her, but she'd never believed that her body was so undeniably hot it caused men to lose control of themselves. Seeing Will this nervous—ostensibly because of her boobs—was strangely empowering. And rather erotic.

"I'm just going to clip it in the middle so it's closest to your mouth," Will explained as his hands manipulated the shirt's thin fabric. They both knew she wasn't wearing a bra.

"Okay," she said barely louder than a whisper.

They watched as he attached the microphone clip, neither one remembering to breathe. Emma suddenly understood why so many people had affairs. Not being allowed to kiss someone really did make you want to kiss them even more.

"How's that feel?" Will asked as he took a step back, breaking the moment before it turned into something they couldn't take back.

Emma tested out the placement by turning, twisting and pretending to pack. "It's good. Thank you."

"No problem. Just doing my moderately paid job." Will went over to his laptop to hit Record; Emma was officially on the record.

"If you help me with the kitchen, I'll also let you do the medicine cabinets," Emma offered as she handed Will a box.

"Deal. Would love to know what's holding that bizarre mind of yours together."

"I keep all my psychotropics in my purse, thank you very much."

"Damn," Will replied with a grin. "So where is all this stuff going? Your parents' house?"

"Some of it. But I'm sending most of it to storage units. Until we figure out what to keep and what we won't need."

"'We' meaning you and Matt?"

"Yeah," Emma said, avoiding his gaze. "I think the plan is I'll move into his condo after the wedding and then we'll look for a house together in the New Year."

It seemed fitting that if she and Matt were going to wait to have sex they might as well wait to move in together to make the marriage part feel even more special. So what if that was unconventional in the modern era? That was basically the theme of their entire relationship.

"Things seem to really be working out between you two," Will said in an incredibly neutral voice. It was as if he had declared that the sky is blue, or fire is hot, and he had no personal opinion about it. But in Emma's experience, people rarely didn't have an opinion about something.

"They are," Emma agreed.

This was clearly her opening to share the big news. Yet unlike her first engagement when she couldn't stop herself from thrusting her ring finger in everyone's face while squealing, she was having a hard time getting the words out.

Bracing for impact, Emma cleared her throat of nonexistent phlegm and sputtered, "He even officially proposed the other night."

Emma turned to look at Will just as the glass he was packing slipped out of his hand. It shattered all over the floor.

"Shit, sorry… Just my way of saying congratulations, I guess," Will added sheepishly. "I always break stuff when I'm excited for other people."

"What a cool habit," Emma replied with a grin, selfishly relieved that he seemed frazzled instead of ecstatic, "Let me go get a broom."

After Will insisted on being the one to sweep up the mess, they took a break on the couch and shared the one remaining LaCroix in her fridge. She made sure to split it evenly into two of the remaining glasses so she could drink at her own pace.

"I don't think I'm handling this very well," Will said unprompted.

"Handling what very well?"

"You being officially engaged or whatever."

Emma nodded, not knowing what to say next. Her ego wanted to hear him profess that he had made a big mistake and couldn't stand the thought of her with another man. But her heart didn't like to see Will hurting.

"You thought it would all have blown up in my face by now?" Emma teased to lighten the mood.

"Honestly...yeah. Or that you would have come to your senses or something. Not that Matt isn't a catch. He has a great handshake and a hundred-and-twenty-thousand-dollar car." Will laughed at his own observation, but it sounded forced.

"Is it making you rethink—" Emma stopped herself. She wasn't sure if she was breaking Matt's trust by even entertaining this type of conversation. But she also felt like she needed to know Will's answer, or it would plague her like a fire ant trapped inside her brain. "Is it making you rethink turning me down?"

Will let a bunch of air out through his mouth as he considered how to answer. "No. Because even if we want similar things in the end, I think we just disagree too much about how to get there. You move fast and I'm more like a sloth with nowhere to be." Will then proceeded to do his best sloth impression with his arms and face. It was rather good.

"How many sloth videos do you watch on average?"

"Not many. Ten to fifteen a week."

Emma smiled. "I think we both made the right choice. Crushes come and go all the time. Just because we have chemistry doesn't mean we have to freak out or end the podcast."

"Wait, do you *still* have a crush on me?" Will asked with his eyebrows raised and a smirk forming on his lips.

Of course I do, you imbecile, Emma wanted to shout. Instead, she replied, "I'm not answering that one on mic."

"Oh, I turned the recording off once I broke the glass. There is only so much of myself I can share with the entire world. Even if it makes me a hypocrite."

Emma shrugged. "We're all hypocrites. The goal is to just slowly lower your amount of hypocrisy over time. But good luck finding anyone who doesn't contradict themselves in some way or another."

"That's a good point. You make a lot of good points."

"Annoying, right?" Emma joked as Will laughed. She wondered if she'd ever fully get over how much she loved the sound of making him laugh. Maybe once she and Matt had a kid— pregnancy hormones were known to change a person. Which led her to another thought.

"What about you? Are you back on the apps?"

Will gave her a look, trying to figure out if she was setting a trap.

"It's okay. If we can talk about my engagement, we can definitely talk about your dating life."

"You sure?"

"Absolutely," Emma lied. She'd always wanted to be the kind of girl that didn't get jealous. Unfortunately, she was the kind of girl who briefly cried after learning through Facebook that her middle school boyfriend had gotten married before her.

"I've been on the apps a bit. Nothing really to report there. But Anika has been trying to set me up with one of her friends."

"Why haven't you let her?"

"I don't know. Seems like it might be messy if things don't work out."

"Messier than this?" Emma asked as she gestured between the two of them.

"Fair. I guess I'll ask for her friend's number. Got to do something to keep me occupied while you look for a house with your soon-to-be husband."

"Hobbies are important," Emma agreed even though the thought of Will with someone else made her nauseous.

"I guess we should get back to work," Will announced as he stood up and went to restart the recording. He sat down at the dining room table and leaned into a mic that was still attached to his computer. He transformed into his producer role as he asked, "So Emma, does moving out of your old apartment feel significant or symbolic in any way?"

"Yeah, it kind of feels like physical evidence that I'm moving on." She started to pack up the contents of her coffee table. "It's weird but seeing my body take action has been helpful. It reinforces that I'm starting a new life."

"And how do you explain an adult below the age of eighty-five owning so many animal statues?" Will asked with mock seriousness, all evidence of their charged moment already gone, and their friendly banter reinstated.

Instead of answering, she threw a small wooden goat at his head. The mic caught it crashing into the wall behind him.

Twenty-Five

"HOW WAS YOUR WEEK?" EMMA ASKED TWO OF HER FA-vorite clients. Maria and Claire were a married couple who were struggling to juggle their careers, two children and Claire's ailing mother, who had recently moved in with them. Thankfully, they had managed to get themselves into therapy before things got too bad, which was always a blessing—especially for the therapist.

"It was good," Claire said as she shared a suspicious look with Maria. Sometimes Emma's clients seemed to forget that Emma could not only hear them but see them.

"Good in what way?" Emma asked, assuming the look indicated a return of their much-missed sex life.

"Did you get engaged?" Maria blurted out.

"Oh," Emma replied, startled, before remembering she had a brand-new ring on her finger. "I did. Good eye."

"I told you it was real," Claire said to Maria. "You owe me ten bucks and a bubble bath."

"I'm a little lost…"

"Your engagement video came up on my TikTok," Maria

explained. "A big account I follow reposted it, but I thought maybe it was a prank or something."

Emma nodded, trying to keep her cool. She knew some of her clients had probably seen the post—especially after people started pulling it from YouTube and sharing it on social media. Within twenty-four hours of releasing the video on her channel it was already her most-viewed piece of content by a long shot and it had only grown from there. Her Instagram DMs were filled with messages from pretty much everyone she had ever met. Most people seemed happy for her. The rest were furious that she was "making a mockery of marriage for attention." It was one thing for random people to have opinions about her love life. It was another for her clients to know so much about her. But that was the cost of being mildly famous online.

"Why did you think it was a prank?"

"I don't know," Maria replied, clearly uncomfortable. "You just don't seem like the type to do something like that. You've always seemed…"

"It's okay, you can say it."

"Reasonable? I guess it's just hard to imagine you marrying someone you barely know at a wedding you planned with someone else. Seems like a no-no for a couples therapist."

"I think it's awesome," Claire chimed in. "You both seemed super happy, and your fiancé is gorgeous."

Maria, the more jealous of the two, rolled her eyes.

"I even sent it to one of my friends who just got dumped and she said it 'reignited her faith in humanity.'"

"Taylor said that?" Maria asked skeptically.

"Yep. Our very own Emma is inspiring people to not give up. I love it."

Emma smiled while keeping her eyes on Maria. She knew that if Maria lost respect for Emma as an individual, she wasn't going to trust Emma as her therapist.

"I'm sorry to have popped up on your feed like that. I know it can be unsettling to see me outside of my professional setting."

"It is a little weird," Maria offered.

"Absolutely. I once saw my college therapist throwing up in a bar. Took a bit of time to repair that relationship."

Both Maria and Claire laughed, which was a relief. Emma hadn't lost them completely.

"If you want to ask me any questions to address concerns you might have, I'm happy to answer them," Emma said with more confidence than she felt.

Self-disclosure was always a tricky thing to navigate with clients. The mental health field had moved away from the idea that therapists should be entirely blank slates who reveal nothing about their personal lives or experiences. The days of silent analysts sitting behind clients on fainting couches were mostly gone. Many clinicians, including Emma, even believed there was a benefit to occasionally sharing parts of themselves with clients. It helped strengthen the therapeutic alliance and shift the power dynamic away from an imbalanced expert/patient to something more equal. The tricky part was knowing how much to share and when.

Emma had misjudged this ratio before and even lost a client after revealing how many times she'd been ghosted while using dating apps. Emma had hoped to make the client feel better about her turbulent dating history, but it just made her think Emma was a loser—and apparently no one wants professional advice from a loser. After that learning experience, Emma had stayed on the conservative side of self-disclosure, but she worried that if she didn't address the elephant in the room Maria wouldn't get over it and it would prevent progress.

"I don't really know if I have any questions necessarily. But it does make you seem kind of unhinged."

"Maria!" Claire exclaimed as she swatted her wife's leg.

"No, it's okay. I want you to be honest with me. What about

it seems unhinged?" Emma got the dreaded word out of her mouth without betraying how much it triggered her. She had spent her entire anxious existence worried that she was one bad day away from blowing her life up and losing control of herself. But, so far, she hadn't done anything she couldn't recover from. She hoped Operation: Save My Date wasn't about to be the exception.

"Like what kind of person doesn't just cancel their wedding and move on?" Maria asked. "It makes you seem desperate or something."

"Desperate? Have you seen the guy she's marrying? Have you seen the huge rock on her finger? If that's desperate, sign me up," Claire said with a smirk. "Now can we get back to figuring out what to do with my mother because she is driving me bonkers?"

"That we can do," Emma said, knowing she was likely never going to see them again. She could tell she was no longer a trusted resource for Maria and would maybe even become a point of contention in their marriage. Emma would send an email with referrals after the session so they wouldn't feel guilty about switching therapists. It was more important that they got the help they wanted than staying with Emma out of politeness or guilt. Plus, Emma had a huge waitlist of potential clients to pluck from. Apparently, some people *wanted* a super-public therapist who took big swings in her personal life—at least in Los Angeles.

Emma trudged up the stairs of her family home in search of her mom. Matt's second cousin was having a baby and he had tasked her with buying a present to bring to the baby shower in San Diego that weekend. There wasn't a registry because the mom-to-be liked to be surprised. This seemed like a terrible idea, but Matt had found it charming—probably because he wasn't the one who had to find a useful gift that somehow no one else had thought of.

"Mom!" Emma called for the third time. Debbie was an excellent gift-giver, and Emma needed her advice. If she could find her.

Emma was about to fling open her parents' bedroom door when she heard what sounded like whisper fighting. She took a few steps closer and realized her parents must be inside their walk-in closet. Emma knew that if they had purposely gone into hiding to yell at each other, she should give them privacy. But she was too curious to behave. She slowly opened the bedroom door and tiptoed over to the closet.

"I just need some space," Debbie hissed. "You're everywhere all of the time."

"It's my house," Alan hissed back. "Where do you want me to go?"

"Why is that my problem to figure out? I'm not your mother."

"No. My mother actually wants me around."

"Come on. Don't take it so personally."

"What? That my wife can't stand being around me? You're right, why would I care about that?"

"Alan—"

Before Emma could react, the closet door flew open and Alan stormed out. He looked horrified to see her there.

"Sorry," Emma sputtered, "I was just looking for Mom."

"She's by the sweaters," Alan replied before heading out of the room.

Emma debated making a break for it until she heard Debbie say, "You can come in." She entered the closet to find her mom sitting on the bench they'd installed to help Alan put his socks on. Her mom looked like she was about to cry. Debbie never cried.

"What happened?" Emma asked as she took a seat.

"He wants me to teach him how to knit."

This was not the answer Emma was expecting. So she waited for more. She'd learned early on in her training that if something wasn't making sense, not replying right away often compelled people to fill in more details without her having to ask.

"I don't want to teach him how to knit," Debbie explained. "Knitting is *my* hobby that I do by myself or with my knitting friends. But somehow, I'm the bad guy because I don't want us to merge into one entity that is never apart for longer than a bowel movement."

"At least you get to poop in peace," Emma replied, but Debbie was too upset to laugh.

"I *hate* hurting his feelings, but I don't know how to get through to him without being blunt."

Emma nodded; it was a cycle she had noticed growing up. Alan would do something to annoy Debbie. Debbie would try to get him to stop. He would ignore her complaints until Debbie blew up at him, and then both of them would feel hurt and misunderstood.

"Retirement is a big adjustment. You two will figure out a new way to be with each other."

"Maybe," Debbie said, sounding dubious. "Or maybe I'll just be annoyed for the rest of my life."

Emma watched as her mother stood up and walked away, likely to finish processing her emotions unobserved. For the first time, Emma felt worried that her parents' marriage wasn't as indestructible as she thought. It was an unsettling feeling and she wanted to put it to bed before it spun out of control in her mind. She fished her phone out of her pocket and after a moment's hesitation made a call.

"Hi," Matt said. "Everything okay?"

"Sort of. Do you have a minute or are you busy?"

"I'm busy, but I always have a minute for you."

Emma smiled. She realized it was the first time she was leaning on Matt for emotional support for something outside of their own relationship. This was the type of exchange that could make or break couples, and she hated that she knew that.

"I'm worried about my parents," Emma explained, giving Matt the play-by-play of her last ten minutes. "What if I've been so caught up in my own shit, I haven't noticed that they're falling apart?"

"I don't think you have to worry about that. They've been married a long time."

"That doesn't mean anything. I had a client in her eighties file for divorce last year."

Matt laughed even though Emma wasn't sure what was funny about having to navigate the dating scene again after sixty years. It sounded like a plot of a horror film.

"They're your parents. Not your patients—"

"Clients. We call them clients. It helps minimize the unequal power dynamic and gives people agency in their own healing."

"Okay, good to know," Matt said kindly. "I just don't want you to stress yourself out. Just because you've seen things not work out for your clients doesn't mean your parents are going to get divorced."

"You're right. It just freaked me out. I think I'm still waiting for the next terrible, life-altering thing to happen."

"Kelly always used to say, 'The smallest seed of faith is better than the largest fruit of happiness.'"

"What does that mean?"

"Honestly, I'm not totally sure. She'd use it whenever I was worried about the future. I think it's from the Bible or something."

It wasn't, Emma quickly learned through a Google search. It was by Thoreau.

"I'm so sorry but I have to hop on a call. Can we talk later?" Matt said.

"Yes, definitely. Thanks for listening."

"Of course. Try not to worry about it anymore."

Emma held back a scoff. Trying not to worry about something only made her worry more.

Twenty-Six

THE BABY SHOWER WAS A SUCCESS. JACKIE HAD COME through with a suggestion for a monogrammed diaper bag that looked cooler than most regular purses. Matt's cousin had loved it and his extended family had welcomed Emma with open arms. Emma and Matt had spent the weekend together in San Diego and it was finally starting to feel like a real relationship—except for the whole lack of sex and nudity part.

Emma wasn't used to having to bring her pajamas into the bathroom to change, but she didn't want the first time Matt saw her naked to be her attempting to pull up her pants. He had ended up following her lead and they made it the whole trip without crossing any boundary that wouldn't be allowed in a PG-13 movie. It sort of felt like they had jumped decades ahead in their relationship, from dating to being an old married couple who went straight from dinner to bed without any funny business. Emma had hoped the waiting-until-marriage pact would add a tantalizing element to their months-long foreplay, but it suddenly seemed like if the main course was off the table, Matt wasn't that interested in snacking. It was almost a full-time job not to take it personally, especially considering she'd worn her fancy pajamas.

Now that Emma was back in Los Angeles, she was once again confronted by the fact she had to finish her book. She'd somehow managed to make her way through the majority of Michelle's edits but still had absolutely no idea what to do about the last chapter. In the original draft, chapter eight had been nothing short of a tribute to her love for Ryan. She'd interviewed him for it, and they'd discussed how they planned to "keep the spark alive" and prioritize their union above everything else. The pages were laughable now, but it did feel pretty satisfying to have it in writing that Ryan once said, "We make a great team." It was nice to have proof of his hypocrisy.

What kind of teammate ditches their partner without any warning? Not a good one. She hoped whoever he dated next was ready to be left hanging and humiliated.

Unless he married his next girlfriend, and their implosion hadn't been about his secret fear of commitment but his dislike of Emma specifically. This possibility still caused Emma physical pain to think about, which was why she had been doing her best to avoid it. But her defense mechanisms weren't working properly anymore, and she could feel her mood sinking into despair as she physically sank onto her bed. She needed to figure out how to write about what had happened without traumatically reliving it. Maybe if she could figure out a way to spin it into a lesson or something. People loved reading about turning hardships into life lessons. Normally, Emma pushed back against the internet-fueled need to learn something from every horrible experience, but if the capitalization of trauma would help her finish this book, she could sacrifice her morals for a few thousand words.

She just needed to figure out how to do it. And that might require a little help.

★ ★ ★

"Well, don't you look fancy," Will teased as Emma approached his table. Once he had agreed to meet for a brainstorming drink, Emma hopped into her car without bothering to change out of her ripped leggings and big comfy T-shirt that she only now remembered had a vaguely Florida-shaped stain near the hem. She assumed it was a good sign she hadn't thought about looking presentable for Will; her crush was clearly on its way out.

"I'd roast you back, but I'm too thankful you're here," Emma replied as Will stood up to hug her. As his arms wrapped around her waist, it felt like someone had given her crush chest compressions—it was very much alive and well again.

Why does he have to smell so good all the time? she wondered. *Does he have no shame?*

"Anything for my favorite ex-slash-coworker."

"Wait, does that mean I am your favorite ex *and* your favorite coworker? Or just your favorite ex-slash-coworker?"

"Great question. That I will not be answering," he said with a smile. "What's the big book emergency?"

Emma groaned and looked around for a waitress. They had met at one of the painfully cool breweries near Will's place downtown. It had a big outdoor area and horrible service. Emma tried to make eye contact with an employee who purposefully turned the other way.

"Basically, I need to rewrite the entire last chapter. And my editor wants it to be about Ryan but—"

Emma felt all the oxygen vanish from her body. In a single instant she was reduced to her most basic form. She was no longer a human, but a wild animal trapped in front of its most lethal predator. Nothing had come close to preparing her for this moment. Nothing.

"Emma? Are you okay?"

Emma gave the slightest shake of her head to indicate that

she was far from okay. Being okay was now a distant memory that felt more like a dream than her recent reality. If only she could force her body to spontaneously combust to escape her fate. A fire alarm would work too if she ran fast.

"What is going on?" Will asked, increasingly concerned.

"He's here," Emma whispered.

"Who, Matt?" Will turned around to look. Emma was too frozen with dread to tell him to stop. She watched in horror as her ex-fiancé waved and headed toward their table. Ryan was dressed in his favorite Patagonia jacket and what appeared to be new khaki pants. Emma, having been in charge of the laundry, was intimately familiar with his wardrobe.

"Oh fuck, is that Ryan?" Will asked as he turned back around.

"Get me out of here," Emma growled.

"How?"

"Get me out of here, now!"

"Hi," Ryan said as he appeared at the head of their table. "I thought that was you."

Emma looked up into the face of the man she had once planned to spend the rest of her life with. His eyes were still hazel, and his neat beard still covered the scar he'd gotten on his chin from playing flag football as a kid, proving that he had continued to exist without her. Emma's body longed to embrace him while her mind screamed that she was in danger. She felt conflicted about what to do next. So she did nothing.

"I'm Ryan," he said to Will after Emma had failed to respond.

"I know," Will replied icily.

Emma felt a surge of affection for Will. She wasn't going to have to get through this interaction alone.

"What are you doing here?" Emma asked. If he told her he was on a date, she was going to throw up—and not metaphorically. Her chronic acid reflux was already acting up from stress.

"Grabbing a drink with my boss." Ryan gestured over his shoulder to a forty-something guy completely absorbed by his cell phone.

"Did you need something?" Will asked, catching Ryan off guard. As an unfailingly polite person, Ryan was not used to being met with anything other than civility and smiles from strangers. It thrilled Emma to see him being poorly received by someone.

"I just wanted to say hi. I'm happy to see you're doing well."

"Why do you think I'm doing well?" Emma asked with an aggressive raise of her eyebrows.

"I just figured…" Ryan gestured at Will as if the presence of another man absolved him of any responsibility for his past behavior. He obviously hadn't been staying up late consuming her Neutral Third Party content like she had hoped. If he had, Ryan would know Will was actually her podcast cohost and she was currently engaged to a man with some of the best teeth she had ever seen.

"You figured what?" Will inquired, providing excellent backup.

"I'm not looking to start anything. I just wanted to say I'm glad to know we've both moved on. We obviously made the right decision—"

"*We* didn't decide anything. You left me."

"I don't think it was that simple. Things had been off for a while."

"Is that why you proposed? Because things had been off?"

"No, of course not. But I think we both realized we weren't compatible in the long term."

"I don't recall realizing that," Emma replied. "Maybe you had that conversation with someone else."

Ryan put up his hands as though he was being unfairly attacked. "Listen, I just came over to clear the air. I guess that was a mistake."

"Seems like you've made a lot of mistakes lately," Will said. "Have you considered, I don't know, apologizing?"

Ryan shook his head as if he was the only sane person in the room, which infuriated Emma. She might be the one with an anxiety disorder, but at least she wasn't the selfish asshole who refused to take any responsibility for his actions.

"I'm gonna head back. Have a good night," Ryan said as he turned to leave on his high horse.

"Wait," Emma shouted louder than she intended to.

Ryan tentatively turned around. While Emma had initially froze upon seeing Ryan, she could feel her nervous system waking up and shifting into fight mode. She knew this might be her one chance to tell him how she really felt and reclaim some control of their narrative.

Emboldened by opportunity, Emma stood so she could face Ryan properly as Will sat back to watch, a pleased smirk on his face. It was rather fun to have a hype man.

She looked up into her ex-fiancé's exasperated eyes and declared, "Whether you're willing to admit it or not, I know you came over here to prove to yourself that you haven't done anything wrong. That you aren't the villain in this story but some sort of benevolent fortune teller who prevented a disaster by leaving me with no explanation. I want to tell you right now, *none of that is true.* Yes, I am moving on. But you don't get to take credit for that. You don't get to blow up my world and then take ownership over the renovation. *I* am the reason I am going to be okay. Not you."

"I never said—"

"I'm not done," Emma replied. She took a deep breath to help nail the landing. "I need you to understand that I am not mad at you because you broke up with me. People are allowed to leave relationships if they don't serve them anymore, that's couples therapy 101. I am mad at you because you had so little regard for my feelings that you didn't even involve me in your decision. You didn't give me a chance to work on whatever you secretly decided I needed to work on. And you didn't have the courage to stick around, even for a second, to help me pick up the pieces of the life we built together. The moment you determined I wasn't the 'right' girl for you was the moment my existence and emotional well-being no longer mattered because all you care about is yourself. And *that*, Ryan, is why you are a piece of shit who doesn't deserve to sleep at night. No matter what your doting mommy tells you."

"Fuck yeah!" a woman's voice rang out.

Emma turned to see that half of the brewery was staring at her and Ryan, completely engrossed in their drama. The table right next to them, serendipitously filled with college-aged girls in sorority T-shirts, even started to clap. Will immediately joined in, along with about a dozen other people.

Emma felt a swell of pride as Ryan turned bright red. Unsure of what to do, he made a break for the exit as some people cheered his departure, leaving his boss alone and confused. It was the kind of public humiliation that would normally make Emma feel racked with guilt. Right now, though, she felt too good to feel bad.

Will stood up and wrapped his arms around her. "That was absolutely terrifying," he whispered in her ear. "I've never been more impressed."

"Thank you."

She felt the same way about herself.

"Let me get you a drink," Will said as they entered his apartment. "We need to keep celebrating."

"First, I must pee." Emma raced toward the bathroom.

After leaving the brewery they'd stopped at another bar to process what had just happened, and Emma's bladder was dangerously full. They'd decided to go back to Will's for financial reasons after two rounds of twenty-five-dollar cocktails. Emma was still riding the high of having said exactly what she wanted to say in exactly the way she wanted to say it. She'd spent many sessions telling clients that closure was something you had to give yourself, but *holy shit* did it feel good to tell Ryan the truth to his face. She'd long suspected that he had rewritten the story of their breakup in order to live with himself. Not that that was unusual. People hated feeling like they were bad, so they often went through elaborate mental gymnastics to justify their behavior to themselves and the people around them.

Good luck not feeling bad now, Ryan.

As Emma washed her hands, she tried not to wonder how Ryan had explained his abrupt relationship-ending behavior to his friends and family. She could only assume they all thought it was her fault since everyone loved Ryan. He was *such a nice guy*. But seeing him tonight made her question if her assumptions about him had been wrong from the beginning. Sure, Ryan presented as a grounded, incredibly kind, rational person. But Emma had technically only met him less than two years ago. For all she knew, Ryan could be the kind of person who regularly blew up his life. She'd had a roommate like that in college—before the roommate had dropped out of school to pursue something akin to environmental terrorism. Except Emma knew Ryan's whole family and no one had mentioned this kind of pattern.

Who was the real Ryan? The man who once asked her to be his girlfriend in a mailed letter because she'd jokingly said he should put his request in writing, or the self-centered asshole who'd just tried to gaslight her into thinking their breakup had been a mutual decision?

Maybe accepting that she would never know the answer to that question was the last step in finally getting over him.

"Everything okay in there?" Will shouted. "Because I just found some novelty schnapps that I think we should drink immediately."

Emma opened the bathroom door to find Will standing in the hall with a huge grin on his face. He proudly held up a bright blue bottle of alcohol and said, "It's blue raspberry, which doesn't even exist in nature."

Emma laughed and headed toward his couch. "Why do you have that?"

"Inside joke with my college friends. We always try to gift each other the grossest alcohol available. I got this bad boy for my thirtieth birthday."

"Oh good, the blue raspberries will be nicely aged."

"Exactly. You get it."

Will joined her on the couch and reached for the two shot glasses he'd already put on the coffee table. Emma suddenly noticed what was also in front of them.

"Oh my god," she exclaimed. "Unicorn Laura!" Emma grabbed the hand-painted plate that Will had strategically placed on top of his pile of *New Yorker* magazines as a surprise. "You've had her this whole time?"

"Yep. I picked her up after our date. I kept planning to give her to you but then it felt weird after we stopped hooking up."

"She's beautiful," Emma murmured as she gently stroked Laura's colorful mane.

"She's yours, if you still want her. You've earned it."

"Thank you," Emma said with tears in her eyes. It was an emotional night, and the alcohol was clearly catching up with her. She should probably stop drinking before she did anything stupid, but being responsible all the time was an unrealistic expectation to put on herself. Plus, she was morbidly curious to see what the blue concoction tasted like.

"This one's for you." Will handed her a shot and Emma saw that the glass was from Amsterdam. The one in his hand was from Chile.

"Is there anywhere you haven't been?"

"Of course. I refuse to go to Glendale on principle."

Emma laughed. Glendale was about forty minutes away and completely lovely. "Why?"

"Just to be contrarian and have something ridiculous to say at parties. It makes people furious." Will raised his glass and clinked it against Emma's. "To Laura!"

Emma braced herself and opened her mouth. The chemical smell hit her before the extremely sweet taste. She forced herself to swallow without gagging, which was a real feat.

"Wow," Will said as he smacked his lips. "That's the worst one yet. And my old roommate once bought me Belly Button Beer."

"Please tell me that's not what it sounds like."

"Then I will tell you nothing at all."

Emma laughed again. She always laughed when she was with Will. Men spent so much time at the gym to impress women with their ripped abs, but nothing got Emma's juices going more than a sick burn or clever callback. She'd fallen for many a loser solely due to their text banter.

"Should we do another one?" Emma asked. She knew it was reckless to get wasted with a guy she maybe still had feelings for when she was engaged to someone else, but Emma wasn't going to let herself cross any line she couldn't come back from—even if she felt herself inching closer and closer toward it.

"Absolutely," Will replied as he reached for the bottle only to be distracted by the sound of an incoming message on his phone. He took it out of his pocket and a painfully familiar smile broke out on his face. It was the smile of someone who had a crush. "Sorry, one second."

Emma watched as Will carefully typed out a response. She felt her chest tighten with jealousy.

"Who are you texting?" It was hard to self-censor after blue raspberry schnapps.

"You know that girl Anika wanted to set me up with?"

Emma nodded, not liking where this was going.

"We've hung out a few times. She's a graphic designer and she keeps sending me these self-made memes about sound engineers—" Will stopped talking when he looked up and saw Emma's face. Clearly it had betrayed her specific instructions to *appear chill*.

"What's wrong?"

"Nothing," Emma squeaked. "I guess I didn't realize you were dating someone."

Will turned to face her on the couch, putting his phone down on the table. He had the makings of a smirk on his lips. "You're the one who told me to go out with her."

"I know. I just hadn't realized it had already happened. Multiple times." Emma reached for the bottle in an obvious attempt to change the subject. "Let's do another one."

Will quickly grabbed the bottle before she could get it. "Not so fast. I want you to admit that you're jealous first."

"Why? Are you a sadist?"

"Maybe. Or maybe it's just nice that the tables have turned."

"I have no idea what you're talking about," Emma said as she lunged for the bottle only for Will to deftly hold it above his head.

"You have to say it or no more schnapps."

"Oh no, whatever will I do without the synthetic taste of a fake fruit," Emma cried as she stood up from the couch. "I guess I'll have to make do with all that nice wine in your kitchen."

But before Emma could execute her plan, Will sprung up to block her path. They were now wedged in between the couch and the coffee table, and his face was only a few inches from hers. She could smell the mix of alcohol and sugar on his breath. Will took a step closer, and Emma took a step back. He then took another step closer, and Emma couldn't seem to get her legs to work.

"Tell me why it bothers you that I'm seeing someone," Will said barely louder than a whisper.

"I can't," Emma whispered back. "We shouldn't talk about it."

"I thought therapists say you should talk about everything."

Emma slowly shook her head back and forth as he crept even closer. The combination of multiple drinks and the intoxicating smell of what she had come to identify as Will's shaving cream gave the whole interaction a dreamlike quality. Emma wasn't sure if she was really in Will's apartment or if she was tucked away safely in bed. Because if it was somehow a dream, she could get away with anything. And she desperately wanted to misbehave.

"Emma," Will said, reaching his arm out to tuck some of her unruly hair behind her ear.

Without thinking she grabbed his hand and held it to her face. His skin was warm and more familiar than it had any right being. He took her gesture as an invitation to close any remaining space between them. He used his hand to tilt her face up toward him.

"Tell me if you want me to stop and I'll stop."

Emma said nothing, which really said everything. She watched as Will let what remained of his guard down. They locked eyes and she could see how much he wanted her, which was both thrilling and terrifying. She felt the same unignorable need flowing through her body, but she also heard an alarm bell going off. If she kissed Will right now, she wouldn't be able to live with herself. There was no level of mental gymnastics that would justify her cheating on Matt, not after everything he had been through.

So just as Will's unfairly soft lips were about to hit hers, Emma pulled back. "Wait."

Emma grabbed Will's arm so he wouldn't think she was rejecting him. "If we're going to be together, we should do it the right way."

Will looked at her, confused. "What do you mean?"

"Well, for starters, I need to break up with Matt. And you

should probably let that graphic designer know that you're about to marry someone else."

Will pulled away from her as if he'd been shot. Or flashed by someone he did not want to see naked. "Whoa, Emma. I think there's been a misunderstanding."

Emma felt a terrible sinking feeling in her chest. She wondered how many more times she would completely misread someone's feelings for her before she died. She'd started young, mistaking her kindergarten crush's valentine as a declaration of love when really his mom had forced him to make one for everyone in the class—including the pet hamster. Thank god no one had paid attention when she idiotically professed her love for him on the playground.

"What exactly did I misunderstand?" Emma said, with a sharp edge to her voice.

Will had the decency to look guilty. "I don't want you to think I've changed my mind about the whole Save My Date thing."

"Then why did you try to kiss me?"

"Because I like you. And I think you wanted me to."

"Hold on, you can't blame this on me. You know how much I care about getting married and following through with my plan. My dad literally paid the final deposit on all the flowers *today*."

"And *you* know how much I hate the idea of getting married just so you can have the same elaborate wedding you planned with someone else."

"I obviously thought you had changed your mind."

"And I thought you had changed yours. Otherwise, I would never have almost kissed you."

Emma and Will stared at each other, neither knowing where to go from here. As the remaining drunkenness left Emma's body, she felt a wave of relief that she hadn't sacrificed her relationship with Matt for another failed attempt to make it work with Will. She couldn't keep doing this to herself. For whatever reason, this J.Crew-wearing, world-traveling, incredibly sarcastic podcast producer seemed to be her new Achilles' heel. If she wanted to successfully move forward with her life, it wasn't safe to be around him.

"I don't think we should be alone together anymore."

"Okay," Will agreed.

"Obviously we have to finish the podcast." The show had been in Apple's top one hundred since it had come out, making it a runaway hit. Even in her emotional state, Emma knew it would be fiscally and professionally irresponsible to quit in the middle of the season. "But we should record the rest of it in studio. With Anika."

"That's a good idea."

"And we shouldn't text or call each other anymore. Only email."

Will nodded.

"And I'm not going to take Laura. Because of what she represents."

Will seemed confused about this one but Emma knew it wasn't smart to keep such a fond memento of their time as an almost-couple. She didn't need a constant reminder of what might have been.

"Whatever you want."

"It's not about what I *want*. It's about what we need to do to finish the show and not ruin my relationship with Matt. Because he's a great guy. A *really* great guy."

"And I'm not a really great guy?"

"Honestly, Will, it doesn't matter what you are anymore."

Twenty-Seven

WHEN HER PHONE RANG AT SEVEN FIFTEEN IN THE MORN-
ing, Emma was already awake—because she'd never fallen
asleep. She'd spent the entire night beating herself up for almost kissing someone who wasn't her fiancé. The one silver
lining of her broken engagement was that everyone agreed
she had the moral high ground. It was a nice and noble place
to live, and she wasn't sure if she had to give it up now that
she was an almost-cheater. Out of all the agonizing emotions
Emma had experienced the past few months, it turned out that
guilt was the worst one.

As she reached for her phone and saw an unfamiliar number,
Emma debated sending the call to voicemail. But a judgmental voice in her head told her that the least she could do was be
nice to a telemarketer now that she was officially a bad person.

"Hello?" Emma croaked. She coughed to clear her morning phlegm.

"Is this Emma Moskowitz?" A rather brusque voice asked as
if Emma was somehow already wasting her time.

"Yes, may I ask who's calling?"

"This is Lanie Reyes with *The Amanda Sharpe Show*. We had

a last-minute guest cancellation this morning and we were wondering if you would be willing to come on today to talk about—" Emma heard the sound of papers being shuffled "—Operation: Save My Date. Amanda has been listening to your podcast and would love to share the unique idea with her audience."

Emma shot up in bed. Amanda Sharpe was an icon. Since starting out as a child actor, Amanda had managed to star in countless movies, start a wildly successful athleisure company and launch the most popular daytime talk show since *Oprah*. Amanda also seemed super nice in a relatable way, like she just so happened to be super successful and wasn't that wonderful?

Being interviewed on *The Amanda Sharpe Show* launched people into stardom—or made them the most hated person on the internet for forty-eight hours. It was the definition of exposure.

"Emma, I'm going to need you to tell me yes or no."

"Yes, yes, of course," Emma exclaimed. "I'd be honored."

"Great. If you give me your email, I'll have my assistant send you all the information. We'll need you in the Burbank studio by one."

"No problem. I'll have to reschedule a few clients but—"

"Can I have that email?"

"Yes, sorry," Emma replied as she rattled it off.

"See you soon. Don't wear a pattern," Lanie said before hanging up.

Emma immediately let out a squeal of excitement. Amanda Sharpe wanted to interview *her*. Maybe she wasn't such a terrible person after all.

"There just isn't enough time," Jackie declared as the three Moskowitz women stood in her custom-made walk-in closet. "Even if I managed to find the right outfit, there isn't time to dye her hair."

"Why do I need to dye my hair?" Emma asked as she stood mostly naked in front of her mom and sister. She'd spent the past thirty minutes trying on different nonpatterned outfits to no avail. They either looked terrible or caused her so much discomfort she couldn't think straight. It was further proof that being fashionable was a nightmare.

"You have a few grays," Jackie said. "I've been meaning to tell you."

"I don't think anyone will notice," Debbie replied. "The camera won't be on the top of her head."

"We have to be prepared for everything."

"I don't care if people can see I have gray hair. It's a natural part of aging gracefully."

Jackie looked at Emma as if she had just suggested cutting off her toes and sticking them in a blender to live longer. "I can't deal with your ridiculous ideas about embracing wrinkles and cellulite right now. We need to find you something to wear."

"I might have something," Debbie offered. "I brought it with me just in case." She dug into her large Longchamp tote bag and pulled out a black, knee-length dress with capped sleeves and large gold buttons down the front. It was simple and gorgeous. Emma reached for it and was surprised to find it was made of a deliciously soft knit.

"Why have we never seen this before?" Emma asked as she unzipped the back to shimmy into it.

"Probably because I haven't worn it since you were born. It was a work dress."

Emma pulled the fabric over her head—her pear-shaped body made stepping into dresses impossible because her butt always got in the way. As she pulled it down, she immediately knew their problems had been solved.

"What do you think?" Emma asked with her arms out to show it off.

"I love it," Debbie exclaimed.

Jackie took a bit longer in her assessment. Emma held her breath as her older sister's eyes scanned her body. She understood that she was no longer a person but a product about to be unveiled to the public.

Jackie deftly adjusted the sleeves before declaring, "I think it will work."

"Oh, thank god," Emma and Debbie said in unison.

A few grueling hours later, Emma and Jackie were sitting in the green room for *The Amanda Sharpe Show*. Emma had only wanted to bring one guest backstage so she wouldn't feel overwhelmed, and Jackie had insisted that as Emma's manager she should be the one to go. Emma had no idea Jackie *was* her manager, but after sitting through two hours of hair and makeup she didn't have the energy to question it.

"I thought they'd have better food," Jackie complained as she looked over the show's offerings. The room was rather small, and Emma suspected there must be a larger one for bigger guests. Not that that bothered her; she still couldn't believe she was important enough to be sitting in Amanda Sharpe's less-important green room. When Emma called her book editor to tell her the good news, Michelle had shouted a flurry of positive expletives followed by at least five reminders to mention her upcoming book.

Matt, on the other hand, hadn't seemed to understand the significance of the news, not being in Amanda's target fan base. Still, he was happy Emma was so happy. He'd even offered to blow off work to come watch the taping in the studio with her parents, but Emma told him it would make her too nervous. In reality, she wasn't quite yet ready to face him after her reckless and devastating night with Will. She'd had to stop herself multiple times from sending Will a photo of her next to a cardboard cutout of Amanda she'd found in the hall. They had a whole elaborate bit about the power of cardboard cutouts. You had to be *pretty* important to get one of those. Maybe one quick text wouldn't be the end of the world—especially considering she was on the show to plug their shared podcast...

"Knock, knock," a familiar voice rang out from the doorway. Emma looked up to a thirty-something woman wearing a headset and one of the coolest outfits Emma had ever seen: a dark green velvet pantsuit with a Rilo Kiley band T-shirt underneath, paired with bright white platform sneakers. Emma sent out a silent prayer to the universe that she would one day be the kind of person who could pull that off.

"So glad to see you're settled in. I'm Lanie—we spoke on the phone. Amanda just wanted to check if there was anything off-limits when it comes to the interview. She never wants her guests to feel attacked or violated." Lanie spoke flatly, as if she was repeating this speech for the thousandth time and no longer attached any actual meaning to the words coming out of her mouth.

"Oh," Emma replied as she looked at her new manager for guidance. "I don't think so?"

"Emma's happy to discuss whatever Amanda wants to talk about," Jackie said confidently. "We're just excited to be here to spread the word about nontraditional ways to find fulfilling partnerships in the age of apps and ghosting."

"Great, I'll let her know," Lanie said as she left to deal with something else.

Emma turned to Jackie, impressed. "Did you just come up with that?"

"I've been working on how to pitch you as a guest. Once this episode comes out, I'm sure more places will want to talk to you."

"How are you so good at this?"

Jackie shrugged. "I know how to google. And I like to watch *Entourage* when I'm working out."

"Emma, we're ready for you," Lanie's assistant called from the hallway.

Emma stood up and smoothed out her mother's dress. She nervously spun her enormous engagement ring with her thumb as she made her way to the stage. There was no going back now.

"Let me just say, I am *so* excited to have you here," Amanda Sharpe gushed to Emma, who was doing her best to sit upright despite the deepness of the couch. "One of my friends sent me your podcast and I was immediately like, okay, I need to talk to this girl. Maybe she can help me find a husband. Or, I guess, *another* husband."

The crowd laughed with glee. Amanda was delightfully candid about her three divorces. Emma chuckled along too, trying to stay grounded in what felt like an out-of-body experience. Amanda was somehow even more charismatic and charming in person.

"I'd be honored to help. Something tells me it wouldn't be that hard."

"I guess I don't have a problem getting married. I just can't seem to *stay* married," Amanda admitted with refreshing self-awareness. "Which brings me back to your story. After being left by your fiancé, you decided to keep your wedding date and find a new groom. And you've been sharing the entire journey through your YouTube channel and your new podcast. There's been a lot of pushback online suggesting that this is some sort of publicity stunt or a misguided attempt to avoid being single. But as a licensed couples therapist and relationship expert, you say there is a method to your madness?"

"I sure hope so," Emma joked before immediately regretting attempting to be funny on live-to-tape TV. A wave of relief washed over her when she heard at least some of the audience laugh, including her father, who was seated in the front row. "I know that at face value, Operation: Save My Date seems like an extreme experiment destined to fail. But committing to marriage early on in a relationship isn't a unique idea. We see plenty of cultures who practice arranged marriages and know of many people in the military who tie the knot quickly before a deployment. There really is no evidence to suggest that the amount of time you date someone directly correlates with the well-being or longevity of your marriage. What matters more, in my opinion, is that both people have a willingness to work on things and a similar conceptualization of what it even means to be married in today's society."

"And it seems like you have found both those things with your new fiancé." Amanda turned in her chair and gestured toward the large screen behind them. A photo of Emma and Matt with their arms around each other at his second cousin's baby shower appeared. "Look at that man! He is gorgeous. Let's give Emma a round of applause for bagging him—I would marry a stranger too if he looked like that."

The audience clapped and cheered louder than Emma expected. She felt her face flush with embarrassment, slightly worried that everyone thought Matt was too good-looking for her. "I definitely got lucky."

"Can you tell me the moment you knew Matt was The One?"

"I actually don't believe in 'The One.' Part of why I wanted to do this was to prove that we are all compatible with a bunch of different people. We don't need to get hung up on our exes or unrequited loves when it's more productive and fulfilling to focus on finding a connection with someone else—someone new."

"I love that," Amanda said as she curled her legs up on the couch and leaned closer, giving the impression that they were just two ladies gabbing in an apartment instead of on a freezing-cold soundstage. Even though Emma knew Amanda was purposefully creating an illusion of intimacy to make her open up and produce better TV, Emma could feel the tactic working. She let herself lean back into the couch cushions.

"I find it so interesting to hear you use the word *prove*," Amanda added. "Do you feel like you're just doing this for yourself? Or is there a part of you that is motivated by giving your audience a happy ending? I know you and your podcast cohost, Will Stoll, seem to disagree on this front."

Emma tried not to visibly bristle at the mention of Will. "That's a good question. If I'm being totally honest, it's probably a mix of both. I want people to know that you don't have to give up on love just because one person in the world no longer loves you. And I also want to move forward in my own life and start a family."

"Hmm," Amanda said. It was startling how ominous a simple sound could be. "I guess I just view marriage as a deeply personal choice. So my antennas go up when I hear you talking about your future marriage as anything more than a private decision between two people who love each other."

"I hear you. But people get married for all sorts of reasons: familial pressure, financial stability. If other people happen to get something out of my marriage too, even if it is just a bit of hope, that seems like a good thing."

"Sure," Amanda agreed as she shifted even closer. "And maybe I'm just feeling protective or projecting, which you all know I love to do. I just don't want you to lose sight of what's right for *you*, simply because you don't want to let other people down. Like I did when I agreed to make a sequel for *The Fisherman's Daughter,* even though I knew it was a terrible script. It currently has score of seven on Rotten Tomatoes, by the way."

More uproarious laughter from the crowd. This woman could start a proper cult if she wanted to.

"But what the hell do I know?" Amanda asked as she reached out and patted Emma's knee as consolation for questioning her life choices in front of millions of people. "You're the relation-ship expert. And I'm still in love with my second ex-husband."

Emma forced a smile and wondered how much longer she'd have to look like a total idiot before they cut to a commercial break.

Twenty-Eight

"THAT WAS WONDERFUL," DEBBIE GUSHED AS SHE ENVELoped Emma in a hug.

"Absolutely fantastic," Alan agreed fervently. They'd all driven to the studio together and were now reconnecting in the enormous parking garage. Emma, confused by their positive reaction, wondered if they had somehow watched the wrong show or been drugged against their will.

"Really? I thought it was a disaster."

Jackie, who was already trying to share clips of the taping on Emma's social media—even though she wasn't supposed to—looked up long enough to roll her eyes. They already had this conversation in the green room, the bathroom and on the way to the car.

"Oh my god, Emma, it wasn't a disaster. She was just asking questions. That is literally her job."

"Sure, but all of her questions made it seem like I was making a huge mistake," Emma complained. Debbie and Alan exchanged a look.

"Do *you* think you're making a huge mistake?" Debbie asked gently.

"No. Not at all. I mean, you know Matt. He's amazing."

"*So* amazing," Jackie confirmed, slightly salivating at the thought of her future brother-in-law.

"Then it doesn't matter what some talk show host thinks," Debbie replied. "You did a great job up there and I could tell the audience liked what you had to say. You had them hooked."

"I guess I'll choose to believe you," Emma said. Maybe she'd been so afraid of looking foolish, her perception was skewed. And even if it wasn't, there wasn't anything she could do to save herself now. Delusion was the only option.

"Good," Debbie replied as she opened the car door. "Because it's time to get some celebratory ice cream."

Approximately thirty minutes later, the family settled into a table outside their favorite artisanal ice cream shop. As Emma licked her black-raspberry-chip cone, she tried to assess the state of her parents' marriage. The ride over had been filled with backseat driving and a fair amount of bickering over what legally constitutes tailgating, but that was par for the course. Since walking in on their closet fight, Emma was more curious about their interactions outside the exacerbating confines of a motor vehicle.

"Did you get my email?" Alan asked Emma as he slurped down some coffee chip. "The band needs to know your first dance song by the end of the week."

Alan had graciously taken over the majority of wedding planning so Emma could focus on finishing her book and launching her podcast. It turned out he had a real knack for details and badgering people to get back to him—not that either was surprising after thirty-eight years as a high-powered attorney.

"What was your first dance song?" Emma asked.

"I don't know if we had one," Debbie replied. "The whole shindig was just to make your grandmother happy."

"That's not true," Alan protested, forever defensive over Emma's demanding grandma. "We both wanted a wedding."

"Yes, but not one at a stuffy golf club surrounded by people we barely knew. I would have been happier in a field somewhere."

"Who has a wedding in a field?"

"Plenty of people."

"I'm sorry ours was such a disappointment because it was inside," Alan said with bite. The conversation was quickly veering into dangerous territory.

"Oh, come on. Neither one of us would have chosen that type of wedding if we'd had the money to pay for it ourselves."

"If you say so," Alan replied.

Debbie looked at her daughters for backup. "Is this *The Twilight Zone*? Have you *ever* heard either one of us talk fondly about our wedding?"

"I don't think I've ever heard you mention it. But I did spend my entire adolescence tuning you out," Jackie replied.

"I've seen some bad pictures. And I think I knew Grandma planned it all," Emma offered.

"See," Debbie declared as though she had just officially won a presidential debate. "I'm not saying anything we haven't both said for almost forty years."

"I never said I hated our wedding," Alan said standing up from the table. "But I'm sorry you feel that way."

"Where are you going?" Debbie asked, confused.

"For a walk."

"Here?"

"Yes."

"Are we just supposed to wait for you?"

"No, I'll find my way home," Alan replied confidently.

As he took off down the street, Debbie looked panicked. "He doesn't even know where he is."

"He has his phone," Jackie said. "He can call an Uber or something."

"Your father doesn't know how to do that. He's going to end up lying on the sidewalk dead from dehydration."

"Then maybe you should go after him?" Emma suggested gently, only for Debbie to sit back in her chair and cross her arms defiantly.

"If he wants to throw a temper tantrum, I'll let him."

Oh lovely, Emma thought. Things were even worse than she'd feared.

"The oven's on fire!" Emma shouted as flames sprung up from the sheet pan inside. "I told you I didn't know how to cook!"

Matt, who had been working on the couch, ran over to confirm that the oven was in fact on fire. "Oh shit!"

"I'm so sorry! I don't know what happened."

"It's okay. Let me get the extinguisher." Matt reached into the high cabinet over the fridge and extracted a never-been-used extinguisher still wrapped in its packaging. He struggled to open it.

"Can you get the scissors?"

"No," Emma sobbed. "I don't know where they are!"

"It's okay," Matt said as he managed to pat her shoulder while grabbing a steak knife to expertly tear through the plastic packaging. He then put the fire out with a large spray of whatever is in fire extinguishers.

Emma felt her heart start to slow down. She wrapped her arms around Matt in gratitude. "I can't be trusted to prepare hot food. I tried to warn you," she mumbled into his chest. She was both embarrassed and annoyed that her first attempt at oven-fried fish had literally gone up in smoke.

Emma had arrived at Matt's place expecting to order in like they normally did, only to find a batch of fresh groceries and a hand-written recipe waiting for her. Matt explained his mom had sent the recipe for her famous fish fry and he'd had groceries delivered from Whole Foods so Emma could make it for them while he finished a report for work. Emma tried to convince Matt that she was hopeless in the kitchen but he wouldn't listen. Apparently Kelly had once said that his mom's recipes were "idiotproof" so she had nothing to worry about.

But now the kitchen was on fire, which didn't bode well for Emma's intelligence.

"Please don't tell your mom about this," Emma pleaded as Matt attempted to take the still-smoking sheet pan out of the oven. "We can just tell her it was so good we forgot to get a photo."

"We don't need to lie to my mom—hold on." Matt held up a long rectangle-shaped box. "Did you put the fish on wax paper?"

"Yes…"

Matt laughed as Emma waited for him to explain the joke. "Wax paper is flammable. You have to use parchment paper in the oven."

"No one mentioned that in the recipe," Emma countered.

"Wow. I guess you *really* don't know how to cook," Matt said with a smile. "Don't worry. My mom was a teacher for twenty-five years. She'll help you learn in no time."

Emma nodded, wondering if she had somehow expressed a desire to learn how to cook in her sleep or if Matt simply couldn't imagine having a wife who barely understood how to use a microwave. In Emma's defense, some of the fancy ones had too many settings.

"Let me go grab us something from the Thai place," Emma offered. "I don't think any of this is salvageable."

"Are you sure? We can have food delivered."

"I need some fresh air. On account of all the smoke inhalation."

"Fair enough. I'll get my usual."

"You got it," Emma replied, glad she at least knew how to order chicken pad thai.

As Emma walked out of the building and wrapped her sweater tightly around herself, she noticed a familiar blonde pacing by the door. She squinted to get a better look just as the blonde turned and made eye contact. They both gasped.

"Kelly?" Emma asked even though she knew the answer. She'd done enough Instagram stalking to be able to recognize Matt's ex-wife anywhere in anything. Right now, Kelly wore a formfitting white collared shirt tucked perfectly into a floral pencil skirt with what had to be at least three-inch heels. It put Emma's yoga pants and comfy sweater to shame.

"Oh my god. Emma, right?" Kelly looked mortified. "You must think I'm a total stalker."

"No. No. I just recognized you and—" Emma could see tears welling up in Kelly's perfectly green eyes. "Are you okay?"

"Not really," Kelly croaked before slumping down onto a bench. Emma was glad the normally nosy valets were nowhere to be seen.

"Did you need to talk to Matt?" Emma asked as she sat down next to her.

"You aren't mad that I'm here?"

"Not yet," Emma joked. "But let me know if I should be."

Kelly's mouth turned upward without quite hitting the threshold for a smile. "I saw you on *The Amanda Sharpe Show*. Pretty much everyone I've ever met sent your clips to me."

Emma winced. It couldn't have been fun for Kelly to see her ex-husband's new fiancée announcing their relationship to the world. "I'm sorry."

"Don't be. None of this is your fault. I'm the one who ruined everything." Kelly looked over at Emma. "I'm assuming Matt told you what I did?"

"He mentioned there was infidelity but didn't get into too many details."

"I don't know what I was thinking. I'm not a cheater. I *hate* cheaters. But it's like the infertility and constant disappointment rotted my brain. I just needed to escape for a night and not think about anything important or real. I wanted to feel like a woman again and not just an inhospitable womb. Does that make any sense?"

"I certainly think so."

"Well, Matt didn't. No matter what I said or did he couldn't get past it. It's like his perception of me totally changed and I was suddenly some horrible stranger who *wanted* to hurt him."

Emma understood Kelly's pain. It was awful when someone you loved could only see the worst version of you.

Kelly sighed and rubbed her red eyes. "Even after we signed the divorce papers last week, I thought he would change his mind. I know that probably sounds delusional but Matty and I... We just go together. I can't imagine being with anyone else."

Emma nodded, not sure what to say. It felt inappropriate to give her normal spiel about the myth of soulmates and Kelly's ability to be compatible with thousands of random people. It would come off like she was trying to get rid of her.

Luckily, Kelly kept going. "But when I saw you on the show yesterday, I panicked. I realized that if I didn't do something right away, he might really be gone."

Emma nodded again. She knew the feeling. She also knew that every time she had tried to do something to get someone to stay, it hadn't worked.

"Do you want me to let you in to see him?"

Kelly looked at Emma like she might have a concussion. "Why would you do that?"

"Because it's not my place to stop you from talking to him. And if he'd rather be with you that's something we both deserve to know."

"Are you having second thoughts or something?" Kelly asked skeptically.

Emma tried to keep her face neutral even though the disaster in the kitchen had caused some doubt to creep in. What if Emma wasn't domestic enough for someone like Matt? Was she really going to have to learn things like the structural difference between parchment and wax paper to keep him happy? She was busy enough as it was.

"No," Emma managed to reply convincingly. "I just don't want to keep things from him. Even if the thing is you."

"Wow," Kelly said. "You're way nicer than I wanted you to be."

After a moment of silent consideration, Kelly stood up from the bench as Emma followed her lead. "I shouldn't be here. Just promise you'll take good care of him."

Emma nodded. She put her arms out for a hug and Kelly, seeming to surprise herself, leaned in and took it. Emma could hear Kelly sniffle as she said, "Don't let him eat anything with red food dye in it. He'll say it's fine but then his chin will itch for the rest of the day."

"Understood. No Twizzlers or red velvet cake allowed."

As they broke apart, the two women smiled sadly at each other. In another world, Emma suspected they'd be friends. But in this one, they would probably never talk again.

"Did someone order a pad Thai made by an actual professional?" Emma announced as she walked back into Matt's condo. The takeout smelled delicious and it helped soothe her nerves for what was likely going to be an uncomfortable conversation.

"That took forever." Matt dashed into the kitchen, giving Emma a quick kiss on the head before tearing open the plastic bags. "Was there a long line?"

"Not really," Emma replied even though there was one man in front of her who'd become indignant upon learning a Thai restaurant didn't make Chinese lo mein. "But I did bump into Kelly on my way out."

Matt, who had been in the middle of ripping the cover off his noodles, whipped around to face Emma. "What? Where?"

"Right outside the building. I think she was pumping herself up to come in."

Matt's eyes shot toward the front door, his usually calm demeanor out the window. "Is she still here?"

"No. We talked for a bit and she decided it was better to leave, I guess."

"What did you talk about?"

"Oh, mostly geopolitics in the arctic circle," Emma joked to lighten the mood, but Matt just looked confused. "I'm kidding. We talked about you. I guess she saw me on *Amanda Sharpe* and was worried she was going to lose you."

"*Lose* me? We're already divorced."

"I know. But I think she's still hoping to win you back."

Matt shook his head in lieu of a verbal response. Emma noticed the pain on his face and wasn't sure if it was pity for the woman he once loved, or turmoil over whether to run after her or not.

"Did you want to talk to her?" Emma asked gently.

"There's nothing to say." Matt grabbed two forks and handed one to Emma. "Let's go eat."

Emma followed him over to the couch. "Not to be a total therapist, but how do you feel about her showing up here? It must feel weird to know she's still actively fighting for you."

"You have nothing to worry about, okay?" Matt said impatiently. Like Emma was being ridiculous for harping on something that had literally just happened. "I can't trust Kelly anymore, so it doesn't matter how I feel or don't feel. I have to move forward."

Emma nodded as she poked her fork into her Pad See Ew with soft tofu. That wasn't exactly the loving reassurance she was looking for. "How is the book going?" Matt asked in a clear attempt to change the subject.

Unfortunately, he had just shifted them into another touchy topic. After Emma and Will's brainstorming session had been cut short by running into Ryan and then almost kissing each other, Emma had been avoiding her manuscript like the plague. She felt like a pilot who'd studied flying all her life without being taught how to actually land the plane.

"I'm struggling a bit with the ending," Emma confessed, annoyed that her eyes were beginning to water. Clearly her body was more upset about her writer's block than her mind had been letting on. But maybe it was good to open up and let Matt help her through what was beginning to feel like a creative crisis. Especially now that she didn't have Will to lean on for that part of her life anymore.

"I'm sure you'll figure it out," Matt said with an encouraging pat to her knee. "You're really smart. Just sit down and pound it out."

Emma feigned a smile. "Yeah, I'll try that."

Matt smiled back, pleased to have solved the problem. Emma didn't need to tell him he'd only made it worse.

Twenty-Nine

"I THOUGHT WE COULD START OFF BY READING A LISTENER'S email," Will said in his podcasting voice, which was basically his regular voice with better enunciation.

"That sounds fun," Emma replied even though she would rather be anywhere else. It was their second studio recording session since their almost-kiss and it took a surprising amount of mental energy to keep things strictly professional. It helped that Anika was watching their every move—even if she had no idea she'd been awarded the role of unofficial chaperone.

Will consulted his show notes and began reading. "Confused in Connecticut writes, 'Hi, Emma and Will. Big fan of the show. Love your chemistry.'" He cleared his throat, as if the compliment had almost gotten stuck on its way out. "'I'm writing in because I'm forty-two and recently started dating someone new. Everything is going great, and my boyfriend and I have even started discussing marriage. My only concern is that he still talks to his ex. Not just once in a blue moon but almost every day. Should I be concerned that he hasn't moved on, or should I believe him when he says they're just good friends?'" Will looked up. "Emma, you want to take this one?"

"Sure," Emma said, even though the question hit a little too close to home.

She almost wished Matt still talked to Kelly instead of just talking about her all the time. Her recent visit hadn't put a stop to Matt's mentioning her. If anything, she seemed to come up even more now.

"Look, there are plenty of people who can stay friends with an ex in a healthy way. And there are also plenty of people who use friendship as an excuse to hold on to their romantic connection."

"How is Confused in Connecticut supposed to tell the difference?"

"I was getting to that part."

"Sorry," Will said with his hands up. All the lingering sexual tension between them had quickly morphed into frustration and annoyance since their almost-kiss. Now that they couldn't touch each other's mouth, it seemed they were at each other's throats.

"I think the best way to tell is to try to figure out his priorities. As his partner, you should come first—"

Will scoffed, breaking Emma's momentum.

"What?"

"They just started dating. Why should she take precedence over the rest of his life?"

"Are you being serious, or are you just trying to disagree with me for fun?"

Will held back a smile. Emma was beginning to suspect Will took some sort of sick pleasure in their new, near constant arguing. There was a theory in her profession that couples who fought all the time had a better chance than couples who sat in silence.

Not that we're a couple, Emma reminded herself.

"I just don't see why having a new girlfriend means he has to give up a major friendship," Will retorted, as if he'd checkmated her. "People are more than their romantic relationships."

"If you had let me finish, you would know that wasn't where I was heading."

"My mistake," Will said with an unbearably frustrating grin. Frustrating in that he clearly wasn't sorry. And unbearable in how attractive it made him look.

"I was going to say that it might be worth having a conversation with your boyfriend about how this friendship makes you feel and take note of how he responds. If he gets super defensive and says he's not willing to discuss establishing *any* boundaries with his ex, that's a signal that your feelings aren't his priority. And that's a red flag."

"So it's a test?"

"It's a knowledge-building exercise."

Will laughed. "You'd make a good politician."

"I'd say thank you, but I know you don't mean that as a compliment."

"I just think that if you don't feel secure in your relationship, that's something *you* need to work on independently."

"Even if you have a good reason to feel insecure?"

"Like what?"

"Like your girlfriend talking to her ex every day."

"I don't think that would bother me."

Emma let out a mixture of a scoff and a laugh, which perfectly described how she often felt around Will. "You're impossible."

"Or am I exceedingly simple, and that has somehow become confounding in today's day and age?"

"No, it's definitely not that," Emma replied with a grin. "But I'm starting to think you don't have a realistic understanding of what it means to be in true partnership."

The sound of two gunshots suddenly reverberated through Emma's head. Both her and Will instinctively ducked, afraid for their lives.

"Sorry," Anika's voice said through their headphones. "I was playing around with sound effects. You know, *shots fired*."

"I like the instinct. Hated the result," Will said, rubbing his ears.

"I think I had it turned up too loud," Anika replied as they watched her tinker with some knobs through the glass wall. "My bad."

Emma and Will caught eyes and laughed. For a second it felt like they were on the same team again.

"You were saying...something rude, I believe?" Will had a mischievous twinkle in his eye.

Once again, he surprised Emma with his lack of defensiveness. Most people would have taken their imagined near-death experience as an excuse to change the subject.

"I wasn't trying to be rude," Emma explained. "I just noticed a pattern and then I mentioned that pattern in a rude way due to poor social graces."

"Strange apology accepted. Although you do seem to forget that I was in a four-year-long relationship, so clearly I know *something* about partnership."

"Mm-hmm," Emma said unconvincingly.

"What now?"

"It's nothing. Just a hunch."

"Like a good hunch or one that makes me look bad?"

"We can move on."

Will groaned, his curiosity getting the better of him like always. "Well, now you have to tell me."

"Okay," Emma said, sitting up in her chair. "You say that your ex left you out of the blue for a fellowship in England, right? And that she didn't even ask you to come?"

"Right. Thanks for bringing that up."

Emma ignored his sarcasm, determined to not be distracted by Will's wit. "When you first told me that, I thought, *Wow, what a bitch*. But now I wonder if she was just operating under

your relationship rules. Where everyone is out to protect themselves and neither one of you is expected to consult the other
about big life decisions, because doing so would mean losing
your individuality. And when I think of it *that* way, it's like *of
course* she took the fellowship and *of course* she never asked you
to come because she knew you'd say no. You weren't going to
give up your life plan for anyone. Even your long-term, live-
in girlfriend."

Will squinted his eyes as if that would help clarify things.
"So you're saying it's my fault that she left? Because I created
an environment where she felt like she couldn't even ask me
to come?"

"It's just a hunch. But basically…yeah."

"Fuck," Will replied, the fire fizzling out of him. "You
might be right."

Emma stared at her phone, debating whether to check in
with Will. Even though he had agreed with her rather harsh
assessment of his love life, she still felt bad for being so blunt.
They weren't allowed to text or call anymore, but a kind email
from a concerned colleague wouldn't break—

"He's here," Matt said, startling Emma out of her internal debate. She looked up from her seat at Le Pain Quotidien
and saw their wedding photographer making his way toward
their corner table. Phoenix Cody, with his man bun and hulk-
ing figure, had come highly recommended by the only one
of Jackie's friends who was over thirty when she got married.
Matt had liked his documentary style, which was good because Emma had already paid Phoenix's initial deposit before
they had even met.

"Matt and Emma, I presume?" Phoenix asked in deep regis-
ter with a touch of Southern twang. According to his website,
Phoenix had come to LA by way of Louisiana to fulfill his lifetime goal of "capturing people's souls on the most meaningful

day of their lives." He also modeled on the side and had some sort of brand affiliation with a juice company.

"So great to meet you, man. I love your work," Matt gushed, standing up and extending his arm for a firm handshake. Emma followed suit, trying not to wince as her fingers were engulfed in Phoenix's enormous palm.

They all settled into their chairs and the requisite small talk about parking difficulties before Phoenix dived into business. "As we discussed on the phone, I want to make sure we're all on the same page and I capture the right moments on your big day."

Emma forced herself to nod along with Matt even though it seemed pretty obvious what Phoenix was supposed to capture; the wedding ceremony and the various guests came to mind.

"Emma, let's start with you." Phoenix rested his elbows on the table and cradled his head in hands like she was the most interesting specimen in the world.

His intense eye contact made Emma squirm. It was one thing to talk about romantic relationships as a trained professional, or even *with* a trained professional like her therapist. It was another to earnestly and openly talk about her own mushy feelings in a public café with a perfect stranger. This was what she meant when she'd told Imani she wasn't a romantic.

"What can you see in Matt that makes him different from every other beefcake out there?"

Emma turned to Matt as his cheeks grew red from the compliment. It was a good question and Emma felt guilty that a rush of answers didn't immediately spring to mind. Maybe it was the pressure to deliver that was getting in her normally loquacious way. She let out an awkward laugh that only showcased her growing embarrassment.

"Take your time," Phoenix responded. "It's a lot of feeling to put into words. That's why we have cameras."

This man takes his job very *seriously,* Emma thought before forcing herself to address the question. "Matt is probably one of the nicest people I have ever met. He treats everyone like he already knows them, putting everyone at ease. And he's also very good at making eggs." Emma threw the last part in even though he'd technically only made her eggs once. It might have been a fluke.

Phoenix stared at her for a moment with what Emma could only describe as a look of deep disappointment. The silence lingered like a toxic gas until he asked, "Anything else?"

Emma looked at Matt, who offered her an encouraging smile. "He has very strong legs. But I guess that will be hard to showcase under his suit."

Phoenix ignored her attempt at a joke and turned his focus to the groom-to-be. "What about you, Matthew? Why did this young woman take your breath away?"

Emma stifled another laugh. Phoenix seemed incapable of talking like a normal person and was instead trapped in the stereotype of an overly sensitive artist—which wasn't that unusual in Los Angeles, but was still hard to stomach.

"Oh, well," Matt said as he squeezed her hand. "Emma's a great listener. She has a lot of empathy. And she's an amazing caregiver."

Emma felt her body tighten up. It wasn't that what Matt was saying was wrong—everything he mentioned was something she took pride in. It's just that they weren't the first things that came to mind when she thought about herself. Traits like *hilarious* or *ambitious* seemed more accurate coming out of the gate.

"Amazing caregiver. I love that," Phoenix replied as Emma tried not to focus on the less glamorous associations with that word. She hoped Matt wasn't mainly excited to marry her because he knew she'd be willing to wipe his butt when they got old. Obviously, she'd do it, but it wasn't like she was excited about it.

"If you could only keep one image from the wedding, what

would you want it to be?" Phoenix asked with his standard gravitas.

"I thought contractually we were allowed to keep them all," Emma joked.

"I think he's just trying to figure out what we care about," Matt explained gently.

"I know. I was just...being silly." Emma smiled at Phoenix, who gave her a condescending grin in return. *So much for bridal privilege*, she thought.

"I think I have one," Matt said with a bit of excitement. "I would really want a photo of our entire family. My side, her side, all together with the kids and grandparents. Like one of those photos everyone can hang in their living room."

Phoenix nodded encouragingly. "Multigenerational. The past sowing the way for the future."

"Sure," Matt agreed good-naturedly. "What about you?"

"I guess your answer makes sense," Emma replied. "Weddings are about community and not just the couple."

Matt grinned, glad to be in agreement. He put his arm around her, hugging her close despite their separate chairs. Emma tried not to feel slighted that his answer hadn't been their first kiss or their first dance. Or even one of those cheesily staged first-look photos.

But then again, Matt already had all those pictures with someone else.

Thirty

———————

"I JUST NEED TO GRAB MY COMPUTER FROM THE OFFICE and then we can go to lunch," Emma explained to her parents.

They were currently being icy with each other in the front seat of Debbie's Volvo. Things had been increasingly tense since Alan stormed off at the ice cream shop a few weeks ago—a failed attempt at getting his wife's attention. Debbie seemed fed up with Alan and Alan was clearly wounded by Debbie's distance. They hadn't played a single game of cribbage in weeks, breaking a daily tradition Emma had grown accustomed to since moving back home. Something had to change, and it had to change fast.

Plus, focusing on someone else's relationship problems always made Emma feel better and more in control of her own life. But that was just a bonus.

"Do you want to come in with me? We got some new artwork I think you'd like," Emma fibbed.

"Sure," Debbie said as Alan unbuckled his seat belt next to her. They all climbed out and followed Emma through the door into the waiting room.

"It's right through here," Emma lied again as she directed her parents into her shared office.

Imani looked up from her seat in the therapist chair and smiled.

"Imani, hi," Debbie exclaimed, always happy to see her daughter's closest friend. "I hope we're not interrupting anything."

"Not at all. I was actually waiting for you."

Alan and Debbie looked at Emma in confusion. She gestured for them to sit on the couch. They reluctantly obliged.

"What's going on?" Alan asked. "I thought we were going to Olive Garden."

"I know you did," Emma replied as she perched herself on the arm of Imani's chair. "And I'm sorry for the misdirect but I didn't know what else to do. I'm really worried about you two."

"You're worried about *us*? Why?" Debbie asked, completely lost.

"Because you aren't prioritizing each other anymore. Ever since Dad retired, your dynamic has been off, but neither one of you wants to properly address it."

"Oh, honey," Debbie replied, "I think you're overreacting. We've been married for a very long time. There are always bumps in the road but it's nothing to worry about. Right, Alan?"

Instead of answering, Alan shrugged.

"What is that supposed to mean?" Debbie demanded, already annoyed and reverting to defensive mode. Alan wasn't providing the backup she'd expected.

"I don't know. This feels…different. Like you can't stand to be around me."

"Oh my god, just because I don't want you breathing down my neck all day doesn't mean I can't stand to be around you."

"When you put it like that, I guess I have nothing to worry about," Alan replied sarcastically.

Debbie opened her mouth to retort but Emma put up a hand to stop her. "Before you keep going, I am going to excuse myself and turn it over to Imani to help facilitate your discussion."

"What?" Alan and Debbie shouted in unison.

"It's not ethical for me to run a session with my own parents."

"It's also not ethical for me to run a session with my best friend's parents," Imani clarified. "So, I need to make it extremely clear that I am not here as a therapist and you are not here as my clients. We are just three people who are going to have a constructive conversation that no one will ever mention to my licensing board."

"This is ridiculous," Debbie protested. "I'm sorry Emma roped you into this, Imani, but we are perfectly capable of resolving things by ourselves. Not that there is anything we even need to resolve in the first place."

"Why don't we just give it a try, Debbie?" Alan asked gently. "I know you think therapy isn't for you but how can you know that when you've refused to try?"

Emma restrained herself from giving her father a fist bump. She had tried to relay the exact same argument to her mother countless times only to be stonewalled. Debbie loved the idea of therapy—but only for other people.

"Because I know I don't want to talk about myself with a total stranger," Debbie countered. "It's not in my nature to share on command."

"I'm not going to make you share anything you don't want to," Imani said kindly. "I'm just here to be a neutral third party if the two of you get stuck or want another perspective. We can always give it a try and if you don't feel like it helped, Emma will do your laundry for a month."

Emma shot Imani a look. It was the first she was hearing of this plan, but she had to admit it was a good one. "I'll even iron your T-shirts."

Alan playfully poked his wife in the arm. "You've got to admit, that is a good deal."

Debbie sighed and turned to her husband. "How important is this to you? On a scale of one to ten?"

"Nine-point-five."

"Wow. Okay." She turned to Imani. "I'll give you one hour."

Emma stood up, thrilled that this had somehow worked out. "I'll come back then." Her parents nodded, one more cheerfully than the other.

Emma knew it was frowned upon to force someone into therapy—especially under false pretenses. It was also extremely unlikely that anything would be solved in a single session. But none of that mattered since all Emma really wanted was for her parents to stop avoiding their issues and start talking. They had somehow made it forty years without fully understanding the inner workings of each other's brains. It was time to learn.

"Is there anything I'm not doing that you wish I would do?"

Matt looked at Emma strangely from behind the wheel of his car. They were on their way to the final tasting at their wedding venue, a gorgeous hotel and event space in Malibu called Calamigos Ranch. When Emma and Ryan had first visited the spot a little over a year earlier, they had been blown away by the big trees and chic rustic decor. They'd even fantasized about coming back to the resort each year on their anniversary. Emma, who hadn't been back in person since, hoped it would somehow feel just as special with Matt—or at least not super uncomfortable.

"What do you mean?"

"All this stuff with my parents has just reinforced how different people can be. You might need things that haven't even occurred to me. I thought I'd ask."

Her parents' off-the-books session with Imani had been more successful than anyone could have expected. Debbie seemed to finally understand that even though it wasn't true, Alan saw her need for alone time as a painful personal attack. And Alan started to come around to the idea that it wasn't helpful to take all of Debbie's actions so personally. Nothing was said that hadn't been said before, but something about saying it in front of someone else, in a neutral territory, made it easier to listen. Funny how that worked. They'd even agreed to see another therapist Emma knew from grad school for a few more sessions as they worked the kinks out. It was a therapy success story, and it made Emma want to flex her own communication skills with Matt.

They also hadn't said anything to each other in twenty minutes and Emma was getting pretty bored. Matt was a wonderful, kind, incredibly good-looking man. But he wasn't much of a talker.

"Huh," Matt said. "I can't think of anything. What about you?"

"Oh, come on. I can't be the only one to say something. That's not fair," Emma teased.

"So you do have something?"

"Nothing huge or anything."

"What is it?"

Emma debated if she should share or not. On the one hand, she didn't want to hurt his feelings. On the other, she needed to learn how to be more honest with Matt without fearing rejection.

"I guess sometimes I worry that we are going to run out of things to say to each other."

Matt laughed until he realized she wasn't joking. "Why would we run out of things to say?"

"Because it happens sometimes. Haven't you ever seen two old people at a restaurant eating their entire meal in silence? That is my greatest fear."

"Really? I've always thought it was nice. They're so comfortable with each other that they don't even have to talk."

"But I love to talk. It's one of my favorite things to do."

"Then we can talk."

"What if we run out of stuff to talk *about*? What will we do then? People can die from boredom, you know."

"Is that true?"

"Not really. But it isn't good for you." Emma wasn't sure why she was getting so worked up. This was supposed to be a productive conversation, not a triggering one.

"Is this something you've always worried about or is it something you're just worried about with me?"

"I've always worried about it. But I've also never dated someone who would *want* to have a silent dinner. I guess that scares me a little."

"Hmm," Matt said with an unreadable look on his face.

"What?"

"I guess it scares me that you view silence as such a bad thing. I find it peaceful. Sometimes Kelly and I would just sit out on our porch and watch the sunset without saying a word."

That picturesque scene was quite literally Emma's nightmare. She shuddered at the thought of being left to her own thoughts for thirty-two to thirty-seven minutes, depending on her location and the time of year.

"Do you think I talk too much?" Emma asked, even though she knew nobody should ever ask a question they don't want the answer to.

"Not too much. Just a lot." Matt quickly glanced at her to make sure he wasn't in trouble. "I really don't mind though. Unless I'm trying to work or something."

Emma suddenly felt like her seat belt was strangling her. She pulled at it anxiously, only for the stiff fabric to remain in place, sucking the life out of her as a rush of worry took over her brain. Was she unintentionally setting herself up for a lifetime of fear that her husband was just *tolerating* her whenever she opened her mouth? Because given her chatterbox personality, that seemed like a big issue.

"Did Kelly not talk a lot?"

"No, she talked. It was just different."

"Different as in better?"

"Why are you asking that? Are you trying to start a fight?"

"No. I'm trying to figure out if we're forcing something that shouldn't be forced."

As the words left Emma's mouth, she knew there was no turning back. She had said the scary thing—the thing they made sure to never acknowledge or mention—out loud. They would either come out of this conversation stronger than ever or not together at all.

"Do *you* think we're forcing it?" Matt asked with concern.

"Please just answer the question," Emma replied, exasperated.

Matt sighed. "I think we're still in the figuring-each-other-out phase. But that doesn't mean we're forcing it."

"How long did it take for you to figure Kelly out?"

"That was…"

"Different?"

"Yeah. We're both from the Midwest. We both have big families. It's like I already knew her or something."

Emma nodded; she had recently felt the same way. About someone else.

From the moment she'd met Will she'd been able to be her full self. She'd cracked jokes. She'd spoken her mind. She felt understood in a way that shouldn't be rare but always was. There was no *forcing it* when she and Will were together. Someone was always talking—often both of them at the same time.

And just like that, a light bulb exploded in her head.

"I think you should pull over."

"What?"

"I think you should pull over."

"I can't. We're halfway up a mountain." Matt made a good point. They had left the Pacific Coast Highway behind and were now weaving their way up Kanan Dume Rd. It wasn't a road for the faint of heart.

"Up there. You can pull over there." Emma pointed to a scenic overlook ahead.

"That's on the other side of the road."

"Just do a U-turn."

"Are you serious—"

"Quick, turn now! No one is coming," Emma screamed, causing Matt to panic and swing the car around. They came to a screeching halt dangerously close to the edge.

"That was not okay!" Matt exclaimed in the closest thing to a yell Emma had ever heard from him. "We could have died."

"I know, I'm sorry." Emma scrambled out of the car.

"What are you doing?" Matt demanded, climbing out after her. They stood facing each other over his Porsche Panamera. "What the hell is going on? Are you having some sort of—"

"Psychotic break? No. I don't think so. But I was starting to have a full-blown anxiety attack until I realized we don't have to do this. We don't have to get married."

Matt's confusion quickly turned to hurt. "Where is this coming from? Because I like to watch sunsets and not talk all the time? Or did Kelly say something the other night that turned you off?"

Emma shook her head. When Matt had shut down their conversation about Kelly's late-night visit, Emma had tried to convince herself it was because Kelly no longer meant anything to him. But now, in light of her own epiphany, it was glaringly obvious.

The real reason Matt couldn't talk about Kelly was because she still meant too much to him.

"Kelly didn't say anything bad. She's still in love with you and I don't want to be the reason you two aren't together."

"You aren't. I was already getting divorced when we met."

"I know, but that was a mistake. You shouldn't throw away what you and Kelly have over one mistake."

"She *cheated* on me."

"One time, under duress! I'd bet good money she'd never do it again."

Matt shook his head in frustration. "This doesn't make any sense. I thought your whole thing was that there is no such thing as soulmates, and we can be happy with a bunch of different people. Do you not agree with that anymore?"

"No, I do."

"Then why do you keep acting like Kelly is the only person for me when I—" Matt stopped himself.

"When you what?"

"I was going to say 'when I love you' but I realized we haven't said that to each other yet."

"Exactly." Emma was glad that Matt had gotten to the heart of their issues himself, even if he hadn't meant to. "*Why* haven't we said it yet? We're engaged and we've been together for a few months. Most regular couples would have already said it at this point."

Matt shrugged. "Nothing about us has been regular."

"Sure, but that doesn't explain why it's been so easy for us to wait until marriage to have sex. Shouldn't we want to rip each other's clothes off? Have you even thought about how weird that is?"

"If sex is your big problem, we can have sex right now. The windows are tinted. I can lower the seats down. Just get in."

"Matt," Emma said gently. "You know that won't solve anything. The whole point of Operation: Save My Date was that if two people have a certain level of chemistry and compatibility they can make a marriage work even if they don't know each other for a long time. But what if we don't have enough chemistry or compatibility?"

Matt hung his head, showing his first sign of defeat. "I really wanted this to work."

"Believe me, I did too. And so did my book editor."

Matt chuckled as he wiped his eyes. "Maybe I messed things up by not letting us sleep together. That could have prevented us from getting closer."

"Maybe, but I doubt it. We tried our best, but you need a spark to start a flame. And it just wasn't there."

Matt nodded. It was a relief to know that underneath all his certainty, he had felt the same lack of connection. Perhaps if neither of them had properly been in love before they would have thought what they had together was enough. But they each knew what it was like to be fully tethered, in your heart and in your mind, to another person—and this wasn't it.

"What now?" Matt asked gently.

"I think you should get in your car and you go find Kelly."

Matt barked out a laugh. It was maybe the loudest one she'd heard from him yet.

"I can't just show up and ask for my ex-wife back. We're divorced, remember?"

"Why not? I know you think you've moved on, but as someone who has spent a lot of time with you recently, I can assure you you have not." Emma watched as Matt's mind attempted to reject this uncomfortable news. She needed to help him see the truth. "You talk about Kelly all the time, Matt. It's like she's still living in your head with you. Like you never let her go. And that's okay because she clearly never let you go either."

Matt sighed, his resolve to forget the past weakening. "I've never been divorced before. I didn't know how much it was supposed to hurt. Or how hard it should be to move on." He looked at Emma, his face painfully hopeful. As if he couldn't sustain another blow but was somehow still willing to fight. "You really think Kelly and I could make it work this time?"

"In my professional opinion, you can't guarantee anything

when it comes to love," Emma replied truthfully. "But in my personal opinion, yes. Absolutely."

Matt rubbed his face, still slightly in shock. "This is insane."

"I think you mean *bananas*. Insane is derogatory for people with mental illness."

"Sorry."

"Don't be. I should have told you that a while ago, but I was too busy forcing things." They smiled at each other.

"Let me drive you home."

"That's okay. I'm going to call an Uber. There's somewhere else I need to go first."

Matt raised his eyebrows.

"If it works out, I'll fill you in."

"Okay," Matt replied as he climbed back into the driver's seat.

Emma walked around the car to say a proper goodbye. "I'm sorry I dragged you into all of this."

Matt reached out and took Emma's hand. He gave it one sweet kiss before letting it go. "Don't apologize. Unless Kelly kicks me out."

Emma laughed. "I highly doubt that will happen."

Matt crossed his fingers and closed the door. She watched as he drove off down the road. In less than six months, she'd lost another fiancé.

Except this time, Emma knew exactly what to do about it.

Thirty-One

ONCE MATT HAD DRIVEN AWAY, EMMA QUICKLY REALIZED she didn't have strong enough service to call an Uber, so she had had to make the perilous trek down the mountain on foot. Not a single passing car had offered her a ride, but two separate ones had honked angrily and loudly questioned her sanity.

They don't know the half of it, Emma thought as the reality of her actions began to sink in.

Had she really just made the ginormous decision to blow up her personal and professional life because her seat belt felt too tight? Or had the seat belt's sudden tightness been a signal that she was feeling trapped and needed to free herself of a situation completely of her own making?

By the time she reached the main road and had cell service, Emma had decided on the latter. So what if her audience was going to lose all respect for her and her book was likely to get canceled? Emma had done the right thing for herself—and for Matt. Amanda Sharpe would be proud of her, if she remembered Emma at all. Daytime TV had a lot of guests.

When she finally made her way to Will's apartment building, she was tired, hungry and more than a bit sweaty. As Emma prepared herself to knock and open herself up for yet another potentially brutal rejection, the door swung open.

But instead of seeing Will, Emma found herself face-to-face with another woman. She was about Emma's height with short blond hair, large green glasses and a sleeve of tattoos on her right arm.

"Oh, hi," the woman said, not at all fazed to find a stranger on the other side of the door as she reached down to grab a package from the welcome mat. Clearly this woman didn't have a high startle response like Emma, who would have screamed.

"Hi, I was just looking for Will."

"Will? There's no Will here. It's just been me and my birds for the last ten years." As Emma started to question her entire reality, the woman laughed. "Sorry, couldn't resist. Let me get him for you. I'm Camila, by the way."

"Emma."

"Nice to meet you," Camila said as she went back into the apartment and shouted, "Will? Emma's here to see you."

"What?" Will's surprised voice rang out. It didn't sound happily surprised either.

What the hell am I doing? Emma wondered. She'd already blown her chance with him—multiple times. Why had she thought she deserved another?

As Emma debated making a break for the elevator, Will appeared in the doorway. His blond hair was slightly messy, perhaps from recent intercourse with Camila, and he didn't look pleased to see Emma.

"What are you doing here?"

Emma wasn't sure how to respond. She wanted to reach out and inappropriately stroke his cheek or burrow her head into his neck. She wanted to declare she'd made a huge mistake and that they should book a weekend trip in Palm Springs to make up. She wanted to move past this part and get to the stage where their disastrous beginning was just a funny story they told at cocktail parties now that they were so solid as a couple. But nothing about Will's stance or his face or his overall vibe implied he felt the same way.

"I… Never mind," Emma sputtered, the lack of food in her belly clearly impacting her brain. She took off down the hall at a fast clip before things could get any worse.

"Emma!" Will shouted, causing her to break into a jog.

After thirty-two mostly mortifying years, Emma had finally exceeded her embarrassment threshold and needed to immediately move to the woods, leaving human civilization for good. She hit the elevator down button five times and begged for it to open before Will reached her. She could tell by the sound of his footsteps that he was closing in.

"Will you just wait—"

The elevator finally arrived and Emma thrust herself inside. She desperately searched for the right button to close the door, only for Will to beat her to it. He stepped into the claustrophobic metal box with plenty of time to spare.

"Want to tell me what's going on?"

"Not really," Emma replied as the doors closed. Neither one of them made a move to press a button. As the uncomfortable silence wore on, Emma realized that Will was using her own favorite trick to get people to talk—he was waiting her out.

"Your girlfriend seems very cool. I like her cat-eating-a-plant tattoo. Is she the one Anika set you up with?"

Will nodded. "Thanks. But she isn't my girlfriend. We're just dating." Will cheekily turned to Emma to explain, "Dating is when two people take time to get to know each other before deciding if they would like to move forward into a more serious commit—"

Emma whacked Will in the stomach. "I know what dating is."

"Could have fooled me," Will teased.

"Why didn't you mention things were getting more serious with her?"

"It's pretty new. And I was trying to keep things professional and email only."

Emma nodded in understanding. She felt some of her tension ease now that she knew Will was still technically single. It meant she might still have a chance. It also meant she needed to open her mouth.

"I broke up with Matt," Emma nearly shouted.

Will looked at her with concern, which was not the reaction she was hoping for. She'd have preferred him to break out into a celebratory song. Or at least crack a smile. "I'm sorry to hear that," he said instead.

"Are you?"

"Of course. I know how much you wanted it to work out."

She really had. But now Emma wanted something more. "I'm the one who ended it. I realized that we didn't have enough of a connection to make it work. Operation: Save My Date is only feasible if there's enough chemistry to begin with. I didn't have the wrong plan, but I did have the wrong guy."

Emma reached for Will's hand just as he moved it to run it through his hair. She wasn't sure if the move was deliberate or bad timing.

"When did you have this big revelation?" he asked, his voice frustratingly neutral.

Emma glanced at her watch. "About an hour and a half ago. I would have gotten here sooner but I miscalculated the power of AT&T's cellular coverage."

Will sighed, which felt like an emotional punch to the throat. "I can't keep being your backup plan, Emma. You can't run to me every time it doesn't work out with someone else and you're too afraid to be alone."

"That's not...that's not what's happening."

Based on Will's extremely closed-off demeanor, Emma likely

only had one shot at making this right. She took a deep breath and dived in. "When we first met, I was terrified. I didn't want to give up on love, but I was also trying to figure out how to mitigate my risk. I thought if I found someone who valued marriage as much as me, I wouldn't get hurt again. But there is no way to avoid getting hurt. That is simply part of the deal when you sign up for a relationship. You're basically saying, 'I like you enough to let you destroy me.' The only way putting yourself out there like that is tolerable is by trusting that if you *do* get destroyed, or heartbroken, or left randomly on a Monday night with no explanation, you will be able to pick up the pieces and keep going.

"When Ryan left me, it felt like my second strike, with all my previous relationship failures mixing together as the first. I felt like I had *one* more shot in me and if it didn't work out, I'd have to accept that I don't have whatever it takes to be loved for a whole lifetime. I thought I couldn't handle any more heartbreak and I didn't want any more proof that something was wrong with me."

Will opened his mouth but Emma held up her hand. "I'll take questions at the end," she replied before taking another deep breath. "So, when I met you and you refused to take the leap with me, I thought it meant you didn't care about me enough. That if I had been someone else, someone more worthy or whatever, you would have thrown caution to the wind and bought a tux."

"I already own a tux."

"Please let me finish."

Will raised his hands in surrender.

Emma tried to keep going but had lost her train of thought. "What was I saying?"

"That if you were someone else, I would have agreed to get married at a wedding meant for another guy."

"Right. Exactly. But then, as I continued to get to know

you, it became clear that the real issue wasn't *me* but the very idea of you marrying *anyone* so quickly."

"I told you that many times."

"I know, I know. And I would have listened if I had had the capacity to think rationally. But by that point there was too much outside pressure to make the plan work—not to mention my brand-new abandonment issues thanks to Ryan. The whole thing felt too high-stakes for me to back out with the world watching. Especially if I wasn't even sure if *we* would work. In my defense, you do seem to have a problem with commitment."

"It's not a problem so much as an issue."

"That's the same thing."

Will shrugged. She had him there.

"Anyway," Emma continued as they stood stagnant in the unmoving elevator, "for those various reasons I decided to take the easy way out and move forward with someone who I thought would never leave me if I stayed faithful and put in the work. It didn't hurt that he looked like a Greek statue come to life."

Will rolled his eyes at this, as Emma intended. Even in times of strife, it was impossible not mess with him.

"The problem, William," Emma said as she took a bold step toward him, "is that he wasn't you."

Will looked at her skeptically as she kept going.

"You aren't my backup plan. You're my first choice. And to prove that to you, I'm willing to risk never getting married if it means we get to be together."

Will raised his eyebrows in disbelief.

"Yep. You heard me. I'm talking no quick engagement, no ominous wedding deadline. Just two people taking the time to see if this connection is as good as I think it is. And if I'm wrong, so be it. It won't mean that I'm an idiot who doesn't understand how relationships work. It'll mean I'm human. Maybe even a *brave* human, depending on how you spin it."

"Are you being serious? You'd be okay with us *never* getting married?"

"Well, I mean, I'd hope that after a certain amount of time—and once you feel comfortable, of course—we could *discuss*—"

Will's lips crashed into Emma's before she could finish her sentence. Without hesitation she gave herself over to him, running her hands through his hair and inhaling his intoxicating scent. Their entanglement felt both deeply thrilling and achingly familiar. Emma had somehow missed touching Will even more than she'd realized. But as he reached his hand up her soft shirt, the elevator doors pulled open, revealing a tattooed woman with big green glasses.

"Ah, so that's where you went," Camila said icily from the elevator bank. Will quickly pulled away from Emma as his face turned red.

"Camila, I'm so sorry—"

Camila put up her hand. "I don't want to hear it. I just want to go home, post about this on Reddit and order expensive takeout."

"That's fair," Emma replied as Camila walked into the elevator. "I'd do the same. Except I don't really understand Reddit's interface—"

"Can you get out of there already?" Camila asked, exasperated.

Will and Emma jumped back into the hallway.

"You can bill me for that takeout if you want," Will offered gallantly as the doors closed. Their final image of Camila being her middle finger.

"I guess we deserved that," Emma said as guilt started to take hold.

Luckily, Will quickly washed it away with his mouth.

Thirty-Two

August 29

EMMA FELT HER EYES FILL WITH TEARS AS SHE STOOD under the chuppah in front of roughly one hundred and fifty people. She contemplated discreetly wiping her face but worried she wouldn't be able to hold her huge bouquet of flowers with only one hand. Alan had clearly gone for the VIP floral package, and while her bundle of peonies was gorgeous, they were a bit cumbersome. Emma checked to see if Jackie was also struggling, but her big sister was too busy smiling at the bride and groom.

Alan and Debbie looked radiant as they held hands and gazed into each other's eyes. No one would suspect they had already been married for forty years. Emma was so grateful her mom was finally getting the wedding she'd always wanted. Even if it had originally been planned for someone else (and then someone else again).

As the rabbi helped the happy couple renew their vows, Emma looked out into the sea of people and immediately found who she was looking for. Will was seated in the front row and the moment they made eye contact he grinned and gave her a little wave. Even though they were only boyfriend and girlfriend, Emma felt confident she'd never have to go to another family event alone again.

The past few weeks had been the happiest of her life—despite the barrage of online harassment and social media commentary about her life choices. Jackie had helped Emma film a video explaining her decision to officially call off her wedding and her engagement to Matt. Jackie had also pitched ending said video with a surprise cameo from Will to give viewers the happy ending they'd been rooting for—even it didn't come with a ring. During the six minutes and seventeen seconds of footage, Emma did her best to take ownership over her mistakes (getting engaged to Matt despite their lack of connection), while openly sharing her joy over her new relationship. A lot of people were excited to see their two favorite cohosts announce they were officially an item. A lot of other people thought it was "disgusting" and "the end of feminism."

But, as Jackie put it, "At least you've given people something to *keep* talking about." It helped Emma's morale that Amanda Sharpe had reposted her YouTube video with the caption "You go, girl!" Emma's social media following had never been larger. Apparently, controversy was catnip for chronically online people—even if that meant she'd had to stop reading the comments for her own mental health.

Luckily, spending less time obsessing over other people's opinions meant Emma finally had the space and perspective to figure out how to end her book. She'd written a new last chapter that detailed in excruciatingly vulnerable detail what it was like to realize your partner didn't love you anymore. She shared all the horrible, masochistic thoughts that had gone through her head and how her broken engagement had made her question if she would ever get her own "good enough" relationship. But instead of leaving the readers feeling sorry for her or questioning her credibility as a relationship expert, Emma had managed to reframe her story and leave them with a feeling of hope. "One person falling out of love with you doesn't make you unlovable: it makes you human," she wrote. "When things don't work out, all you can do is try again. And then maybe a third, fourth and fifth time because you owe it to yourself to not give up."

During a surprisingly positive editorial call, Michelle had convinced Emma not to mention Operation: Save My Date in her current manuscript, because the podcast was doing so well there was already discussion of a second book based off the show. It felt surreal to have so many good things happen in a row after a series of calamities, but Emma knew better than to question how long this high would last. She was too busy enjoying it.

Emma had started this whole experiment with the sole goal of being the one in the big white dress on August 29, but as she watched her parents joyfully exchange rings, she knew she was right where she should be.

"You may now kiss your wife," the rabbi announced as the crowd erupted into applause. Alan grabbed Debbie and dipped her as far as her bad back would allow. She came up for air laughing and yelling at Alan for using so much tongue. Emma dropped her bouquet so she could clap loudly with both her hands.

"Have you talked to Matt yet?" Emma asked Jackie as she joined her at Table One during the reception—a table that was notably set for six and not five. "He seems so happy."

Jackie followed Emma's gaze to the bar where Matt and Kelly were canoodling. No one would suspect they were technically divorced. Emma had invited them on a whim, hoping they could find a way to all stay in each other's lives after going through so much together. She'd been shocked and pleased when they'd accepted without question. Not that she should have been surprised; Midwesterners were famously skilled at making potentially uncomfortable situations incredibly comfortable.

"During cocktail hour," Jackie replied with excitement. "He told me they're eloping next month. She's smart to lock him down when he looks like that in a suit."

Emma laughed. "Chris doesn't look too shabby either." She gestured to her brother-in-law, who was currently busting out his best moves with her nieces on the dance floor. They involved a lot of shoulder movements.

"Oh my god, he's so embarrassing," Jackie groaned, despite the smile on her face.

"I have something for you." Emma pulled her phone out of her clutch and tapped the screen a few times before passing it to Jackie.

"What is this?"

"It's your new YouTube channel. I got you the domain Youtube.com/YouDoKnowJackie. You can change it obviously, but I thought it might be cute."

"Why would I need a YouTube channel?"

"Because your talents shouldn't be wasted all on me. And mommy influencers get a bunch of free perks."

"You think *I* should become a mommy influencer?"

"Or beauty. Whatever appeals to you more."

"What if it was more of a lifestyle channel? That way I could share my workouts *and* my haircare routine."

"Even better. I'll send you the log-in details."

Jackie didn't reply because she was already too busy making notes on her phone, including "Ask Chris to get his teeth whitened."

"Sorry to interrupt the party," Alan's voice suddenly boomed over the speaker system. Emma looked up to see both her parents sharing a mic on stage with the band. "But we just wanted to take a moment to thank you all for being here."

"At first we felt silly throwing such a big party when we've already been married for so long," Debbie added. "But then we realized we'd already paid for it so what the hell."

The crowd laughed. The original intention of the day's festivities weren't a secret to anyone, including one of Ryan's second cousins who had already booked the trip to Los Angeles over a year ago and had still wanted to attend regardless of who was getting married. Emma was relieved to see he seemed to be having a great time.

"Weddings are always a beautiful thing," Alan continued. "Especially when they have an open bar." He paused for more laughter, like a true showman. "But if our youngest daughter, Emma, has taught us anything, it's that the real beauty is what comes *after* you say 'I do.'"

"So, with that in mind, we'd like to invite Will Stoll up onto the stage."

Emma felt a wave of anxiety rush through her body as Will appeared and took the mic.

"Hello, everyone. I'm Will, Emma's boyfriend." The familiar sound of Will's voice helped Emma realize she'd misidentified her feelings. It wasn't anxiety coursing through her. It was excitement.

"Oh my god, oh my god," Jackie murmured next to her. Emma grabbed Jackie's hand and locked eyes with Imani, who was by the dessert table with that supposedly straight, technically married girl from her gym as her date. Emma's best friend raised her eyebrows and grinned, signaling her approval. If even Imani supported whatever was about to happen, Emma knew she was doing something right.

"I know this day is about Alan and Debbie," Will continued. "But when I told them what I was planning to do after tonight, they insisted I do it now so they could watch." From the side of the stage Alan gave a big thumbs-up. "Emma, do you mind coming over here?"

Emma stood, her heart pounding, as Jackie frantically whispered, "Fix your bangs!"

The walk from the table to the stage only took a few seconds but Emma finally understood what it meant for time to slow down. She kept her eyes on Will and only briefly stumbled over someone's shoe before righting herself. Once she was planted in front of the stage, Will jumped down and joined her, the wireless mic still in his hand so everyone could hear.

"Emma, I know you said you were willing not to get married if it meant we could be together."

Emma nodded, too afraid to say anything and potentially ruin her third proposal in one year.

"And I love that you were willing to make that sacrifice for me. As everyone here knows, when you first pitched me the idea of getting married today, after I had only known you for a few weeks, I thought you were—to put it like you would—totally bananas."

Emma laughed, already wiping the tears off her face.

"I'm ashamed it took me this long, but I now *finally* understand what you have been trying to tell me this whole time. You weren't looking for a replacement groom. You were looking for someone to spend your life with. Someone who would show up every day, not because they signed some paperwork, but because marriage actually means something to them—to him—to *me*.

"I know what I'm about to do is a huge risk. There are going to be a lot of people out there that won't understand why we are 'rushing things.' Fortunately, though, I am no longer one of them. Because Emma Moskowitz, you deserve someone who will take the leap with you. And I feel unbelievably lucky that I get to be the guy to do it."

Will knelt down on one knee and pulled a ring box out of

his suit jacket. He opened it up, revealing a thick gold band with diamonds sprinkled throughout it.

It wasn't an engagement ring. It was a wedding ring. Emma covered her mouth to stop herself from screaming with joy.

"So, Emma, will you marry me? Preferably sometime this week?"

"YES!" Emma exclaimed as she wrapped herself around him.

As their lips found each other and the crowd erupted in applause, Emma knew with uncharacteristic certainty that out of all the husbands in all the world, she would choose Will over and over again.

Epilogue

Ten months later

OFFICIAL TRANSCRIPT OF EPISODE ONE

Emma: Hello and welcome to the very first episode of our brand-new podcast, *Operation: Marriage*. I'm Emma Moskowitz, a licensed couples therapist and the author of the upcoming book, *The Good-Enough Relationship*, which will soon be available in bookstores near you.

Will: And I'm Will Stoll, an award-winning podcast producer and Emma's husband.

Emma: You might know us from our previous podcast, *Operation: Save My Date*, which won Will some of those awards he just mentioned.

Will: After we wrapped that adventure up a few months ago, which included Emma and I getting married at city hall in a twist ending, we started talking about what we wanted to do next.

Emma: I suggested a series on bats, but Will said it was better to stick with what we know.

Will: Actually, I think I said that you didn't know anything about bats other than that they look like tiny puppies with wings. Which isn't exactly enough to carry an entire season.

Emma: Either way, we found ourselves, as newlyweds, gravitating toward a show about the inner workings of marriage in today's society.

Will: Why do some marriages work while others—

Emma: Combust.

Will: And how can we make sure ours falls into the first camp?

Emma: Over the course of the next ten episodes, we will be interviewing married couples, divorcees, relationship experts and researchers to try to figure out what makes a marriage stick.

Will: And on top of all that Emma and I will be attending couples therapy together because Emma is a shill for her own industry.

Emma: I think what you meant to say is that couples therapy is a great resource for anyone who can afford it. And this feels like a good opportunity to shed some light on what actually goes on in sessions when it's used as a preventive measure instead of as a Hail Mary.

Will: Sure. That too.

Emma: But before we dive in, we have to take a brief break for our sponsor, JointTaxes.com. Why file your taxes alone when you can file them together? Get married before December 31st and save!

Rustling of papers.

Emma: Is that the actual ad copy? I can't say that. It's ridiculous.

★ ★ ★ ★ ★

Acknowledgments

To my kind and brilliant editor, Lynn Raposo. You are everything an editor is meant to be and somehow more. Thank you for believing in my idea, gently shaping it into something better and teaching me how not to overdo it in my dialogue. I feel endlessly grateful to get to continue collaborating with you.

To my agent, Stacy Testa, whose tenacity is the backbone of my literary career. Thank you for helping me break into this new and incredibly exciting genre. I have never felt more supported and heard than when I am celebrating (or complaining) with you.

To my manager, Matt Sadeghian. Thank you for pushing me to evolve while remembering who I am. I can't wait to see what the next ten years of our partnership brings.

To my parents, Ruth and Ken Raskin. Thank you not only for giving me this idea but for helping me heal enough to write it. I quite literally could not have done this without you. I hope you get to renew your wedding vows one day soon in real life.

To my husband, John. You know that I don't believe things happen for a reason. But if they did, you would be that reason.

And finally, to anyone who has ever had their heart smashed on without a second thought. Keep going. It's worth it.